The Elite Crimes Unit is a covert team within Interpol that specializes in taking down the world's top criminals—and then offering them a deal. Because sometimes a history of bad behavior can be a very good thing . . .

Jack Angelo is clearly off his game. First his wallet gets lifted—by a pregnant woman, no less—on the ferry to Finland. At his hotel, he's seduced by a sexy redhead who takes him for a ride, too. And when he finally starts casing the bank he's supposed to rob, yet another female fouls things up. All he wants is to complete this assignment for the ECU to save himself and his family. Little does he know that the women who keep interfering are actually one woman—who's about to show him just how outmatched he really is . . .

Known as "The Chameleon," Saskia Petrovik is a mistress of disguise tasked with watching the new recruit as he meets up with his high-level crew of thieves. She has no problem getting under the covers to pull off an undercover job—especially with the man known as Gentleman Jack. But multiple identities can cause multiple problems, and in these dangerous circles, the temptation to show her true self could change a deceptive affair into a deadly one . . .

Visit us at www.kensingtonbooks.com

Books by Michele Hauf

The Elite Crimes Unit
The Thief
The Forger
The Chameleon

Published by Kensington Publishing Corporation

The Chameleon

The Elite Crimes Unit

Michele Hauf

LYRICAL PRESS
Kensington Publishing Corp.
www.kensingtonbooks.com

Lyrical Press books are published by
Kensington Publishing Corp. 119 West 40th Street New York, NY 10018

All Kensington titles, imprints, and distributed lines are available at special quantity discounts for bulk purchases for sales promotion, premiums, fundraising, and educational or institutional use.

To the extent that the image or images on the cover of this book depict a person or persons, such person or persons are merely models, and are not intended to portray any character or characters featured in the book.

Special book excerpts or customized printings can also be created to fit specific needs. For details, write or phone the office of the Kensington Special Sales Manager:
Kensington Publishing Corp.
119 West 40th Street
New York, NY 10018
Attn. Special Sales Department. Phone: 1-800-221-2647.

Kensington and the K logo Reg. U.S. Pat. & TM Off.
LYRICAL PRESS Reg. U.S. Pat. & TM Off.
Lyrical Press and the L logo are trademarks of Kensington Publishing Corp.

First Electronic Edition: December 2017
eISBN-13: 978-1-5161-0200-6
eISBN-10: 1-5161-0200-2

First Print Edition: December 2017
ISBN-13: 978-1-5161-0201-3
ISBN-10: 1-5161-0201-0

Printed in the United States of America

3 6109 00535 3393

Chapter 1

The distant shore of Finland loomed closer. The ferry windows revealed a crisp gray ocean, chunked here and there with icy slush slabs, beneath a sharp azure sky. This was the last leg in a three-day journey from London to Hamburg, to Copenhagen, to Stockholm, all by train. Flying was out of the question. Jack Angelo liked to keep his feet as close to the ground as possible. There wasn't enough alcohol in the world to get his feet that far from earth. The exception being this ferry, but he'd been sipping ginger tea since boarding sixteen hours earlier.

That he was eager to set foot on land after this cruise across the Baltic Sea was putting things mildly. To avoid the anxiety that clung to his neck like an alien being, he'd eaten in the dining room (dry toast and fruit), gambled a bit (he was up sixty quid), and in the lounge he'd had a few shots of something called Salmiakki. The bartender had said it was a Finnish favorite—was supposed to taste like salted black licorice.

It had looked and tasted more like tar, Jack thought now as he regretted that third shot, which still roiled in his gut.

A sudden gust of wind beat against the windows and rocked the ferry. As frigid and icy as Helsinki promised to be, he should have worn a winter coat. The dress coat he wore over his suit was warm enough for London's winter, but not below-zero tundra stuff. And while he'd never been across the ocean to visit the Finns, he knew that the country was not a place any man who did not want his bollocks to permanently freeze should visit in January.

Opportunity had provided an assignment in Helsinki, and necessity required he not complain. He would be in proximity to a new beginning. He had to take this chance, even if it was more forced than he desired.

He was sitting in an aisle seat, next to a very pregnant young woman with dyed black hair who kept shifting in the seat and biting her fingernails. They were soon to arrive at Helsinki's Katajanokka Harbour, but this was the first time he'd sat for more than twenty minutes or so.

With all his seat mate's commotion and occasional groans of discomfort, Jack hoped she wouldn't give birth before then.

"Headed in to Helsinki?" he asked the woman.

"Yes, to meet my fiancé. He wants to live in Finland. We've been here two years, off and on. But I don't know. I'm more of a London girl myself." Her accent sounded like the Queen's English to Jack. There were so many accents in the city. Even he had trouble understanding the cockneys who dropped their letters. "I'm not so keen on this big wobbly boat, are you?"

"Ginger tea." He tapped the empty paper cup he'd set in the cup holder.

"What does that do? Calm you down? Whew!" She shifted again. "I think this baby just kicked my kidneys. Oh! Did you feel that?"

The boat had lurched, probably cresting against the sharp whitecaps the captain had told them they'd experience on this cold and windy morning.

"It's okay. We're almost there," he reassured in a calm voice that managed to surprise himself. "I bet we'll be docking in ten minutes."

"Brilliant." Managing a weak grimace, her hand smoothed over her stomach. "What about you? You sound like an Irishman but you've got a bit of something else going on in there. Heading home or visiting?"

He smirked at her assessment. The Italian in him gave his Irish a run for the money sometimes. "Just a short visit."

"Where you staying?"

"Huh?"

"I know a lot of the hotels. Worked at a few of them as a maid. You would not believe the things people leave behind in their rooms. I'm talking DNA evidence, you know?"

Jack lifted a brow. They were fast headed toward TMI.

"Sorry. I know too much about some things a person shouldn't know much about," she added. "I like to observe. Take everything in. Anyway, you going cozy or fancy?"

He waggled a hand before him. "Maybe middle ground. I'll decide when I plant my feet on land again."

She nodded. "I suggest the Hotel Hop. It's nice and cozy, and the sheets are clean. Trust me on that one. It's tucked at the northern suburb of Toukola. Quaint little village feel to it, so there's not a lot of noise. That is, if you want to be away from the bustle of the city. Helsinki is so cosmopolitan, you know? And the hotel has outdoor hot tubs, too. Don't let the cold freak you. Ten seconds of frigid is worth it for the soak in steamy water. Ah, bloody babies."

She gestured that she was going to stand. "I need a bathroom break. This bloke keeps playing MMA fighter with my kidneys."

She pulled herself up by the back of the seat in front of her, and then stumbled, or maybe all that weight hugging her belly toppled her off balance. With a sudden swing, she caught her hands against Jack's chest and her long black hair brushed his face.

"Ah shite. I'm so sorry, mister."

"No problem. You okay?"

"Yes. Sort of. Don't ever let anyone tell you having a baby is easy." She pushed up to stand, using his chest as leverage. "You smell nice. Like ice and pine. I'll be right back."

He smiled to himself as she wobbled down the aisle toward the bathrooms, and wondered how such a small woman could get so large. Her belly circumference must equal her height. Would she fit in one of those tiny bathrooms? For her sake, he hoped the fiancé would find her a nice warm climate to settle down in and take care of his family well. Family should be a man's focus. Always.

He'd probably check out the hotel she suggested. He liked it when the minor, extraneous decisions were made for him, leaving him to concentrate on the task at hand. And away from the bustle of the city? Sounded perfect, especially since he'd need to keep a low profile for his current assignment.

Knowing his penchant for avoiding air travel, The Elite Crimes Unit had dispatched him three days ago. Travel expenses were always covered. His assignment? Infiltrate a crew of bank robbers and learn what it was, exactly, they were stealing. They'd committed a heist, of sorts, a few weeks ago in a small but elite Belgian bank. According to an inside source, it had been a clean job, four crew members, two hours in and out. Except. Nothing had been taken from the bank. No cash, no security bonds, not even a hack into the bank's clientele database. They'd walked in, had gone through all the motions of robbing the place, and then had left. With nothing.

Or had they?

It was Jack's job to find out, and to be there when it happened again.

He did love a good heist. Had participated in half a dozen successful endeavors himself. Successful meaning, he and his crew had most definitely walked out with cold, hard cash.

He'd been born into the business. Heists, extortion, and occasional smuggling jobs were the Angelos' means to a living. Family was everything to Jack, and he'd learned that a man protected family before himself always.

That included a father with a heart condition who would never survive a decade behind bars. So when Jack had been arrested for a petty traffic violation and taken into Scotland Yard for questioning—and Interpol had been sitting in the room—he had known the jig was up. He would not give up his father for his participation in a two-year smuggling job that had shifted almost a billion pounds' worth of AK-47s from Iraq to the US. So Jack had been sent to Brixton prison for ten years.

Two years served had given him a lot of time to think. When The Elite Crimes Unit had offered him a get out of jail free card in exchange for working off his remaining eight years, Jack had considered it. They hadn't asked him to give up his father. Or to divulge information about the crimes any in his family had committed. But to work on the opposite side of the law? He'd almost said no. Had crossed his arms and watched as, after the final ultimatum, the Interpol agent with the long blond hair and ice in her eyes had stood and left the interrogation room. The door had closed.

And Jack had wondered if he'd done the right thing. Certainly he could endure another eight years on the inside. But.

And the but had occurred on the way out of the interrogation room. He'd been handcuffed, a dark hood had been placed over his head, and he'd been knocked out. He'd come to in the back of a van, parked in the East London cemetery. Right next to his late sister's grave.

The promise of his tombstone right next to hers, had decided him. A man couldn't continue to protect his family if he was six feet under. Or in prison. He'd agreed to work for the ECU. The last three years had been... not terrible. And he'd been able to keep up a covert line of communications regarding his family's activities, though he'd never risk speaking directly to any of them.

And then he'd gotten the information about his brother, Jonny, three days ago. The idiot was in trouble.

Which was why Jack had agreed to take the job in Helsinki. It had almost been a gift, landing on his radar but hours after learning about Jonny.

Checking his wristwatch, he realized ten minutes had passed. A glance out the windows proved the ferry had already docked. He hadn't noticed their arrival. Not a heavy jolt or even a horn to announce their docking. He swung a look over his shoulder toward the bathrooms. Still in there? It had been a long time. Maybe he should check on her?

He slapped a palm over his heart, where he kept his wallet and—something felt wrong. After digging in the inner coat pocket, he came up empty. No wallet. He'd had his passport in that pocket as well. What the bloody hell?

"Really?" She'd pickpocketed him?

Bursting up to stand and striding toward the bathrooms, Jack knocked on the door and called, "Ma'am? You in there?" No answer. He pushed the door and it opened to reveal an empty bathroom and... "Oi."

A false belly had been abandoned on top of the toilet. It had large, foam breasts attached to it as well.

"Of all the—" The last time someone had tried to dupe him they'd walked away bleeding. What the hell? He'd never suspect a pregnant chick, that was sure. "Clever. But just for a wallet?"

He spied the leather wallet sticking out of the trash bin and pulled it out. Three hundred euros—he'd exchanged pounds in Stockholm—gone and... He didn't keep anything else of value in it save a lock-pick set. That was gone as well. He opened the cabinet beneath the tiny sink and tugged out the bin. Nothing inside but wet paper towels. No bloody passport.

The ferry captain announced disembarkment could now commence, and Jack soared down the aisle, checking faces and not seeing the dark-haired woman. She could have already made an escape, for the doors opened and everyone stood up, blocking him from reconnaissance.

"Damn it!" He scanned through the windows but the thick crowd did not offer up the thief.

The day was getting off to a right terrible start.

* * * *

Even after entering the warmth of the four-story building, he still shivered. Jack stood before the reception desk at the Hotel Hop, waiting for the pretty receptionist to book him a room. Her red hair spilled over one green eye and a sigh lifted her breasts beneath the sheer red shirt that was strategically unbuttoned to reveal cleavage.

He could use some of that.

"Just a visit?" she asked in a tired tone.

Jack startled out of his stare. But she'd seen the trajectory of his gaze. It was about as close to flirting as he ever got. "Of course. You don't think I'd purposely stay in this ice box?"

She smiled, but it was weary. "Would you like a ground level room or higher up?"

"Ground level is good." Always made for an easy escape. Not that he planned any escapes. Not yet.

She handed him back his ferry receipt, which he'd used for ID after telling her he'd been robbed. It had been easy enough to clear customs at the docks thanks to his ECU credentials, but from here on he was just another visitor. When he'd given her the receipt, she had shrugged, laughed and, with a look over her shoulder—keeping an eye out for management?—had said she'd take care of him. And that promise hadn't been empty but rather had ended with a seductive wink. Thankfully, he had memorized his ECU-issued credit card number. That always came in handy.

"If you don't mind me saying..." He leaned onto the desk. "You look about as happy to be here as I do."

She blew a sweep of soft hair from her face. "I'm ending an eighteen-hour shift. Can't wait to tilt back a whiskey and head home."

"The whiskey here in the bar?"

"It's remarkably good," she said with a nod toward the bar down the hallway. "Stop in before you head to your room. I will meet you there?"

Now that was an invitation he could get behind. And since he wasn't scheduled to get "vetted" by the leader of the bank crew until later this evening, he'd take her up on it.

"I'll have a drink waiting for you. Thanks." He tucked the room key in his front pocket, winked at her, and strolled toward the bar.

He was not a man to ignore the obvious. A chat in the bar with a lovely bird? Great way to ease his apprehensions about this job. Not that he was nervous. It was different this time. His life would change. And he'd never be able to look back.

The receptionist arrived five minutes later and slid onto the creaky wooden bar stool beside him, tilted back the entire two fingers of whiskey, gestured for another, and then finally turned a smile up at him. "I'm Rachel. And you are my lunchtime fling."

"Is that so?" After two servings, he was feeling the whiskey. It was strong enough to "put the hair on his back," as his father would say. Hell of a lot better than that tar shite on the ferry. "You do know my room number."

"I put you at the end of the hallway. Quiet down there. And maid service is at the opposite side of the building right now. You had enough to drink?"

Sexy and to the point. He did like this woman. Jack's gaze dropped to her cleavage, which was much more apparent now that another button had been freed. "Absolutely."

They made it into his room in a flurry of kisses and scattered overcoat and suit coat. Hands moving over her breasts and down her narrow waist, Jack lifted Rachel up and pressed her back to the wall. She kissed him deeply and hungrily. This was not a shy flirtation. They both meant business.

A glide of his hand over her thigh and between her legs found her panties were...not there. What kind of welcome to the city had he stumbled on?

"Oh, Jack, yes! Slam me against the wall!" She moaned into his kiss as his fingers explored her wetness. Slick and hot, he wanted to feel her all about his cock now.

She tugged his tie loose and started to unbutton his shirt, but gave up and shoved it up to slap a palm to his chest.

"Pants off," she said between furious kisses. The fingers of her other hand raked across his scalp, where he kept his hair shaved at a quarter inch. "Hurry!"

He was all for fast and furious. Pants down, Jack plunged his hard-on into the softest, hottest, most welcoming escape from the day he'd ever known. All the back-numbing travel slipped into a distant memory. Even the humiliating pickpocket incident ceased to matter. Groaning roughly, he thrust into her heat, and thumbed at her nipples through the bra he hadn't taken the time to remove. He would come *like that*, but he wanted to ride this bird a bit longer.

He lifted her by the arse and carried her to the bed, wobbling with his pants about his ankles. Landing them both on the bed, they disconnected briefly until she greedily pulled him back inside her and locked her legs about his hips.

"You certainly know what you want," he muttered.

"A quickie from the biggest cock I've had in a while."

He'd take the compliment. He did have a sizable—

"Oh!" She was coming and he was surprised by that. Most women needed more stimulation. Again, he wasn't about to argue. But it was time for him to catch up. So he gave a few more thrusts and surrendered to the immense and satisfying release as she spilled out a short but effusive cry. Her spasms milked him to a satisfying orgasm. He slammed into her and shuddered above her.

Hell. Yes.

Oi.

Collapsing on top of her, then rolling to the side, Jack fisted the air triumphantly. "Welcome to Hel-freakin'-sinki."

She laughed and slid off the bed, flipping her thick red hair away from her face. Disheveled suited her beautifully. Her dark lashes fluttered over bright green eyes. "Can I use your bathroom, my big Irish bull?"

"It's all yours, Red." Jack closed his eyes.

Now he took a moment to toe off his shoes and let them drop to the floor. After gliding a hand down his abs, he gently gripped the base of his spent erection. It was a comfort hold. The shudders of orgasm still lingered faintly, and a squeeze of his rod milked them for a few sweet moments.

"Thanks, Jack Angelo," Rachel called from the hallway. From his position on the bed he couldn't see her. "I'm going to head home now. Have a great stay here in the city."

Her quick escape didn't bother him. Too much. They'd both gotten what they'd wanted. Jack closed his eyes and settled in the aftereffects of orgasm.

It must have been half an hour later that he snorted out of sleep and realized he'd dozed off. He sat up on the bed, laughing because his pants were still around his ankles. His dick was limp but happy. Standing and pulling up his pants, he decided he'd rent a car and drive into the city proper, pick up some new clothes and warmer gear, and have a bite to eat before tonight's meeting. He also wanted to check out the bank that intel told him was the target.

He strolled into the bathroom to take a piss. Glancing over the fake marble vanity as he did his business, he hissed at the sight of what sat there. Zipping quickly, he picked up the passport set open like a birthday card to display the inside. *His* passport.

"What the hell? How did she?" Jack slapped a palm to the hard vanity.

Had the two women been somehow working together? The pregnant chick *had* recommended this hotel. Bloody Christ, he'd allowed himself to be duped by two women in less than half a day. What was wrong with him?

"You're already off the clock," he muttered about his failing instincts. "Stay sharp, Jack. One more job. And then you're out. For good."

He tucked the passport in his pocket, then headed out.

Chapter 2

Jack handed over the application for a safe deposit box to the thin man behind the desk, who nodded effusively as if he were headbanging to a beat no one else could hear but him.

"Thank you, Mr. Angelo." His chopped Finnish accent was interesting to Jack, but he liked it. "I will take a moment to look through this. Then we can take you into the safe room and let you deposit your items. We do thank you for choosing Aarnivalkea Pankki to trust with your goods."

"You seemed like a right friendly place," Jack said, "what with the big potted plants a man can see through the windows. A touch of summer, I say, is what I needed."

"You are not happy with our cool weather?"

Cool? That was the understatement of the day. The weather station had reported a temperature with a single digit for the rest of the week. Jack had not stopped shivering since stepping off the ferry.

"Not exactly, no. But like I told you, my daughter has decided to move to Helsinki with her fiancé. She's expecting a little one, so I'll be visiting quite often. I have some things I'd like to keep safe here."

"Very good. Well, it looks like everything is in order. I'll go find a box number and key for you; then I'll walk you down to the lower level. Give me a moment."

Jack nodded, then spun on the chair to take in the lobby. There were no inner offices that he could see from this vantage. Along the wall opposite where he sat, five cubicles hosted account managers and others sitting before desks. The vast lobby featured a marble floor impressed in the center with a bronze medallion displaying a flame. Probably the country seal or somesuch.

He wasn't familiar with Finland. He rarely ventured farther north than Germany, despite his job forcing him to travel the world. By train, automobile, or boat, that is.

There were six teller windows, but at the moment only one was helping an elderly gentleman. It was a quiet bank. But it was known in certain circles as one of the elite, a place where the rich and famous discreetly kept their millions, and billions.

It was also the place the crew intended to hit next, according to the inside source who had reported to the ECU.

Interesting choice, Jack thought. In its own small and unassuming way it was simply a friendly neighborhood bank. On the other hand, this was the sort high rollers sought to keep their valuables. Nothing flashy. Not an institution that had previously failed or gone under due to the crash in 2008 that had begun in Switzerland and spread worldwide.

He was supposed to meet someone from the crew this evening and get vetted to meet the man in charge, Clive Hendrix. The ECU had a limited dossier on him, and suspected the surname wasn't real. Again, the info was thanks to the inside source. Was this source a part of the crew? Jack hadn't been told. But if someone was working for Clive *and* informing to the ECU, Jack would be able to sniff him out.

Neither had he a name for the person he was to meet. He'd only been told she was a she, and that she would find him.

While he appreciated the cloak and dagger and the need to know situation, he could do with a bit of detail. He was flying blind here. And while he was accustomed to keeping one eye over his shoulder, the bollocks-shriveling weather had him focusing on whether a man's jewels could freeze and fall off.

"Here we are, Mr. Angelo."

The banker in a crisp brown suit stood behind him. Slender and boasting wide, rough red knuckles on his over-sized hands, he waited. Jack stood and shook his hand. Firm handshake. But then company execs were often trained to perform just such confidence-inducing gestures.

As the banker signaled, he followed him toward the bronze doors that led to the safe deposit box vault room; a woman called out to Jack. He didn't even notice how close she was until he felt her clutch at his arm and hug up against his body.

Thick, cloying perfume made him cough as he turned to shuck her off. Rarely could he smell a woman's perfume, so she must have poured it on. She clung to his arm with glossy red-lacquered nails.

"Jack, darling, I finished at the shop across the street and didn't want to wait for you out in the car." Bright red lipstick provided a focus point on a pale, thin face that fluttered dark lashes and featured a beauty mark to the right of one of her turquoise eyes. "Mercy, it's cold out there." Her accent was American. Maybe a touch of Texas? "Oh, darling, now I get to see you put away my pretty things."

Who the hell was this woman?

The bank manager paused by the bronze doors and eyed the woman cautiously and then Jack.

She wore a tight-fitted red top and skirt, and hugged her breasts against his chest. A tug at his yellow tie with those glossy nails, and she fluttered her lashes up at him. "You're on," she whispered. "Show me what you got."

He was…on? Wait. Was *this* his vetting?

"Mr. Angelo?" The manager waited.

"Uh, yes. You said the room was down the stairs?"

"Right this way. Shall we?" He pulled open a door and the stairway turned to the right.

"Let's both of us go in, sweetie," Jack said as they followed. "Wouldn't want to leave my darling sitting out in the frozen car, would I?"

She cooed and pawed at him in a manner that he'd normally want to shove away. No one touched the tie. Unless of course, he had her pushed up against a wall. But if she knew him—she'd called him by name—then he could only guess she was the one he was supposed to meet.

Hadn't he been duped by enough females today? It couldn't happen again. The odds were impossible. But he'd remain cautious.

As they landed in the basement and followed the manager down a marble hallway, she clung to him and wobbled on heels that must have been half a foot high. She was still a head shorter than him. And, bloody hell, that perfume was strong. Always surprising to notice for a man who'd had his nose broken so many times it had damaged his sense of smell.

How had she known to find him here? He hadn't told anyone where he was going today, or that he'd intended to visit this bank on the sly to familiarize himself with it before stepping into the fray. The ECU wasn't even in on his every move. Technically. They could track him at any moment with the GPS chip embedded at the base of his skull. But the only time they would keep in close contact and alert him to their actions was when he wore a communications device in his ear and had requested their assistance. He'd forgotten to take that along this trip. Not a mistake.

Someone must have been following him. Because this was not a wild coincidence. He had a twitchy—if damaged—nose for things like this.

"We keep our safe deposit boxes separate from the main vault," the banker explained as they waited for a guard to enter the vault combination. "This is the original vault from when the bank was built in 1912."

"Quaint," the woman said.

Jack didn't see any positives in a quaint vault. He wanted security. On the other hand, a thief would not.

"We've installed digital security only in the past year," the manager added. "It's a marvel."

It was a simple digital keypad, as opposed to a rotating combination lock. Jack counted eight bleeps indicating it was a long entry code. A man would need some hi-tech digital tools to crack this one, and it could take up to ten minutes to get inside. Either that, or he could cut through the steel door. Interesting. Not very secure in this modern age of robbers who utilized every technical doodad to their advantage.

"You'll always be escorted into this room. And once inside," the banker continued, "we'll use our keys to open and retrieve your box. You can then select any of the adjoining privacy rooms to view the contents for as long as you wish. The admitting employee will remain close to help you return your box to its secure position and escort you out. Do you have any questions?"

"So many boxes full of pretty things." The woman on Jack's arm cooed as they entered the small vault that was about twenty feet long and only ten feet wide. Three walls were lined with steel boxes in varying sizes. Jack had selected a small one strictly for price and—he didn't have anything to put inside it anyway.

"Do we get to pick which one we want?" The woman strode in her awkward heels up to a wall of boxes and spread her hands over the fronts of them. "I like the big ones."

The manager cleared his throat and when he met Jack's gaze, Jack managed a shrug and a deadpan, "She likes big ones."

"Oh, and yours is the biggest, Jack darling."

She started toward him for what he guessed would be an illicit hug, so he gripped his tie, putting out his elbow in blockade. "Ours is over here, sweetie."

The manager inserted his key into a small box, and waited for Jack to do the same. "We turn at the count of three." He counted and Jack turned, and the inner lock mechanism clicked.

Standard in most medium-sized banks. Not particularly high security to the thief who carried a rotating diamond-bit drill, but enough to keep out ninety-five percent of those who would try hand-picking. Of course, a good old crowbar always seemed to work rather well on these older models.

Jack pulled out the foot-long box and nodded that the banker should show him out of the room. The woman followed behind them, but when they got out into the hallway Jack realized she was still inside. And the bank manager noticed immediately, too.

"Uh, ma'am?"

"I just like to wonder," she called out from inside the room, "what everyone puts in all these treasure boxes."

"You'll need to exit the room now, ma'am."

"Don't rush me!" When one of the security guards entered the room, she tripped out and tugged at her uber-tight skirt. Jack fancied he could see the line of her mons with each step. Well, he did. She was slender and quite the looker. But he didn't like the blatant act.

On the other hand, she was drawing all the attention to her. Which he didn't mind at all.

"We'll take this room here." Jack nodded toward the second room away from the vault, and the woman eagerly walked toward it. He gave her a little shove and then entered and pulled the door shut behind him. The walls would not be soundproof, so he kept his voice low. "Oi. Who the hell are you?"

She clutched his arm and hugged up to him again. This time she dragged her tongue up the side of his cheek, then winked at him. "I'm your sweetie. You forget that so quickly, Jack Angelo? We'll talk about your need to go banking on your own when we get out of here. That wasn't part of the plan. Hurry up, will you? These heels are killing my arches."

Lasering a dead stare on her, he opened the box, and then closed it. Then he gripped her by the upper arm. Her jaw clattered as he gave her a good solid shake. "I don't like playing games, little girl. Who are you?"

He hadn't anticipated the toe of her shoe slipping between his legs and sliding up to nudge his right leg forward. Jack's balance wavered and that gave her the ability to shove him against the wall and notch her forearm up under his chin, pushing roughly against his throat.

"I'm your new watcher, Angelo. Or is it Gentleman Jack?" She shoved her arm harder, making him wince.

Not many knew him by that name. Which could only mean she had details about him. "You the one supposed to meet with me later?"

"Later is now," she said. "And I'm not sure what to think about you, or if I'm willing to vet you to Clive after this bold move. Put the damn box back and let's get out of here." She stepped away from him.

He caught himself and stood, straightening his tie and slapping a hand to the box. With a sneer at the not-so-sexy-anymore woman, he shoved the door open and with a lift of his chin, then summoned the guard to help him return the box. The woman waited in the hallway, tapping one foot loudly and sighing as if this were the longest she'd ever had to wait on a man. Box returned, Jack strode by her, assuming she'd do whatever worked best for her act. He didn't know her. He didn't want to know her either.

His watcher? What the hell had he just walked into?

Once outside the bank, the wind smacked him in the face and he cursed his need to have left his overcoat in the rental car, which was parked half a block up the street. Tugging at his tie, Jack faced the brutal wind and with rushed strides quickly reached the vehicle. He turned the ignition and twisted the heater to high. It was like an icebox in the car, and he shoved his hands between his thighs to warm them.

The passenger door opened and in slid the woman in red. She set a big leather bag on the console between the seats and shook out a long and shivering, "Brr! It's like the tundra out there."

"Listen, lady—"

"Get over it, Jack. Whatever problem you think you have with me, lose it. We're tied at the hip now."

"I think you need to explain—"

And what she did next stunned him more than the fact she'd invited herself into his car. She pulled down her skirt, revealing black lace panties, and long bare white legs—that goose bumped in the freeze—and shimmied it off. Rolling the skirt into a neat tube, she then dug in her bag

A tilt of her head caught his stunned look. "What?"

"Who *are* you? And what are you doing?"

"I just said it was friggin' freezing out there. And I am walking around in a skirt with no nylons! Who does that? Why fucking Helsinki, of all the places in the world?"

Was he supposed to reply to that? He felt as incensed about the climate as she obviously was. But the sudden need to pull down her skirt and get naked in such weather baffled him. And her accent had noticeably changed. It sounded like, hmm…

From the bag, she pulled out a plastic baggie and put the skirt in it, then tugged out another baggie and from that one unrolled some dark pants. Pulling them up her legs, she winked at him as she did so. "Better, yeah? Hey. We were not properly introduced." She offered her hand to him. "Saskia Petrovik."

He took her cold hand, guessing his was no warmer, and shook it. Only because he wanted to make a connection. Nice and firm. Strong, too. And her accent was decidedly Russian.

"Jack Angelo," he offered carefully. "I thought we were supposed to meet in another hour?"

She shrugged. "You on a schedule, Jack? I just took care of what needed to be done. Let's go talk to Clive."

Clive was the man in charge, the leader of the crew. The only person Jack wanted to talk to. And apparently he had been vetted by this woman. In a manner that baffled him.

"Are you part of the crew?"

"No questions until after Clive talks to you." She pulled down the visor and opened the mirror. Peeling away one large flutter of false eyelash from her lid, she winced. "I hate these things. But they distract, yeah?"

Jack was about to say that watching her strip to her panties had been a bigger distraction, but he'd pass on that one. He was too cold to feel any sort of heat in his extremities, especially his dick. Too bad. She had given him a free one, and he'd been too frozen to react.

"Where we headed?" he asked as he pulled away from the curb.

"Northeast. Edge of the city. I'll tell you when to turn. Flip on the radio. There's a great polka station."

He flicked her a wonky look as he twisted on the radio.

"Seriously. It'll put your head in a different place. And don't you need that when the whole world is like a big ice rink and one wrong step will land you flat on your back?"

"Point taken. Polka, it is." Though he much preferred some Queen.

He dialed until he heard the jaunty beat of an accordion, and decided the day's adventure was only getting started. And with this exotic bird at his side, it could prove quite an experience.

Polka and black panties? Oi.

Chapter 3

Clive had set up the crew in an old auto body shop at the edge of the Toukola district, which wasn't far from where her new partner in crime, Jack Angelo, was staying. The garage sported three defunct car bays and an office walled in with corrugated tin. And a working heating system, which, Clive had explained, had been the key selling point.

Saskia, now comfortable since she'd ditched the spike heels and skirt, led Jack into the shop and set her leather bag down by the big, red, wheeled tool bench. Niles stood across the room beside Clive, his ever-present leather jacket collar flipped up against his neck. Both men were discussing something they'd drawn on the oil-stained concrete floor with white chalk.

"They're diagramming the building layout," she offered as Jack looked around the vast space. He'd slipped on a winter overcoat before stepping outside, and beneath that, the suit and tie were impeccable. But a yellow tie? Was the man asking for attention? "Come on, I'll introduce you to Clive and we'll take a look at what they've got so far."

She noted that Jack took in everything, yet he also seemed relaxed, casual. He either put up a good show or really was that laid back. She knew, from experience, that he was quite aware of his surroundings. Except when he'd been drinking.

Clive turned and nodded to her as he left Niles with a stick of chalk and a couple papers in hand. "Sass! You're back early. I take it things went well?"

"Clive, I'd like you to meet Jack Angelo. Jack, this is Clive Hendrix. I found Jack at the Aarnivalkea checking out the safe deposit boxes."

"Is that so?" Clive slapped his palm against Jack's for a firm shake and held it a bit longer than normal.

The man had his quirks. For one, he wasn't a big talker. And never gave out any information that wasn't necessary. Much to Saskia's annoyance.

His silver hair and tanned skin with a brisk line of stubble edging his jaw gave him a fashion model look. He was sexy in a disarming manner, and she hated to admit that because he had to be twenty years older than her twenty-nine.

Jack released the handshake and nodded. "I always like to take a look at the location as a civilian. You know. Before I get involved in schematics and subterfuge. Gives me a different angle."

"I can understand that," Clive said. "Doing your homework. So the things I've been told about you are true. And the suit. So dapper! I'm not sure you'll want to dress so fancy for the actual heist."

Smoothing a hand down the bright tie, Jack said, "Who expects a bloke to rob a bank in a suit?"

Clive conceded with a nod. "Point made. If Sass says you're good, you're good. Right, Sass?"

A wince was always unavoidable when he tossed out the ridiculous nickname so often. "Of course. I'm a good judge of character. You got the layout of the bank drawn out?"

"Yes, though Niles thinks my scale is off. We've got the building plans from the secretary at the city planning office. Niles is killer when it comes to sweet-talking the ladies. Come take a look."

"Jack," Saskia said as they approached the chalk drawing. "This is Niles. He's our tech guy, and, apparently, our resident sweet talker."

The man with skin so dark it gleamed, and a bald pate, offered Jack a hand shake and bowed, offering, "Namaste. You're our muscle and getaway driver, eh?"

"That's what I was hired for." Jack tugged at his tie. "So what's the ETA for this party?"

"Five days," Clive offered. "Maybe four. I've already planned our movement. The only thing holding us back is waiting on a few items."

"Which are?"

"I'll let Sass fill you in. I'm headed out to walk the bank myself. Have an appointment at five with the manager. We'll compare notes tomorrow, yes, Jack?"

"Of course."

"You'll be staying with Sass," Clive said. "You keep an eye on him."

She nodded, but Jack spoke up, "I have a room already. Not far from here, actually."

"No. I like to keep my crew in as few places as possible, and Sass has a sweet little rental in the vicinity. Besides, you're the new guy. Someone has to keep an eye on you. You don't like it? Walk."

Jack crossed his arms, and lifted a brow as Clive filed past and left the garage with a creak of the outer door.

Saskia could imagine his thoughts. They mirrored her own when she'd first met the enigmatic Clive and he'd asked her to stay with Niles. "He's like that. Little to say. Likes to order people around. But he's got the plan right here." She tapped her temple. "We just follow along."

"Is that so?" Jack wandered over to the chalk drawing. "I don't like not knowing the big picture. And such a short ETA? You people must have been involved in planning for some time. If not, there are too many variables that need to be worked out. If everyone isn't on the same page..."

"He and Clive are going to clash," Niles declared as he wandered off toward the garage office.

Indeed. But how would it flare up? Saskia almost hoped to see them go head to head. It would set Clive off and it would show her Jack's true nature. Something she was eager to see revealed. The man was a bit too calm and collected for her. Personally, she preferred her men more volatile with spring-loaded reactions.

On the other hand, cool and calm was a necessity for what they had planned. She was glad to have him on board.

"I guess we're roomies," she offered to Jack. "You know how to cook?"

"I can make a mean lasagna. But do you always follow Clive's directions like a sheep?"

"You wanted in on this crew, Angelo. You want to earn our trust? You gotta follow the rules."

"Yeah, I get it. Test out the new guy. Make him prove his worth."

"But mostly that we can rely on you when the clock is ticking and we need your eyes on the getaway."

"Don't worry about it, sweetie."

Sweetie. Ugh. But it was marginally better than Sass.

"Good. I'm in the mood for a hot homemade meal. Getting tired of microwave pizza. Let's head to your hotel and grab your things; then we'll get you settled at my place."

She strode toward the door, knowing Jack remained where he stood, staring down at the diagram on the concrete. Probably wondering what he'd gotten himself into.

A hell of a lot more than he bargained for, she knew that. And it was her job to make sure he didn't fall off course. Or it would be her neck in the wringer.

"Come on, Jack! If we leave now the car might still hold a little warmth."

* * * *

"It's the Hotel Hop," Jack offered as Saskia navigated the streets.

"I know." She caught his wondering lift of brow. "I am your vetter. I know things about you, Jack. Have to. It's my job."

Okay, then. Of course, she must have followed him to the bank somehow. He settled back and took everything in while the daylight still glimmered on the horizon. They weren't driving into Helsinki's heart. Nor was the bank in city center. But he needed to familiarize himself with the area. At the very least, the people, and the transportation, and the pulse of the traffic. The bank was at the edge of the city so they should be able to avoid rush hour traffic, if it came to that. Not that they'd be working at such times, but he had to know how the city operated at all hours.

"Do they have a tube system in Helsinki?"

"Yes, the metro. Most of the lines are aboveground but they've a few underground. But most important? They have an awesome sportswear store close to the hotel. You want to stop and pick up a warm coat?"

"You think I'm cold?"

"I think you must be a freakin' icicle. Come on, man, my tits are hard as rocks. I hate this weather. Why, of all places, did it have to be Finland in January?"

"Rocky tits, eh?"

"Figured you'd get stuck on that one."

"Is your bra black lace, too?"

"Not wearing one. Which is why they're frozen. What about you? Since you deem undergarments a good topic. Boxers or briefs?"

"Depends on my mood."

"A man of mystery. Gotta love that. So tell me about your nickname, Gentleman Jack. I hear it's because you're anything but a gentleman."

He squeezed a hand over his opposite fist, his jaw pulsing.

"I take offense," he said. "I am extremely gentlemanly. In fact, I always apologize before I push in a bloke's teeth or kick him in the kidneys. Mama Angelo taught me manners and respect."

Saskia laughed. "Oh, the fun we're going to have."

"Is that so? Roughing up blokes is your idea of a good time?"

"If they're deserving? Sure. I like some action tossed in to counteract the muscle-numbing concentration required for safe cracking."

"I find it hard to believe a woman like you can rough up any size man."

"Like me?" Saskia reached across before catching Jack's tie and pulling it hard.

He struggled as she pulled over to the curb, parking. Catching his hand with her other hand, she then head-butted him. He yelped. The move had been unexpected and he wasn't accustomed to fighting women.

She sat back with satisfaction. Jack's skull stung.

"Point taken," he said nastily. "You've a hard head, you know that?"

"It protects my smarts." With a wink, she pulled back into traffic.

* * * *

Once parked, Saskia got out and Jack followed as they strolled through the lobby. No sign of the redhead, but then, she'd gone home and was sleeping off her long shift. He walked at Saskia's side, aiming toward his room. But when he realized she was walking slightly ahead of him—and seemed to know where she was going—a suspicious tingle crimped the back of his neck.

Sure, as she'd stated, she had been following him. To keep an eye on him. And she could have easily followed him to the hotel, maybe even to his room. But he was keener than that. He hadn't sensed a tail when he'd arrived earlier today. And even after his attention had turned to the sexy receptionist, he'd kept his wits and hadn't noticed anything out of the ordinary. It took more than a couple shots of whiskey to confuse his senses.

Only thing he'd sensed was the hot receptionist's sweet arse in his hands as he'd banged her against the wall. Of course, that had ended...oddly. He pressed a hand over the passport he'd tucked inside his overcoat pocket.

Why did it seem that every woman he encountered of late had it in for him? Was it something in the frigid air?

When Saskia stopped at his room door and waited for him to slide in the keycard, Jack's face drained of blood. She knew this room. And the obvious reason was because of what he didn't want to consider. And yet... She *had* put on a disguise for the bank.

She widened her big blue eyes at him, waiting. The receptionist's eyes had been green. Of course, eye color could easily be changed.

Shite. Really?

He slipped in the keycard and pulled it out. The lock mechanism clicked and Saskia pushed the door inside. Jack stalked up behind her as she entered the room. When she turned to speak to him, Jack slammed his hand up under her chin and pinned her to the wall. "Who the bloody hell are you?"

Chapter 4

Now this was the kind of aggression she'd hoped to see in Jack Angelo.

Saskia reacted to the violent shove against the wall. She put up her feet against Jack's hips and kicked him away from her. The man rolled over the end of the bed. Lunging, she jumped on his back and grabbed him by the shoulders. Together they tumbled to the floor. She landed on top of his chest. He grunted as her knee dug into his ribs. A swing of her fist was caught by his hand about her wrist, sounding a smart smack of flesh.

With a deft flip, he slammed her to the floor, shoulders hitting the flat carpeting hard.

"I am not going to fight a woman," he insisted, even as he struggled to keep her from kicking him. A well-placed knee to her thigh compressed the femoral artery and Saskia hissed. "Is this the kind of man you said you wanted? Trying to rile me up, eh?"

"Just defending myself, actually."

He sprang up from her and stepped back. He rubbed a hand along his stubble-darkened jaw. "Who are you working for?"

Saskia rolled to a crouch, then stood and stepped back toward the window. Though she preferred having the door at her back. Why was he so suspicious of her? She had been the one to react to his sudden suspicion. And she'd only physically challenged him to show him he was dealing with a woman who could hold her own. She'd found it necessary over the years. Men always thought they were stronger than women.

It didn't require size or even muscle to defeat a man bigger than her. Smarts and quick thinking always triumphed. And if that didn't work, she could manipulate the shit out of his macho ego. Been there, done that. In this very room.

"You led me right to this room," Jack said.

Right. She'd hadn't been thinking. Stupid move!

"You couldn't have known which room I was staying in."

"I could have," she countered coolly. Then, with a grin, she decided it wasn't necessary to keep up the game any longer. At least, not this particular episode of the play. "Oh, Jack, yes! Slam me against the wall, you big Irish bull!"

He pointed at her, but couldn't get out any words. His lips thinned as his jaw tightened, and the veins in his neck looked ready to burst. If that tie were any tighter...

Saskia watched as recall darkened his gaze and he shook his head. "You?"

She performed a hair-fluffing motion, as if a glamour girl checking her style. "I've been told I make a ravishing redhead."

"With green eyes." Jack's jaw dropped open. Then he exclaimed, "I fucked you!"

"A quickie, but a goodie nonetheless. Now grab your things." She nodded toward the small carryon bag sitting on the table. "We're headed back to my place."

"Wait a minute. I'm not going anywhere with—that means you were also the—bloody hell!"

She sat on the chair before the window. The man needed a few minutes to process. And the way he flexed his fingers in and out of fists and stalked from the end of the bed to the nightstand was indication he could blow at any minute.

Really, he needed to loosen that tie.

"I figured the woman I screwed here this morning was the same as the one on the train. How else had she gotten my passport? Unless she was working with that other woman. But she was a fake. I saw the belly and tits—" He thrust an accusing finger at her. "I don't like this."

"I never asked your opinion of my methods. I was given an assignment to vet you. And I carried it out. Clive handed the passport information to Niles, who did a dark net search on you. I'm not sure what he found, but you passed muster, otherwise Clive wouldn't have accepted you so easily."

"Letting a little girl do his dirty work, eh?"

Saskia straightened, shifting back her shoulders. "I am not a little girl. I am a skilled master of disguise who knows how to get the job done."

Shoving his fists down at his sides, Jack gave her an assessing look that ended with a bob of his head. "That you are." With a heavy sigh, he went about gathering his things into the carryon, then strode toward the door. "You coming?"

That had been much easier than she'd anticipated. He'd accepted her con. Which went a long way toward his trustworthiness to Saskia. He knew how and why games were played in their line of work. He was either playing along now, or could graciously accept defeat.

Either way, she'd stay on guard. Her job security demanded she not let the man out of her sight. It had also been suggested that seduction could be necessary. Not a difficult challenge, especially when he was so handsome. And virile. Mm… She wanted more.

And she would have more.

Let the games continue.

* * * *

Forty-five minutes later they arrived at Saskia's small but long flat, three stories above a quaint main street that edged Helsinki's business district. Jack had unpacked the few groceries they'd picked up and now he rolled up his shirt sleeves and got to making pasta. Not because she'd requested he cook, but because he was hungry. He didn't intend to do anything to please the duplicitous woman.

She was tricky and remarkably skilled with disguises. To have insinuated herself into his path since he'd boarded the ferry at Stockholm had been genius.

Was it possible she'd been on him since before Stockholm? He didn't want to consider it. If so, that could only mean he was slipping. Big time.

Now he had to work with the sneaky Saskia Petrovik. He'd fucked her! She'd been…so good. Soft, hot, and more than willing. As horny as he had been. And that arse in his hands. Whew! How was he supposed to act around her now that he knew?

Cool and calm, Jack. Just keep it together for the next week.

And stay sharp. He would not let that woman fool him again any time soon. Of course, it was no longer in her interest to do so. They were a team now. Had to work as a crew to accomplish the task.

Would he ever be able to follow her anywhere now and not imagine that sweet arse in his hands?

They'd left his rental car behind at the Hotel Hop, because she'd argued that they'd be tied at the hip anyway. Jack had begrudgingly agreed. Now, he stood over the stove, stirring tomato sauce for the lasagna. Cooking took his mind away from all things covert and high stress. And illegal.

Just this one final job, and then he was going to walk away from it all. The Elite Crimes Unit would never willingly let him go. But he had a way around that small detail. Besides, he hadn't a choice. It was do or die right now for the Angelo family, and, despite the do or die promise he'd made to the ECU and vacillating over if it was the right thing to do, Jack couldn't stand by and let things fall apart in his own family. No matter the consequences. And they were grave.

It was around eight p.m., and the sky facing away from the city was already coal dark. Saskia sat on the long and low brown leather sofa, which faced a broad window overlooking the main street below. Streetlights provided illumination on the notebook she scribbled in. Her straight dark hair fell over her shoulders to her elbows. Dark eyeshadow outlined her blue eyes and gave her the look of an Egyptian queen.

He had held that woman against the wall and sunk his cock inside her. It had been a moment of need, of agreed want and desire. Something he hadn't felt guilty for, and normally never would.

But now to know she'd been using him...? How to feel about that heinous bit of information? He should let it slide. And he could. Maybe. But how many other men had she fucked to get what she needed? Did it bother her?

Why the hell did he care? He was not an upstanding citizen. Though while working for the ECU, his focus had been putting away criminals. But it was just another disguise he wore. That of getting along with others, pulling his weight, doing what he was told.

He had to stop thinking about this. It would only drive him crazy, and he needed to keep his cool.

"That smells delicious," she called without looking up from her notebook.

"It's my mother's recipe."

"Your Irish mother made lasagna?"

"What makes you think she was Irish?"

"Well, you've got the brogue. Though, I guess the last name doesn't fit."

Indeed, he did have the accent, though it battled with the Italian in him when he got angry. "My Irish mother learned to make lasagna from my Italian nonna," he said. "I'm half and half. But I got my Italian father's good looks."

"I guess you did."

He paused from stirring the sauce to analyze the tone of that reply. Had it been appreciative? He smiled to himself.

"So what did you get from your mother besides some recipes?" Saskia changed her tactic.

"Her temper."

She turned and looked at him over the back of the sofa. No wig, colored contacts, or disguise. Just plain Saskia. Or was she? Jack wasn't sure how to read her now. Could he ever trust someone so at ease with shifting her mannerisms and looks?

"If you've got your mother's temper, then who taught you to fight? I mean, I was told you're excellent muscle. And I have been at the receiving end of your fist."

"You have not. I pulled my punch in the hotel. Trust me, you'd know it if my fist met your face. Both my parents taught me how to protect myself and to make others understand it's not nice to screw the Angelos over. You like mushrooms?"

"Sure. So you only do bank jobs?"

As an ECU asset, his job required he play a role, fit himself in with the crew to suss out the true nature of their crime. But sometimes he didn't have to lie to create his character. It came naturally. Because, hell, he'd had a lot of experience.

"Not always. Smuggling is a jolly good time."

"And roughing people up?"

"It's called beating the bloody shite out of them. You can call it like it is. I'm a big boy."

"That you are. My big Irish bull." With a wink, she turned on the sofa and bowed her head over the notebook again.

And Jack wasn't sure how to take that comment. That he was a big bull because…? Of his cock? She knew him in ways he hadn't anticipated. He'd been inside her. With his big bull. Heh. Yeah, that's what she'd meant.

Maybe.

Ah hell, she was screwing with his mind again. He had to stop falling into her sneaky games.

Pouring the pot into the sink, he drained out the water and then grabbed a steamy sheet of limp pasta to lay in the pan. Tomato sauce with extra oregano—because he liked to actually smell it—and lots of ricotta. No meat. Saskia had pooh-poohed meat in the store. Whatever. He assembled the dish and put it in the oven.

Then, with just the quiet darkness and the sensual woman seated close with her back to him, he flexed his fingers in and out of fists. Nope. Not going to sit next to her. Felt awkward. And… *Don't think about her arse.*

He swung around the kitchen counter and pulled out his cell phone to look busy. This was a burner he'd picked up in Stockholm. The ECU did not have this number. The text he'd been expecting was there. It detailed a dollar amount in English pounds. The exchange location and time hadn't been set though. They were giving him time to collect a million pounds. Bloody fucking lovely. Jonny had really gotten in over his head this time. The idiot.

A return text wasn't necessary. Jack either complied or Jonny died.

Glancing over his shoulder, he exhaled. *Find your center, buddy. Just hold it together.*

Tucking away that phone, he pulled out the other, which was a fancy smartphone. He scrolled to the solitaire game he often played when he needed to zone out and go mindless to defeat the anxiety that always threatened to come out as punches. He had so much to worry about he could almost relate to those times his mother had cursed him and his brother for going missing for days and leaving her an absolute mess wondering if they were dead and dumped in the Irish Sea.

He'd do right by her this time. Or die trying.

Half an hour later, the lasagna was cut and consumed. Saskia impressed Jack by eating three large squares. He hadn't had a decent meal since the ferry ride. There were no leftovers.

"My thanks to your mother," she said with a wink. "There's something about a momma's boy."

"Oi. I am not a momma's boy," he defended.

"Don't take offense. I like a man who respects women. You could have done some real damage to me in the hotel room." Another wink.

"Beating on women is not my thing."

"What if one came at you with a knife?"

"I know how to disarm an assailant without harming them. Not too much anyway. A little hurt does serve its purpose. Depends on whether or not the woman has pissed me off bloody right."

"I'll remember that for future reference. I'm going to hit the hay. It's been a long day, what with the ferry ride and, seriously, that bladder routine was the real thing. I had to pee so bad waiting for you to finally return and have a little conversation with me.

"You can have the room to the right of the bathroom," she offered as she aimed toward the back of the apartment. "There's fresh sheets on the bed, but no extra blanket. Sorry! The place only provided so many linens. And it does get cold in here at night. I think the building superintendent keeps the temperature regulated to just above freezing. See you in the morning, Jack Angelo. Sweet dreams."

She strolled back toward the bedrooms, pulling the shirt over her head as she did so, revealing her bare back—no bra—which successfully kickstarted Jack's wet dreams for the night.

Chapter 5

Thankful he'd gotten a good night's sleep after days of traveling, Jack soaped up under the steaming hot water. He'd slept like a dead dog, despite the chilly room. Which was why he had the water cranked as hot as possible. First item on the list today? Buy an electric blanket. It would be an expense worth its weight in gold.

Turning to face the water stream, he slicked off the soap from his eyes and mouth. He couldn't smell the soap and just hoped it didn't have a floral scent. Not very manly.

When a hand suddenly stroked up the side of his ribcage, he jumped and yelped. Slapping a palm to the tile wall, he prevented a sudden slip. Turning around in the tub, he faced a very naked, wet woman, who was laughing.

"What the bloody hell?"

She was already soaping up her arms and her tits jiggled as she slicked over them. Nice big handfuls, that. The nipples were red and so tight.

"Only got five minutes of hot water a day," Saskia said. "You're going to have to share, Angelo."

"I don't think so." His hand instinctively moved down to protect his privates. "You're... You're naked."

"Yeah? That's generally how a person takes a shower, smart guy. Move over. You're clean. Let me at the hot stuff while I still have a chance."

"This is not right. You can't climb in with a bloke and think it doesn't matter."

"Oh, come on, Jack. What is the problem? You've already fucked me."

"Yeah, but you weren't naked then."

Her laughter did not alleviate the tense situation. "Think about that one for a second," she said. "You didn't even manage to get my clothes off you were so hot for me."

"As you were for me."

"Oh yeah." She slapped a hand to his chest and curled in her nails.

The erotic dig sparked through Jack's system, and his cock bobbed. He was not going to let her have this round. He couldn't. He just… "Where's the towel? Christ, don't press up against me."

"Why? Mm, you get a hard-on in the shower. Now that is impressive."

With a curse, Jack gripped his erection to keep it from brushing any slick, sensual part of her body. He stepped out of the shower, away from the woman who now hummed a tune as she began to rinse under the water that, indeed, was growing cooler. He grabbed a towel and wrapped it around his waist, but it was short, and his hard-on poked through the gap.

"Christ on a piece of toast."

She was good. He could admit to that defeat. Again.

Stomping out of the bathroom, dripping, he sucked in his breath as the chill air outside the steam-filled room worked to instantly deflate his boner. He left the bathroom door open and waved his hands toward it. Maybe some of the cold air would sweep in on her. She deserved the brisk slap to her senses. And those tits.

Shaking his head, he wandered into the bedroom, thinking a smart man would have not abandoned ship so quickly. He might have even gone round two with the bird who apparently seemed open to anything involving naked bodies. Or even only partially disrobed bodies.

Was it a game? Or something more?

He didn't like to feel off-balance when working with others. And most especially with a woman whom he was attracted to. That woman had the ability to throw him off in spades.

He pulled on a clean shirt, then cursed because he hadn't dried off yet and his wet skin soaked the shirt, making it impossible to tug up the sleeves beyond his biceps.

Dropping his arms, and sighing, all he could manage was a defeated, "Shite."

* * * *

While her main goal had been to take advantage of the hot water, Saskia wouldn't discount catching the man by surprise and setting him off kilter. The look on his face would serve her giggles for days. The instant his gaze had averted to her breasts, she'd noted his erection had sprung upright. Oh, how easy it was to control the male species with but a flash of tit.

She had cornered the bull and made him lower his mighty horns.

Something not quite so satisfying about that win. It felt...stolen. Huh.

As the water quickly cooled, she rinsed her hair and then stepped out just as it turned to fluid streams of ice.

There were no clean towels. The apartment hadn't provided any more than two, and the other was sitting in the hamper waiting for the laundromat. But there was a foldable blow dryer tucked away on a shelf above the vanity. Flipping it on, she blasted the air up and down her body, drying off in the comfort of warm spurts of air.

Noticing Jack had left the bathroom door open, she didn't close it. She wasn't hung up about nudity and certainly she was not a woman to tease a man.

Not a man like Jack Angelo. She'd had a taste of him, and she was ready for the full course. Whenever he was willing to serve it. But she wouldn't push him. Not too much, anyway. But it was a delicate balance, this sharing of the apartment, working together, and her being assigned to tail the man's every move. Alliances would be tested, for certain.

Saskia knew exactly where her alliances stood, and she would not falter from them. She loved her job, and wanted to continue doing it as long as she was able.

Now, to learn just where Jack Angelo stood on the scale of trust and alliance.

Her cell phone rang, vibrating on the vanity. It was Clive. He relayed that he'd received the heavy-duty industrial drill he'd ordered specifically for this job but the shipper was holding on to it and asking for more than the agreed price. Clive wanted to bring Jack along as muscle. He was on his way to her apartment right now.

"I'll send him down in five," Saskia said and hung up. "Jack, darling!"

The man peeked into the steamy bathroom from out in the hallway. He'd put on the suit and tie. She was still naked, but her hair was now dry. He stepped back so as not to look directly at her. Cute.

"Ah, come on, Jack. You never seen a naked woman before?"

He curled around the corner, drawing his gaze up and down her length. With a shrug he offered a forced, "All the time."

Oh, sweet man who was struggling with so much right now. Was it the Catholic in him? With his bloodline he had to be Catholic. All that delicious guilt that she could dip her fingers into and stir into a mess.

"That was Clive on the phone," she said, as she fluffed her hair. Tilting a hip against the vanity, she thrust back a shoulder, which made her breasts jiggle. "He needs your tough guy skills. He's stopping by to pick you up in five minutes. He drives a black BMW."

"Fine. You going to get dressed today?"

She shrugged. "You like me naked?"

With a groan that made her wonder if he wasn't sexually repressed, the man wandered off, but he called out, "I'm going to buy a blanket while I'm out. You need anything?"

"Bring back something to make for supper!"

Hey, if the man liked to cook, she wasn't the woman to stand in his culinary way.

Now, how to get what she wanted from him—more sex, and preferably longer and slower this time—without compromising the job? Wasn't as if sex was off the table. The only trouble was how it would mess with the man's mind if he screwed her again. For the sake of the job, she needed him to be in top form.

Was Jack Angelo like an athlete who needed to abstain before the big event, or would stoking his fire serve him the focus and energy required to pull off the heist?

"I'll have to dive in and take my chances," she muttered as the man closed the door behind him and left her alone and suddenly shivering.

* * * *

Clive pulled the bimmer before a long stretch of sea-weathered and rusted warehouses that were filed in rows before the Baltic sea. This was not a main shipping port but rather an old and forgotten cove that rarely saw any sizable arrivals.

Clive hadn't said much to Jack on the drive here, other than to ask how it was going with Sass. Fine by him. He wasn't a chatty person. And besides, a man could determine more about another man from his silences. Clive was overconfident, but not stupid.

Jack was the first to ask, "Shipment gone bad?"

"The shipment arrived," Clive confirmed. "But the receiver is holding tight to it until I cough up more than the pre-arranged price. That makes him an idiot."

"You've worked with him before?"

"No, and I never will again. This should be an easy pickup. Go in, flash some muscle, walk out with the drill at the price we agreed on. But, like most idiots, they tend to push things beyond their control. You prepared to make the man stand by his word, Jack?"

"Always," Jack offered calmly. It was what he did. Use muscle to show others the wrongness of their ways. It had worked on him, after all.

His father had never missed a punch. He shrugged off his overcoat, then adjusted his tie. "Lead the way."

"I like you, Jack. A man of few words, but your actions speak boldly. I'm glad I took Sass up on her recommendation for you." The man opened the car and got out.

And Jack followed, but now he had that information pinging his thoughts. *Saskia* had recommended him? How did she know him? She didn't. And as far as he knew, the ECU had been instrumental in insinuating him onto this crew. Were his previous suspicions true? That she'd been following him far longer than from Stockholm? Didn't make sense. And his reputation for being a team player on bank heists could have only come from information years ago when he'd been out and working the streets.

He'd have to ask Saskia about that later.

For now, it was time to pull on the thug. Jack buttoned his suit coat and smoothed a palm down his yellow tie. It was frigging cold, but that just helped to keep the sweat from his brow. Right?

He needed a vacation. In Jamaica.

Clive paused at the door and turned to say over his shoulder, "Stay behind me until it's necessary to move elsewhere."

"Always."

He wasn't stupid. As the muscle, Jack kept his eyes on all the players while standing behind the key operator. He'd know when it was his turn to step in. Thanks to his twitchy nose for the suspicious.

They strode inside the blessedly warm building, and a narrow hallway filtered them toward a small room cluttered with ropes of all thicknesses coiled and hung on the walls. Sea-fishing equipment, Jack figured, as he took in an assortment of massive wood pulleys and rusted iron hooks. It looked like a collector's messy stash, not an organized inventory of anything that might prove of use.

Clive stopped abruptly and Jack stopped three feet behind him, hands calmly hung at his sides, as he took in the scene. A small man, no taller than a fourth grader, stood behind a desk with his hands up. Wire-rimmed spectacles made his eyes look five sizes bigger than they were. And the reason for his quiet submission stood before the desk, holding a Beretta 8000 aimed at the small man.

"Busy man," Clive commented.

The gunman quickly swung his arm toward Clive and Jack. His gaze darted. His mouth was stretched tensely. The pistol was a small bit of aluminum and gunpowder, but easy to conceal. "Who the hell are you two?"

Clive put up his hands in placation. Jack kept his hands down at his sides and his attention split between the gunman and the man behind the desk.

"We have an issue with Mr. Koskinen," Clive offered. "Much like, I presume, you appear to have an issue?"

"He stole from me," the gunman blurted out. He redirected his aim toward the short man, but then back at Clive and Jack. "Get out of here. This is my deal."

"I had an appointment with this gentleman," Koskinen said with a nod toward Clive. "You, I did not."

The gunman pointed his pistol toward the ceiling and fired. Building debris sprinkled down to land on the desktop.

Clive turned to Jack. Jack got the message.

Stepping quickly, he swung around Clive and reached the gunman just as he swung the pistol toward him. Catching his wrist and pointing the gun downward, the man managed to get off another shot, even as Jack wrangled an arm about his neck. Squeezing his fingers about his wrist and compressing the bones, the gunman yelped and the weapon dropped to the floor. Jack's firm bending of his fingers backward produced a satisfying *snap*.

Jack twisted the man around to face the wall of ropes and slammed him against a thick coil. His captive spun quickly, his agility surprising Jack, but he was prepared to block the fist that soared toward his face. Kneeing his opponent in the kidneys dropped him to his knees. Bending, Jack grabbed his arm and twisted it behind his back, slamming a foot to his shoulder to force him to lower his head to the floor. He moved his grip down to the broken hand and applied pressure. This time the yowl progressed to a pleading wail.

"Kill him!" the man behind the desk encouraged.

"Whatever issue the two of you have," Jack said calmly, "I'll leave for you to take care of. Clive?"

"Where's the drill?" Clive asked.

"The price is twenty thousand euros," the deskman had the audacity to say.

"We agreed to five, and I am a man of my word. Are you a man of your word?"

Jack crushed the toe of his shoe against the back of his captive's head, while slowly and firmly pressing into the broken hand bone, forcing out a groan from the gunman. He gave his arm a tighter twist, just for good measure. "Sorry about that," he said. "Needed to be done."

"Isn't he a gentleman?" Clive asked no one in particular. "Now hand over the drill or I'll have my Gentleman Jack show you the error of your ways, Koskinen."

"Where's the cash?"

Clive tugged out an envelope from his pocket and tossed it on the desk. The short man eyed it for a few moments. He had nothing to counter that action. And if he were smart, he'd take the cash. Jack didn't see any weapons, though he wouldn't rule out a gun in a desk drawer or taped under the desk.

"Fine. It's over there." He gestured toward a wood crate on the floor beneath a coiled rope.

"Open it for him," Jack said before Clive could make the mistake of looking in the box himself. He twisted his shoe against his prisoner's neck. He should have blacked out by now. For a gangly bit he was hardy.

"Do as the gentleman asks," Clive said.

With a hell of a lot of huffing and sighing, the short man opened the crate with a crowbar and showed Clive what was inside. It was a box for a large machine that would require two men to carry out. Jack did not like that scenario, especially with an idiot gunman waiting to get served what he felt was just. Whatever that was.

"It's good." Clive toed the box. "Doing business with you has not been a pleasure. But I'm going to guess you prefer it that way. Have your idiot help carry it out to the car." Clive turned and strode down the hallway.

Really? That did not leave Jack in a good position. He wasn't about to let this bastard move any more than he already had. Jack flipped the man over and delivered him an upper cut under the jaw. Knocked him out cold.

As he rose, he lunged to grab the abandoned gun. He ejected the magazine. Saw there were only three bullets, and emptied them into his palm. Calmly, he set the gun by the head of the unconscious man, and slipped the bullets into his pocket.

With a nod to Koskinen, Jack said, "Looks like you're the idiot. Help me carry this thing out or I'll pocket the cash myself."

Shoving the envelope in his front pants pocket, the man then lifted one end of the crate, which did have a rope handle on it. Jack lifted the other and led the way down the hallway, listening carefully. Not a sound of any weapon being picked up. But he always stayed alert until the coast was clear. And the coast was never clear until he could not see the people or the place in view.

He was getting too fucking old for this racket. Bruising his fists across jaws, cheeks, skulls, into ribs, and right into the sensitive esophagus. He'd once gotten a rise out of the act of violence. It had simply been what he did. It was all he had ever known. He'd grown up in a violent family.

Beating the shite out of one another was how they resolved conflicts and got taught lessons.

But he'd beaten all his anger out years ago. Honestly, he had nothing left he could summon that would personally offend him.

Now, the act of swinging his fists had become merely a job. One that was becoming harder and harder to be proud of. He could only justify beating on arseholes for so much longer before it all crumbled. His world. His life.

But what waited for him on the other side? Was there another side?

The chill air smacked him as he walked out, and he and Koskinen shoved the crate inside the backseat of the BMW. It just fit.

"And don't come back!" Koskinen said with a flip of the bird to them before he scrambled back inside the building.

Keeping an eye on the building as they pulled away, Jack could only smirk as Clive congratulated him on a job well done.

Indeed. And yet, who had they marked as their enemies now?

Chapter 6

Jack read the note Saskia had left taped to the fridge door: Left for the garage. See you later.

He tapped the note, then tugged if off and let it flutter into the trash bin. Clive had said he'd see him around six, and... It was only three. So. Since his watcher was also absent, he had a few hours to himself.

He tugged out the burner phone and reread the text stating the demand for a one million pound ransom. He wasn't going to waste this time.

* * * *

At sight of Jack leaving her building across the street and strolling down the sidewalk, Saskia slid off the coffee shop bar stool and tossed her paper cup in the trash bin. Pulling down the blue knit skull cap over her short blond hair, she walked outside.

The homeless guy who was begging from his beat-up piece of cardboard square stepped in front of her. "Dude, you got some change?"

She dug into her pocket and slapped a couple two-euro coins into his hand. "Thanks, man!"

Walking onward, she smirked. Satisfied her disguise made her appear a thin man, perhaps a teenaged boy in holey jeans and a thick black down jacket. A knit cap boasting the Finnish hockey team—the Lions—fit snuggly over short blond hair that dusted her ears. She kept pace with Jack as he walked with purpose. He knew where he was going. And she had some idea too. There was a reason she had chosen the apartment in this area of the city. Not only was it reasonably close to the garage, it was in the vicinity of another location that put up all her red flags.

Actually the apartment had been pre-chosen for her before she'd arrived in Helsinki four days before Jack had gotten here. She did what she was told.

If he turned at the next street...

And... He turned right. Good call on the neighborhood selection. Sometimes her employer seemed to have an almost prescient knowing of things.

Crossing the street before a bus that had stopped to let off passengers onto the salted sidewalk, she walked with a swing to her step, how one might if they were listening to music through earbuds and were generally happy with their life.

She was happy with her life. When she was working a job, she was most happy. And this kind of work? It was as if she'd been born to it. Perhaps she had been. She'd learned safe cracking from her brother—may he rest in peace—and witnessing her grandmother's changing styles, looks, and costumes had set her on a lifelong love for assimilating herself into the world in the manner in which she wished to be accepted.

Respected and trustworthy? She could put on a suit, some sideburns, and, with some heavy-duty makeup contouring, she could stand before a board meeting while presenting figures for the latest corporate takeover.

Sexy and smart? The librarian look with a tight pencil skirt, thick glasses, and hair coiled in victory rolls was one of her favorite disguises. It also came in handy when role-playing for sex.

Sweet, innocent and not altogetherthere? She could fashion herself a teenager with little makeup and non-figure-conforming clothing. The times she'd needed to be a kid to wheedle her way into a tense situation and feel out the players were numerous.

Jack turned down an alley, so she quickened her steps and peered around the corner of the brick building where he'd turned. He shifted at the hip to look over his shoulder so she slipped out of view. Waiting a few seconds, she looked again. Almost missing him, his back leg disappeared as he walked in through a doorway.

Hastening her steps, she avoided the slushy channels from cars that had pummeled the snow and ice to soup, and, fully aware of the camera above the door she neared, stepped lightly across the alley to sidle up alongside the door. There wasn't a sign or identifier on the door. And no windows. The camera positioned a foot above the metal door did not sweep, nor would it mark her with her back against the wall. Whoever was inside would know who was coming and allow admittance.

She didn't need to show herself or go inside. If her intel was correct, this was the place of business for a doctor who specialized in adjustment surgeries. Not plastic surgery that could change a person's face and characteristics. Rather, he removed tattoos, or added them, took out teeth and replaced them with a GPS chip and a crown. He even removed tracking devices that could have been placed anywhere on the body. And he charged a pretty penny.

Backing away from the door, Saskia shoved her hands in her coat pockets and kicked at the snow wedged up along the slushy channels as she walked toward the main street. Stationing herself at the building corner, she had only to wait another ten minutes before Jack swung out and walked toward her. He gave no clue that a procedure had been performed, but it had been mere minutes. Nothing had happened, except perhaps a conversation and scheduling an appointment.

Back pressed to the brick building Saskia waited, nodding her head, as if in time to music. Jack turned the corner, remarking her with the side eye, but kept on walking. Just another kid, he must have thought.

When he'd walked a good block away, she swung around the side of the building, and using the relative privacy of the shadowed alleyway, she slid off her black coat and turned it inside out to reveal the white reversible lining. Put it back on. Then she tugged off her cap and wig, and tucked away the hairpiece in the zippered pocket. She shook out her naturally dark hair. After pulling a tiny packet with an alcohol face wipe from another pocket, she then wiped away the makeup from her cheeks that had given her a sunken look.

Turning about the corner, she inspected her work in the window of a pastry shop advertising fresh scones. One last swipe to a streak of contouring along her jawbone and she was back to plain old Saskia. Just another face in the crowd. It was her most difficult disguise, but she never stayed in it too long.

Jack Angelo had made the move she had hoped he would not make. Not that she had a stake in what he did or did not do. But since meeting him, and deciding he was an all right kind of guy? She had to admit, at the very least, she liked him. Didn't want to see him get in any trouble. Because some troubles were devastating, and no man could rise up from them.

And as far as she knew, he would be breaking a promise if he went through with an appointment with the man he'd just visited. She liked her men rough and rowdy, but also, true and possessed of integrity.

Her big Irish bull was making her wonder about him now.

* * * *

Jack arrived at the garage and noted how his shoes crunched over the snowpack. Sounded like he was walking over Styrofoam. It snowed in

London, his home base, and he'd been to Siberia and even Minnesota in the States, but those had been brief visits. Who on God's green earth chose to live year-round in a place like this? Not simply for a visit, but permanently. It was colder than a witch's tit. And that was mighty cold.

Entering the digital code for the garage that Saskia had given him, the metal door popped open and he swept in, rubbing his hands together and mentally marking on his list the need for thermal gloves. Clive's crop of silver hair was nowhere in sight, but there was a light on in the office. Saskia and Niles stood across the garage, looking over the plans drawn on the floor.

"Jack!" Niles greeted him with a thumbs-up. The man did like his turtlenecks, and today's choice of black blended with his skin tone. He wore earbuds decorated with gold skulls, but only one was in an ear, the other swung across his chest.

"You have a relaxing afternoon?" Saskia asked as Jack approached. "Clive has been here for hours."

"He said not to meet him here until six." Jack checked his watch. "It's exactly five fifty-nine. I'm early."

"So you are."

She slid her gaze up and down his body in a manner that said so many things. I've seen you naked in the shower was the first thing. I've scammed you not once, not twice, but three times was the second thing. And the third resulted in that judgy look females always gave a man when they had deemed him not up to snuff.

He didn't need the judgment. And he really didn't need the mind games.

"Niles has plotted our steps from entry through the wall in the accounting office that sits next to the bank to the safe," Saskia explained while pointing it out on the floor drawing. "It's an easy walk. Even the drill through the wall should prove quick with Clive's new toy."

"If you consider two hours quick," Niles chimed in. "That's how long it should take to drill through the office's brick wall and then the bank's reinforced concrete wall, if I've guesstimated the schematics correctly."

"No building plans?" Jack asked.

"I was able to access the floor plans for the entire block through city records," Niles explained. "But the bank plan is vague. To be expected. It meets the standard wall thickness using concrete and brick. And the bank is over a hundred years old, so I expect that thickness. The building materials weren't as strong back then, but they reinforced them with concrete and used a lot of rebar."

"No steel barriers?"

"Not that the floor plans show."

"Then it'll be quicker than two hours with that drill," Jack said. "More like an hour."

"You think?" Niles scratched his head. "I admit this is my first time with this sort of drill."

"I've used something similar before," Jack said. "It cuts through concrete like butter. Just need to have a water source to keep it lubricated."

"There's a bathroom in the accounting office. We'll run a hose from there to the wall."

"Sounds like you've got it all worked out." Jack crossed his arms over his chest. "We should be able to move on this sooner rather than later."

"Are you in a rush, Jack?" Clive pushed the industrial drill on a low cart across the concrete carport and planted it next to where Niles was working on his laptop. "The party's only just begun. Don't you want to stick around and get to know us?"

Jack quirked a brow. Since when did the man suddenly want to chat over tea? He was here for a job. Get in, get out. Get paid. Bye bye.

And in the process he intended to learn as much as he could about the operation and exactly what the take-away was.

"Just kidding." Clive patted the drill. "I say we go in this Saturday. Banks are only open Monday through Fridays here in Finland. It'll allow that one extra day for discovery and for us to get the hell out of this icy Dodge."

"Works for me." Saskia toed the drill. The diameter of it was a foot across, and the teeth were diamond-tipped. "We going to test this monster out?"

"Jack, that's your job," Clive said. "You and Niles form the setup for testing and give it a go. I want to make sure the five thousand, and the broken fingers, were worth it. Sass." Clive nodded toward the office. "Let's talk."

Jack and Niles watched as Saskia followed Clive to the office and they closed the door behind them.

Niles exchanged a raised brow with Jack.

"An office romance?" Jack asked teasingly. But he didn't feel the humor like he should have. Clive didn't seem Saskia's sort. And besides... Well, he probably shouldn't go there.

Niles chuckled. "Unlikely. You do know that if Clive were to hit on any in the crew it would probably be you, mate?"

"What?" Jack's jaw dropped open as he realized what the man was implicating. "Really?"

Niles nodded. "I'm a married man. And Sass is, well, Sass. I don't think you have anything to worry about, though. The man's all business. Still. You do have that rugged bad boy thing going for you." Niles winked. "You ready to drill something?"

The man's choice of words made Jack wince.

* * * *

The office was chillier than the garage, which surprised Saskia. Then again, the main heating ducts blasted air into the vast space, and she didn't notice any vents in here. This tiny room could use a portable heater.

She zipped up her down coat. Her breath fogged before her in intermittent clouds as she waited for Clive to speak. He sat on a creaky chair behind a stack of pallet crates. When they'd moved in, the office had been empty save the chair, and he'd brought in some pallets on which to lay out his papers and whatever else he deemed necessary.

"Is our Gentleman Jack on the up and up?" he finally asked.

Saskia shrugged. "Far as I can determine."

"As far as you can determine? He's living with you. It's your job to figure him out, Sass. Make sure the new guy doesn't work us over."

"He doesn't have much to say."

"No, he doesn't. But he's got a smart right fist. I'm glad I had him along for the pickup today. He truly is the gentleman you told me about."

"Gentleman Jack always apologizes before he puts your teeth into the back of your skull. That's his reputation. But he's also capable of making a mean lasagna." She blew out a whistle and shook her head in appreciation.

"He's a cook?"

"Best meal I've had in over a week."

"You soft on him, Sass?"

"No." Yes. "Just isn't often a woman gets a meal cooked for her. And by a man. I'm not going to refuse."

"I wouldn't either. You've served me well in bringing him into the crew, Sass."

"No problem." Her shoulders relaxed an inch.

"Now, I need you to get something for me before we move on Saturday. It's for a side project of mine that's happened to overlap with this job."

"Anything."

"I know you're an expert in poisons."

"I am." All her alarm bells suddenly started to clang. Of course, Clive would have some intel on her. But only that which had been carefully selected for others to dig up. But still, this subject put up her hackles. Saskia maintained her calm façade. "What's up?"

"Just need a bit of Folidol."

"Folidol?" Scanning her knowledge of poisons, she hit on the old compound that had once been used in the 1970s. "You mean parathion?"

"Yes, I think so. Was once used as an insecticide?"

"Right. When pure, it's a white crystalline solid."

"Perfect."

"It's been banned from use since mid-last century. Very poisonous to humans. It kills upon ingestion. You got a reason to take out a hit on someone, Clive?"

"Like I said, it's for a side project. No questions, eh?"

"That's cool." But not really.

"Is it something you can make?"

"It would be easier, and quicker, to buy some on the black market. Germany is a good shopping spot for such a thing. Might even be able to dredge some up here in the city."

"Can you do that for me?"

He hadn't explained why he needed it. And her light suggestion that he wanted to take someone out had been brushed aside. She wasn't averse to murder—for all the right reasons—and such a poison wouldn't be requested for any other reason than that. "I...will have to look into the availability."

"You've got two days. Don't let me down, Sass."

And she took that as a dismissal.

With a curt nod, Saskia left the room. Outside the closed office door, she bowed her head and breathed in the warm air. It didn't do much to stifle the new shiver that had clutched about her spine. That wasn't from the temperature.

Getting the poison would not be a problem. The problem was this new wrench. What the hell would a man who held up banks possibly want with an insecticide known to kill, and in a horrible and slowly painful manner?

Chapter 7

Locating the parathion was much easier than Saskia had expected. And the ease with which she'd arranged a purchase put a wicked tingle at the base of her spine. She was an expert in handling and creating poisons. Thanks to her grandmother's boyfriend. He'd worked as a pharmaceutical engineer until he'd met grandma Petrovik, and then had turned to creating his own drugs and selling them for top dollar. Yet he'd quickly learned it was easiest and the least noticed by law enforcement to sell poisons instead of addictive recreational drugs.

Criminals were generally the only ones interested in such substances, because the legitimate companies could purchase such poisons in bulk and not be questioned whether or not they were killing humans. The argument was that they were not. The truth was that decades of exposure to chemicals and small amounts of toxins in the food system was slowly killing, if not seriously damaging the health, of millions. And that was how grandma's boyfriend had justified his work. Everyone was doing it.

Since she liked to learn new things, and had a good knowledge of anything that could prove profitable, Saskia had dabbled with poisons under his tutelage. But she had never used or sold them when she knew the result would be a death. Generally, that was the intended result.

So Clive's need for poison troubled her. A side job? She hadn't thought the quiet, methodical bank robber was the murderous sort. Maybe he was selling it to someone else? Possible. But really, what did she know about him? The last job in Belgium had resulted in the crew walking out of the bank empty-handed.

They'd gotten paid, and now she'd been hired for a new job.

Something was missing from that scenario.

Was the poison related to the lacking booty? She couldn't dismiss the possibility that it was. But it made little sense. They weren't robbing the bank during business hours. No one would be inside when they struck. So even if, by some weird chance, Clive intended to use the poison to waylay possible security guards, it just wouldn't happen.

Had he intention to use it on them, the crew? Get inside, open the safe, and oops, spilled some poison. You're all going to die while I make a clean getaway with millions.

That didn't ring true to her. Clive wouldn't be so sloppy. And there was no reason for him to kill off the crew. The financial arrangements had already been made. It wasn't as though they had to grab enough cash to cover everyone's tab. As soon as the job was completed, money would be wired to their accounts in payment.

An odd method of paying the crew when really, grabbing some extra cash while in the vault was as easy. But Saskia suspected that Clive answered to someone higher up, and that someone ordered the heist and wrote out the paychecks. So to speak.

Had poison been a part of that order? No way to know. Even with this disturbing news she intended to see this heist through. She had to, in order to keep her cover and her thumb on Jack Angelo.

Thinking of whom, Jack strolled into the living room and sat on the sofa next to her. She quickly closed the laptop and set it on the floor.

"Making secret rendezvous plans?" he asked with an almost wink. It was one of those looks that implied a wink, but didn't deliver.

"Aren't you the teaser this fine morning? Get an extra jolt of caffeine in your coffee?"

"I recognize a redirect when I hear one. Fine." He'd been stringing the yellow tie about his neck when he'd sat, and now he focused on making the knot. "Not willing to divulge your secret liaisons with all the men you plan to dupe into having sex with you?"

"Don't be an asshole, Jack."

"Does that mean I'm your only dupe?"

She wasn't going to answer that one.

"Okay. What are the plans for today?"

"I have an errand to run in a few hours. Did you and Niles test the drill last night?" She'd left after Clive's request, unable to concentrate on watching the boring turn of the drill for an hour.

"We did, and it's slick. Cuts through concrete and rebar much faster than Niles had anticipated. We've modified our entry time from two hours to one."

"That's awesome. What did Clive say?"

"Not much."

"As usual."

He adjusted the knot of his tie and smoothed a hand down the slick of yellow. Today he smelled like her peppermint soap from the shower. It had a strangely attractive effect on her, made so masculine with his natural intensity.

"What did Clive have to say to you yesterday, alone in his office?"

"Why? You jealous, Jack?"

"Not of a man who prefers other men."

"So you figured that one out?"

"Niles told me. I'm a little slow on the whole gaydar thing."

"Clive is a manly bit of gay. Too bad he bats for the other team. He's one sexy man."

"You think so?" He spread his arms across the back of the couch, not quite comfortable, but more claiming his territory. "What qualifies as sexy to you?"

She shrugged, liking his subtle uncertainty and the way the conversation was veering. It kept the focus off the real concerns. "Stubble and silver hair? I never thought I'd say this, but the combination is major sexy. And just enough of a tan to give him a healthy glow. I think he's a health nut, too. Probably puts down kale and wheat grass shakes, or something awful like that."

"Kale." Jack mocked a shudder. "That stuff looks mean."

Saskia laughed. His assessment of the vegetable was right on. Then she dipped her head and looked at him through her lashes. "But what I also find sexy is not so much hair and stubble." She averted her gaze to his head, which barely sported a quarter inch of dark hair, and he must have trimmed his stubble this morning because it was a mere shadow on his skin. It outlined his square jaw. A warrior's face, he had. Rough, rugged, and the broken nose added the bit of wild that really got her going. "Also a certain confidence."

"So stubble seems to be important." He rubbed his jaw. "Not abs and muscles?"

"Oh, for sure. A well-honed physique is always a nice touch. But the real sex appeal is all in here." She tapped her skull and pulled up a leg to tuck under her other leg, turning on the sofa to face him. "Not necessarily brains or smarts—although, that is a given—but what is going on in the man's head. What makes him tick? What is important to him? What isn't?"

"That's a whole lot of philosophical stuff just to get to sexy," Jack said.

She tapped his shirt cuff. "What makes you tick, my Irish bull?"

He shrugged. "A sizeable paycheck and the promise of a challenge."

"That's what's important to you? Money?"

"Most of the time, yes. But foremost? Family," he said with so much conviction Saskia felt it vibrate in her veins.

"Family. Yeah. Family." Even the family who had taught her to be a criminal? She loved her parents, and couldn't imagine living a life other than the one she grew up in. But she often wondered what life for her might have been like had she grown up in a normal, suburban atmosphere. And if granny Petrovik had not decided to raise her after her parents had abandoned her, following her brother's death. "Did your family teach you the trade? You said something about your parents teaching you to fight for respect."

"You know it. A man is only as useful as the skills he hones. And he's judged on how he treats others. And always respect family. Never let them down."

"You've never let down your family?"

"Never have. Don't intend to start."

"Would you go to jail for family?"

"Already have."

Did she know that? She couldn't recall reading that in the intelligence report on Jack Angelo. "How much time did you put in?"

"Two years."

"And now you're right back to the same life."

"I know nothing else. What about you?"

"Prison time? No. Not yet. And I don't intend to take up space in a tiny cell anytime in the future. I'm damn good at what I do."

"Cocky. I like that." The husky tone of his acknowledgement stirred in Saskia's core. So sexy. He rubbed his jaw. "What do you do, exactly? Besides putting on a costume and duping innocents."

"Like you?"

He nodded with a wince.

"A little of this. A little of that. I like to fight, run grifts, occasionally broker a stolen goods deal. I am a Jack of all trades, if you will. But safe-cracking is my forte. I can't wait to get my hands on the vault. Niles says it's an oldie but a goodie."

"You familiar with the vault?"

"Yes, it's supposed to be a Richardson 2700. It's got a glass plate and a digital interior monitor, but I'm all about the hands-on old-style crack. I've tapped into two previously. Gaining access will not be a problem, Jack. You can trust I'll hold up my end of the bargain."

"I hadn't worried that you would not."

He offered her a small smile. But it was in his eyes that she saw the genuine interest and perhaps even a glint of desire. The man had been giving her the eye since they'd met (even when he'd not known she was who she was). But this look was gentler, maybe even longing.

Saskia leaned in closer until his faint peppermint scent teased at her senses.

"You never kissed me in the hotel room, Jack," she said.

"That was a fast fuck. We were a speeding train wreck."

"You call it a wreck. I call it a good time."

"I agree with the good part." He shook his head. "But to be honest, it feels weird now."

She pulled back from their closeness, suddenly at a loss. "Why? Do you feel some moral obligation not to have sex with me again, because...?"

"In the hotel, you were a means to relieving some exhaustion and frustration over my encounter with the pregnant woman."

"You mean me."

"Right. You threw me with that one. But now, I know you. And this." He waggled his finger between them to indicate what she had hoped could become a kiss. "Things are different."

"Not so much, Jack." She tapped his stubble. He was so warm. Masculine and made of steel. Such a man. "Except the part where I want to know what your kiss feels like."

"You think two people working together should kiss?"

"I've never been one to follow rules. I suspect you haven't either. Rules are for pussies. Yeah?"

"Most of the time."

"And now?" Parting her lips, she teased out the tip of her tongue, waiting for him to answer her call.

"You tempt me."

"Why do you have to resist so much, Jack. Kiss me." She didn't want to beg for it, but then again, that was a surprising turn-on. She leaned in and put her hand on his arm. "Please?"

"You do ask sweetly."

He leaned in and she met his mouth with her own. It was a simple, easy kiss, that teased her to plunge forward and attack him, but Saskia held back. When had she last let a man simply press his mouth to hers? Giving her the luxury to taste him. To smell him. To gauge one another's want with the intensity of contact, skin on skin, mouth to mouth.

She inhaled him and he filled her with dangerous ideas about secret liaisons and not-so-secret ones. And all she wanted was to see what he did next. To let him take control.

Would he dare? Was he the rough and ready man she wanted him to be? He tilted his head, and their mouths twisted, finding a new angle. This time, he opened her lips with his tongue and touched her sigh. He was much more tender than she expected from a man who liked to rough up people. An interesting surprise, especially since her choice of men was generally fast, furious, freaky, or all the above.

She detected a hint of cinnamon on his breath. "You had one of those korvapuusti buns with your coffee this morning, eh?"

"I love those cinnamon buns. Makes putting up with the frigid temps much easier." He kissed her quickly, then sat back.

Saskia immediately regretted the question. She'd given him reason to stop the kiss. "What? You are already bored of kissing me?"

He shook his head. "I could kiss you all day. But I'm still struggling with the right and wrong of it. Shouldn't. I can kiss whoever I damn well want to kiss."

"Damn right."

"But…" He looked out the window and a wince crimped his mouth.

Whatever he wasn't saying seemed to weigh on him heavily. A thoughtful man? Saskia wasn't sure how to handle that. She was more a man in that she couldn't deal with other people's feelings all that much. Give her a quickie, and a relationship focused around good, satisfying sex, and she was happy. Emotions? Who needed all that baggage?

Oh, Jack, you're such a complicated bull.

And complicated had never before turned her eye.

"Right." She stood and wandered toward the bedrooms. "Got to make that run to pick up something downtown. You want to tag along?"

She wasn't sure why she'd asked, but for some reason having muscle along on the poison pickup seemed like a good idea.

"You inviting me for my pleasant personality or my fists?" he called after her.

"Both!"

Chapter 8

"I know this guy," Saskia said as they navigated the busy downtown sidewalks. She had parked the car blocks from their destination.

Jack decided the city was much like London, except cleaner, not quite so much of a bustle, and more cosmopolitan. More orderly, even. Okay, not at all like London. But it was city-like in a manner he hadn't expected. He'd expected tundra and howling ice winds sheering the flesh from his face. The sun was shining today and thanks to the surrounding buildings blocking the wind, he wasn't even shivering. He had to mark that as a good thing.

"By know," he asked, "do you mean in the sense that you've had sex with him without him realizing it was you?"

"You're not going to ever get over that one, are you?"

"Not sure. It was a new one for me. Not too many times a person has managed to get the jump on Jack Angelo."

"I'll take that as a compliment."

"I meant it as such." Moving aside to allow a woman on snowshoes and wielding hiking poles to walk by, Jack marveled at the eclectic crowd. "So. What's the pickup? Is it for the job?"

"Yes, and no. Clive asked me to get it for him. I can't tell you what it is. It's for some deal he's working on the side. Didn't give me details."

"He's got quite the control over you. Surprising."

She cast a glance at him, from under a sleek blond wig, that admonished while it also accepted. "I work well with others, and there's nothing wrong with that. A team player, is that what it's called?"

"Always a good attribute when working on a bank job. Uh, what exactly is the planned take from this job? The heist, I mean."

"You don't know?"

"No." But it was his job to find out. "Don't you think that's a little odd?"

"I'm getting a paycheck, no matter what we walk out of there with in hand."

"Right." Five hundred grand. A meager amount for such a job. On the other hand, how many working-class stiffs could put in a week's work and walk away with half a million? Still. He did have a job to do. "But I would like to know the take."

"Why? Will it change things?"

"Maybe."

She cast him a glance that he read many ways. But mostly, he wanted to kiss that pink mouth again. When she wasn't in costume or sporting false eyelashes, she was makeup free and he liked her best that way. Her lips were plump and soft and, man, he'd wanted to shove her down on the couch and get into a nice, long make-out session with her. It would be rough and rowdy. She seemed to find that appealing. And he had no arguments against it.

But he was troubled by the work ethics thing. Shouldn't be. But the fact it did bother him made him take note. A man was never bothered by something unless he had a reason to be. Figuring out why it troubled him so much, though, was the bitch of it all.

Who in their right mind would push away a woman like the one who strode purposefully by his side? She was smart, talented (in ways that spoke to his born-a-criminal soul) and she had a thing for him. He knew she did. Else why would she have jumped in the shower with him? And she had asked him for the kiss when they'd been on the sofa!

Something was going on between the two of them, and he wasn't sure whether he should push it away, pull it closer, or just stand in the middle and see what happened.

Hell, he was already standing in the middle. The woman bounced off him, then around him, then right into his arms. And it was confusing as all get out.

Oi. Women. A guy shouldn't want to live with one, but he really did like to keep one around for all the good stuff. And Jack believed that having sex calmed him, made him focused and relaxed, especially before a job. Could he manage such with the sexy Russian safe cracker?

He could if he applied himself. And he would.

"Here we are." She veered across the street on a green light toward a shiny steel-sided building. "I didn't tell the client I was bringing someone along. Of course, muscle will be expected. You got a gun?"

"Do I need one?"

"No. I just want to know in case they do a pat down."

"I rarely carry a weapon. My fists provide all the necessary intimidation."

"I believe that. Stay behind me and don't open your mouth, got it?"

He gaped at her, issuing him such a command. But when she winked at him, his affront slipped away and he shook his head. A laugh felt great. The woman had already managed to get inside him. And he liked it.

* * * *

The meeting place was an office building in the center of town. Corporate headquarters, sleek design studios, and hi-brow coffee shops with internet connections populated the area. Lots of steel and glass, which contrasted with the rather quaint and colorful buildings in the district where Saskia was staying.

The six-story office complex was not busy as they strode inside. No security guard at the door, nor was there a reception station on the main level. Of course, there was no reason. Wasn't as though the place was owned by the criminal elite.

Well, it could be, but if so, they'd assumed a normal business mode for this place. Once on the lift, Saskia punched the elevator button for the fourth floor, while Jack assumed a stoic position beside her.

This was the first time she'd gone anywhere with muscle. Made her a little nervous, actually. She was accustomed to protecting herself. And she could. But this was an unfamiliar country and she knew the Finns did not care much for Russians. It went back to World War II. Something about the Russians occupying the country and spreading general mayhem.

She'd pull on an American accent and make this visit a quick in and out. Grab the stuff and leave. Clive had given her an envelope with payment inside. She hadn't opened it. The thickness of the stack of bills felt right. She did not trust the man completely, but for some reason, opening the sealed envelope had felt childish. If Clive were going to screw her over he—well, she hadn't thought about that one until now. But he didn't suspect her alliances. Couldn't.

"You cool?" Jack's voice startled her. She'd forgotten she was not alone.

"Always. Why?"

"Just checking."

He smelled like iced peppermint. And she was not going to forget that less than an hour earlier they'd been snogging on the sofa. But it hadn't gone as far as she would have liked. He was too cautious. She got that about him. Always looking over one shoulder. Never wanting to get caught out.

Didn't mean she had to respect it.

The elevators doors opened with a ding, and she strolled down a long hallway. There was only one door at the end of the hall, and before it stood a man to match Jack's build, and they might have even bought suits at the same shop. No tie on the bruiser though. While Jack flashed his yellow warning tie. She liked to think of it that way. Yield, slow down. You don't want to take it too far with this one.

She smiled as she approached the man at the door. "Got an appointment with your boss," she said in a clean American accent. "He's expecting me."

"Sherri?" the man asked.

She nodded. It was a useful name. Sounded non-confrontational, and a little not-all-there, like an easy mark.

He stepped aside, but when Jack followed, the bouncer barked, "Just the woman."

Saskia turned and met Jack's gaze. The slightest nod from her confirmed she was okay with this. He remained stoic, hands at his sides, but his gaze swept from her face to the other man's face. Then he took a step back and clasped his hands before his crotch. Standard bodyguard *I'm ready, so come on and fuck with me* pose.

Saskia opened the door and stepped inside a conference room walled on the opposite corner with windows. A tall man stood on the other side of a long table, back to her, looking out over the street below. His arms were akimbo, and he was slender. The well-fitted pin-striped suit probably cost him thousands. Of which, she assumed had been a drop in the bucket to him. One of her trusted contacts from years ago had recommended him; he was a pharmaceutical agent. She always expected blatant display of wealth from those bastards.

"Hey," she said, and remained on the opposite side of the long mahogany conference table. Hands down at her sides and head lifted, she showed confidence. "I'm Sherri."

"I know that." The man didn't turn around. His accent was definitely Finnish. A tilt of his head up and to the side showed a closed eye and an almost sun-worshipping desire for the meager light that beamed through the streak-less window. "You bring the cash?"

She tossed the envelope onto the table and it landed with a satisfying *thunk*.

The man turned around. He was handsome, yet the angles of his bone structure were not symmetrical. Sort of an Adrien Brody lookalike. Saskia watched as he slipped long fingers inside his suit coat and drew out a small glass vial as if a magician revealing his secret. He placed the vial on the table before him, then gestured she approach.

So Saskia complied, eyeing the outline of his suit as she did so. It was fitted and she didn't notice a bulge from a gun at his ribs or hip or his waist. There was no reason for this exchange to go sour but she was ever cautious.

Making a swipe for the vial, she sucked in a breath when he caught her wrist. She held the vial carefully, as he squeezed her wrist painfully. If it cracked, she did not want to inhale once the poison hit the air.

"Dude, the cash is all there. You want to count it?"

"I trust you."

"Then what's up? I didn't come for a song and dance. Let me go."

She could take him down by shifting her weight and flipping him over her head, but she didn't want to start a ruckus if it wasn't necessary. She'd play along with his game. For a few seconds.

"You are beautiful," he said in an exact tone that proved he was speaking English for her benefit.

Compliments from the unsavory types generally meant much more than a mere acknowledgement. And the twist about her wrist indicated he wanted her to stay a while.

Thankful she'd worn a wig and that her disguise was secure, Saskia shrugged. "I try."

"But you are also lying to me." He jerked her arm and she stumbled forward. In a move she hadn't anticipated, he tugged the wig from her head. Her dark hair spilled down in a tangle. "What are you? Interpol? KGB?"

"KG—are you crazy? I just like the blond look, is all. Now let go of me, or I will make you."

"Tough girl, eh?" He succeeded in wrangling her up against his chest. His breath smelled like vinegar. His dark eyes were surprisingly chocolate. But not a thing about him appealed to her. "Let's have a kiss, yes, Miss Fake Blond?"

Enough already. "Sure. But only if you can manage it with aching balls."

She kicked up and kneed him in the thigh, missing his groin. He grunted and as he leaned forward, head-butted her.

That hurt like a mother. And it disoriented her momentarily so that suddenly Saskia found herself facing the table, bent over, with one of her arms twisted behind her back. She held the vial of poison in her other hand. And she'd best be cautious with it. Wasn't like she could smash it against the man's face and hope she'd not also take some of the poison into her skin.

At a moment like this, she should call out to Jack. But the tiny niggle that she hated to show him she wasn't up to par kept her from doing so. Struggling as the man leaned against her ass, pressing a hard-on against her, she managed an elbow to some part of him. He swore and she briefly felt the hand about her wrist loosen.

Twisting out of his grip, Saskia pushed against the table, barreling them both backward to land against a steel beam that dissected the floor to ceiling window sections. He clasped her across the chest, squeezing one of her breasts painfully, and lifted her feet from the floor.

Swinging out her arms, she had no traction or means of defense. But she wasn't going to wait for his next move. Reaching high and behind, she scraped her fingernails across the sides of his scalp and leaned forward, toppling them both. She took the brunt of the fall on her knees and shoulder, but rocked to the side and rolled over his body, coming up to stand.

The door opened. The bodyguard peered inside and swore in Finnish.

"Take him out, Jack!" Saskia called.

Then she noticed the glass vial on the floor near her attacker's head. It had been crushed in the struggle. Her fingers clenched. She brushed them swiftly across her pants, hoping she'd not touched any of the white contents. Leaping over his chest to get the hell out of there, she was caught by a pants leg and she tumbled to the floor.

Looking down her body at the clinging monster, she saw he'd rolled his cheek right onto the broken vial. But he couldn't have noticed as his growl was only focused on keeping her in hand.

"Jack, quickly!"

"You are not American," the man said as she kicked at his hand and freed herself.

She crawled away just as Jack entered the room and dodged for the man on the floor.

"Wait!" she called. "Don't touch him. He's got the poison on him."

The man, for the first time, slapped a palm to his cheek and pulled it away to inspect the tiny bits of shattered glass. He swore.

"Run, Jack. Now!" Saskia demanded.

She took off out of the room, jumping over the fallen bodyguard. Jack followed in tow. Avoiding the elevator, she opened the door to the stairs. Behind her, effusive curses from the suited man turned into growling pleads for rescue.

The poison could kill him in less than three minutes. Landing the final floor, she twisted up her hair and then her hood, pulling the strings tight so her hair didn't slip out. Leaving the stairway, she assumed a calm pace with Jack rushing up behind her and paralleling her.

He smoothed a hand down his tie, and opened the door for her as a woman in a long chinchilla fur coat entered and gave them a nod. Jack offered, "Nice day, ma'am."

The chill air smacked Saskia in the face as she veered down the street toward her car. Picking up speed, she ran the last six car lengths and quickly got inside and fired up the engine. Jack slid in and closed the door. He didn't rush to ask if she was okay or check her for injuries. He'd seen her struggling. And he'd seen what had gone down. She was thankful for his silence.

And not. Because right now, she really wanted to swear and beat the steering wheel and then scream at the world. Instead, she gripped the wheel tightly to keep from revealing how much her hand was shaking, and pulled into traffic.

"Well, that was a cock up," Jack suddenly said, breaking the chilling silence.

And all Saskia could do was laugh. It felt good to release her anxiety. Hell yes, it had gone over not at all well. She should have been keener. Anticipated such a tussle. But it was over, and she wasn't going to beat herself up about it. She'd gotten out of there; that was what mattered.

As she stopped at a light, she turned to her partner in crime and nodded. "Thanks for having my back."

"Always."

It sounded good. Like the man would always be there to protect her. But she knew better. It was just another job to him. He'd been doing what he'd trained to do. And so had she.

So why had that encounter shaken her so terribly?

It wasn't because now she had no poison to hand over to Clive. Quick thinking decided she could mix up a fake that would convince him well enough. Nor was it that the jerk in the office had manhandled her and forced her to fight for her dignity. Or that she had come *this close* to touching that poison.

What shook her was an indefinable need for the protection Jack had offered, and which she'd called out for. She'd needed him.

And what would she do when he was no longer there to answer her call?

Chapter 9

Jack held his tongue as Saskia drove directly from downtown Helsinki to the garage north of Toukola. Clive wanted them to run through the plan this afternoon. He could feel Saskia's tension and see it in her tight knuckles that wrapped the steering wheel. She'd been thrown in that office. And more than physically. He hadn't heard the scuffle start, and it was a good thing the other thug had opened the door to look inside. How such a struggle had begun was beyond him, but he was thankful he'd gotten to her before she'd been hurt.

She'd said something about poison? What was that about?

It was for a side job. Yes, he distinctly remembered her saying that, and then telling him no more details.

What Jack most wanted to do right now was wrap her into his arms and kiss her. Tell her she was all right. They'd gotten out of there alive. But would the client send thugs after them? Saskia had lost her wig. They had an ID on both of them. Unless the one man really did die from the poison.

What the hell was she involved in?

It shouldn't matter. He had a job and that was his focus. Whatever happened on the side... Bloody hell, he had to take note of it because he wasn't sure where the heist ended and the poison thing started. If it were key to this investigation he'd better stay on top of things.

The car pulled up to the garage and before Saskia could twist off the ignition, Jack put a hand over hers. "You okay?"

She nodded. "Hell, yes. You think I am not up to a little rassling with a skinny Finnish man in a bespoke suit?"

"I think you can take care of yourself just fine. Suit or no suit. It's the poison I'm wondering about."

"I said no details, Jack."

"I'm cool with that. But I do think I have a right to know one thing. Was it airborne?"

"No, it has to touch the skin to enter the bloodstream. Though, I didn't inhale too deeply anyway. One never knows with such a volatile substance. I don't think I got any on me. At least, I'm not feeling any burning. That would be an indicator."

"You need to take a shower and wash off. Just to be safe."

"I'm fine, Jack. If it had contacted my skin we'd both know it because I'd either be dead right now or my screams would break your eardrums."

He'd heard the man's screams as they'd fled the building. "What's going to happen to the guy we left behind?"

She shrugged and turned off the ignition. "Not my problem. He was an asshole." And with that, she got out and strode inside, leaving him to sit there.

"It becomes everyone's problem if he comes looking for us," Jack muttered.

He considered calling this incident in to the ECU. They could look into the aftereffects of their visit, report whether the client was currently dead or alive, and possibly feed Jack related contacts.

He pulled out his cell phone and texted to Kierce Quinn, the tech operator in Paris, the building name, floor, and a brief overview of the events that had gone on. He ended with a request for an update on the client's condition, and all related ties to Clive Hendrix and Saskia Petrovik. Quinn texted back that he was on it.

Shoving the phone in his suit coat pocket, Jack opened the car door, braced himself against the cold, because he'd not worn an overcoat, and rushed inside the warm building.

Three hours later, the team had rehearsed the entrance through the drilled hole, the walk down the hallway avoiding cameras, and estimated safe cracking times until they had narrowed it to a dozen or so minutes. The target was the main vault on the ground level floor, but as well, the safe deposit vault in the basement. Saskia would man the main vault while Clive worked the one below. The first one to gain entry would be their target.

It was a weird setup, but Jack decided maybe the man didn't have a goal. They'd open what they could and take whatever was available.

He didn't like it. Then again, he had no voice to argue. And he wouldn't. Observing was working so far. Maybe this operation was much more amateur than previously thought. Had the first job netted them nothing because of ill-planning?

On the other hand, Saskia had said she'd gotten paid. Something had to have been taken to cover the crew's paychecks. There was only one way to find out. Keep his mouth shut and his eyes and ears open.

The sky was dark when, satisfied they were ready for the job, the crew stepped outside. Yet Clive called Jack back inside. He was thankful to return to the warmth.

"What's up?" Jack asked.

"You got a vehicle lined up for Saturday?"

"I, uh…" Yeah, that was his job. Normally, he'd be more on the ball. But they still had one more day. "What kind do you want?"

"A van. Something to haul that drill. White."

"White?"

"I've noticed all the local work vans are white."

Jack made a thinking noise. He wasn't so sure he wanted to stand out so much. On the other hand, if he drove it a bit, dirtied it up, he'd blend well with the snowy landscape and, apparently, the rest of the work vans. "I'll look into it. We burning it after?"

"That or crushing it."

"Got it. I'll look into the local junkyards. Anything else?"

"Should there be?" Clive asked.

Yes, there bloody should be, Jack thought. Like more detail on exactly what they intended to walk out of the bank with. "Nope. All's good." He walked out and Saskia drove the rental up to meet him not five feet from the garage door.

Behind him, Clive called to them, "Meet you all at the House Autuuden!"

"The Autuuden? Now what?" Jack asked as he buckled up and Saskia drove the car west toward the main road.

"Means House of Bliss. A hot tub and sauna resort. Clive is big on group bonding before the heist," she said. "Last one we all went to a zen bar and drank sake and meditated."

"Doesn't sound like a party to me."

"Outdoor hot tubs and beer? Should be a better time than humming 'om' and ringing stupid bells."

"Sounds…relaxing. But I don't have my trunks along."

"Don't need 'em." She winked as she picked up speed. "When in Finland we go skyclad, buddy. You up for that?"

"Sure." Maybe. Not really.

With Saskia naked right next to him? What the bloody kind of sexual torture was he walking into?

* * * *

A man shouldn't parade his naked bits around unless there was a woman in the room intent on also displaying her naked bits. Just the man and the woman. No one else. Not a locker room filled with men in all ages, sizes and—ahem, physical attributes. Nor in a frigid land, surrounded by foreigners who didn't seem to give a fig about the other guy's junk.

But still.

The journey from locker room to the wooden walk outside that stretched around a circle of hot tubs was perilous. Jack held the thick white towel about his waist and strolled with as much casual disinterest as he could manage as he passed elderly folk, youngsters, and all kinds that were headed to or from the square tubs positioned around a huge bonfire. Before the others arrived, he slipped into the tub with a subtle removal of towel that hadn't revealed anything he didn't want exposed to the chill air.

He wasn't ashamed of his big Irish bull. It was a fine specimen. According to more than many. But his mother would slap him into the next country should she learn he'd been parading about with it slapping left and right for all eyes to see.

Niles was next. Jack averted his eyes. And Clive and Saskia strolled up a few minutes later, chatting. Clive tossed aside his towel and Jack got an eyeful. He could be thankful the man stood across the hot tub from him because—that would have been eye level and—just no.

Where was the waitress who was supposed to deliver drinks?

Saskia displayed no shame as she slipped into the waters and settled about an arm's length away from him. Ah hell, he wasn't comfortable with anyone in this situation. He was naked. He had no weapons at hand. And the woman who drove him bonkers to fuck was sitting so close, and the water sloshed the tops of her breasts as she laughed and conversed.

And he had a boner, damn it all to bloody hell.

A waitress stopped by with beers for all. Just in the nick of time. Saskia suggested he try the ice beer, and much as he wanted nothing at all to do with more ice, he gave the pale lager a shot. Good stuff. A bit dry, and a little on the champagney side. Interesting. As he sipped, he relaxed, and settled shoulder-deep into the comforting bubbles.

"You got the hose and auxiliary supplies, Niles?" Saskia asked after a couple swallows of beer. She set the bottle on the wood planks behind her head.

"No shop talk," Clive said. "Especially not here." He eyed Saskia admonishingly.

Niles nodded in answer to her question, then tipped his beer bottle against Jack's. "Cheers, right mate? Isn't that what they say in jolly ole England?"

"Something like that. But I thought you were from England. You sound British to me. Where you from?" Jack asked.

"Nigeria. Me mum was born in Sussex and I guess I sound a lot like her."

"Never been that far down in England," Jack provided. "Funny, eh? Lived there most of my life and never got that far."

"But you're an Irishman," Niles said.

"That I am."

"And Italian," Saskia tossed in, tapping the rim of the beer bottle against her lips. "A fighter and a lover, eh?" She smiled at Jack and he beamed at her.

And then he realized his reaction to her was being witnessed by everyone. Clive's brow rose and he tilted his bottle toward Jack in a silent approval. And Niles nodded, smiling to himself.

"So we've established that our muscle man is also a lover," Clive said. "Don't worry, Niles. You still win the title of Mr. Charm."

Niles nodded.

Clive looked to Saskia. "What of our lovely chameleon?"

Saskia sank down in the tub, floating her fingers on the surface. "Just that. A master of disguise. Not much more than that."

"You don't give yourself enough credit," Niles offered. "Do you know how many times you've gotten the jig on me because I didn't recognize you?"

Saskia laughed. "A lot." And again she flashed Jack that secretive—but not so secret—smile in the present company.

Yeah, she'd gotten the jig on him plenty.

"Okay, let's try this. If you had half a million dollars," Saskia said, putting it out to all of them, "what would you do with it?"

Clive set his empty bottle behind him. "Vacation in Belize for a month."

"Is that the going rate for a Belize vacation?" Saskia asked. She shook her head in disbelief. "Spendy."

"But worth it. Especially when they toss in the private yacht." Clive winked. "What about you, Niles?"

"A man might pay off his mother's mortgage then buy himself a real nice sports car. Orange."

"Orange?" Jack frowned. "You want the whole bloody world to notice you?"

"Hell, yes! That's the only reason for having a sports car, isn't it?"

"What would your wife say about that?" Saskia asked.

"Aw, she'd love it. She'd tie a scarf about her hair like those fancy dames from the old movies and put on a big pair of sunglasses and blow kisses to all the old men as we cruised by." Niles's laughter was infectious and the whole group joined him.

Jack felt a toe nudge his leg and slide up the back of his calf. He was just thankful it was obviously from Saskia's direction.

"What about you, Gentleman Jack?" she asked.

He shrugged. "A man might set it aside for emergencies. Family. You know."

"Family," she repeated, and her eyes narrowed. She was thinking too hard about him right now, and he wasn't sure he was comfortable with that.

Jack raised his arm and rallied the waitress back for another round. But for the next two rounds Saskia's gaze held that same preening wonder that seemed to crack open his heart and peer inside. It was discomforting, but at the same time, he kind of liked having her so interested in him.

* * * *

It was midnight by the time they returned to the flat, but Jack didn't feel like sleeping. Not yet. He stood looking out the windows across the cityscape, thinking the sky looked a little…green.

Saskia wandered into the room, grabbed the blanket from the sofa, and wrapped it about her shoulders. Now that her hair had dried Jack noticed it was distinctly not black.

"Another disguise?"

"Blond is my natural color. But I dyed it a few weeks back. Temporary color. It's slowly fading."

"You and the sky are very colorful tonight."

"The sky? Ah. The Aurora Borealis. It was faint out by the House of Bliss. Come on."

"What?"

"Put on a jacket. I'm going to show you something that will blow your mind."

Having his mind blown sounded like an interesting activity, so Jack pulled on his coat and followed Saskia as she slipped on her pack boots, then wandered down the building hallway, blanket still wrapped about her shoulders. At the end of the long hall, she opened the roof access door.

"They're not as bright here in the city." She took the stairs upward. "But you can still see them. When I was out at the garage a few nights ago right before you arrived, they were amazing. And tonight is clear and cold, so it's no surprise you can see them."

She kicked open the metal door and wandered out onto the roof. And Jack shivered, wondering about the woman's fortitude for not even wearing a jacket in what must be pushing below zero temperatures.

With thoughts of hot bubbling water caressing his skin, Jack joined her side at the edge of the roof, facing north. Vivid green lights wavered in the sky at a distance he couldn't measure. Ribbons of light performed a stunning dance for him.

"It's like fire dancing in the sky," Saskia said. "Pretty cool, eh?"

"I've never seen anything like it."

The greens were almost fluorescent and those were edged with gold. A flash of red every-so-often, and then a wash of angel white. God must be practicing his painting skills tonight, he thought.

Jack felt Saskia lean against his arm and tugged her closer. "You should have a coat on."

"This blanket is good. But you are hot. I think the hot tub gave you a fever. If not a hard-on."

Christ. She'd noticed? He didn't want to discuss it. On the other hand...

She leaned in closer, tilting her head against his shoulder. "I'm going to steal some of your body heat, if you don't mind."

"Let's do this." He stepped behind her and hugged her tightly, casting his gaze to the light show in the sky.

It was at once as if a tornado and then an orchestrated light show that might have been painted by a drug-crazed artist. Yet the ribbons flowed and danced and smoked as if fire. And on occasion a flicker of red and orange flittered in with the emerald. And all of it was punctuated by the white stars dotting the black background.

"That's us, you know," she said.

"Huh?"

"Those stars. We are made of whatever makes up those stars."

It was a weird analogy but Jack could go with it. He liked it much better than blood, guts, and bones.

"Some scientist said it. Carl Sagan? Maybe," she said. "We are all made of star stuff. My whole body is a conglomeration of all that stuff up there in the heavens, millions and billions of light years away. Isn't that cool?"

"The stars look very different today," he sang, quoting Bowie.

Bowing his head, Jack nuzzled his face into her hair, wishing he could smell the warmth of the skin behind her ear. He didn't notice the cold so much when holding her. Was he holding a star in his arms? Bloody cool.

"Did you know that the Eskimos have something like forty different names for snow?" she asked.

"Uh...no?"

"They do. It's crazy. I read about it somewhere."

"You seem to have a lot of odd facts in here." He kissed the crown of her head. "What is it I've heard about the way the Eskimos kiss?"

Saskia turned around in his embrace and nuzzled her freakishly cold nose against his. "Like that, I think."

"Yeah, that's it. Your nose is a popsicle."

"Then warm me up."

She kissed him. He wasn't about to argue the benefits of sharing body heat. That was his story. At least, for now.

She pulled him down to keep him close and he didn't mind that either. Her kiss was hot and needy. She knew what she wanted and he gave it to her. Sweeter, more honest, for some reason that really fucked with his most immediate need of simply getting as much from her as he could. Heat, skin, tongue. Yeah, this was a bit of all right.

"We should go inside," he murmured against her mouth.

"And continue what we're doing?"

"Sounds like a plan."

He lifted her into his arms and with one last look to the dancing sky, carried her down and into the warmth of the apartment that he could only appreciate now that he been out freezing his arse off on the roof.

Chapter 10

Saskia shucked off her boots while Jack still held her. He kicked his shoes to the rug by the door. He set her on the back of the sofa. She helped him pull off his coat, while keeping the blanket around her shoulders. When he turned to toss his coat aside, she wrangled him around the waist with her legs and pulled him to her.

"You're an aggressive woman." He leaned in to peer into her eyes. They hadn't turned on a light, but the streetlights offered a sensual ambiance.

"A good match for you, yes?"

He kissed her and his mouth was still a little cold, as was his skin. She smoothed her palms over his stubbled jaw and up over his scalp where the short hairs cushed against her hands. Drawing him in deeply and meeting his tongue with a hot dance, she would show him aggressive.

Gripping his shirt, she was glad the tie had somehow been forgotten. He'd loosened up a little while in the hot tub. And she could have jumped him right then and there after seeing his obvious discomfort at sitting naked around others. Cute. The big hulking bruiser had a shy side.

Her fingers deftly worked the buttons free from his shirt as he angled the kiss and slipped it down her chin to her neck. He licked her up under her jaw and the firm dash of his tongue hit on an erogenous zone she hadn't realized was there.

"Oh yes, that is the spot." She pulled open his shirt to spread her hands over his hard chest. "You are like steel, Jack. I am impressed." She punched his pec gently, and there was no give.

"You want to beat me or make out?" he asked.

"A little of both?"

"Just don't ask me to bring out the whips and chains." He hissed as she leaned in to suck one of his tiny nipples into her mouth. It tightened and she played at it with her tongue. "Don't bite, sweetie."

She paused with her teeth about his nipple, but didn't chomp down. She would have never bitten hard, but a little nip?

He pushed a thumb over her lower lip and shook his head admonishingly. So she lashed her tongue about his thumb and sucked that in. The man tilted back his head and groaned. He thrust his hips forward and she moved up to hug against his big Irish bull.

"I want this." She slid off the sofa and hugging tightly against his body, tilted a hip forward to grind against his cock.

"Yeah?" Of a sudden he twisted her about and she caught her hands on the back of the sofa. His body melded against her backside, and a big, wide hand slipped up under her shirt. "I want this." He squeezed her breast and then pinched the nipple. Saskia leaned her head back against his shoulder, tugging up her shirt to give him better access.

He massaged both her breasts, and nuzzled his kisses at the crook of her neck. There was that luscious hit to her erogenous zone again. Saskia reached behind her and managed to grab his hips. Putting her feet up on the sofa, she ground her ass against his hard-on. There was only one way to go with this…and she wasn't afraid to take control.

Hooking her legs firmly over the back of the couch, she transferred her weight forward, taking Jack by surprise, and successfully flipping him over to land on the cushions. She straddled him. "Didn't see that one coming, did you?"

He pulled her down and sucked her nipple into his mouth, drawing on it, suckling, licking and rendering her speechless. The man really knew how to focus his efforts and to make her body sing. And then he said, "Didn't see that one coming, eh?"

"Keep it coming." Saskia pulled the shirt off over her head and tossed it to the floor. "I will not argue your tactics." He guided her breast back into his mouth. "Your hands have warmed up, and your mouth… This is the best way to keep warm in this crazy country, yes?"

He mumbled an affirmative growl and licked at her nipples. She didn't need him to talk when he was so expert at finding her sweet spots. Saskia shimmied down her leggings and kicked them off, and then she unbuttoned his trousers.

Jack abruptly stopped his sucking and put a hand over hers. "Careful with the zipper."

"Right, big boy. I will be so delicate."

"You? Delicate?"

She took that as a challenge and bent to carefully work the zipper down slowly. The man was going commando and as the zipper teeth parted, the head of his Irish bull rose and begged for attention. Saskia dashed her tongue across the mighty crown. His groan pleased her. And when he was completely freed, she gripped him firmly.

Jack huffed and met her challenging gaze. "I take back what I said about you being delicate."

"You need a good firm hand." She waggled a brow at him. "Yes?"

His positive reply came out as a groan as she shifted her grip up and down his hard, solid length. He was long, but not terribly so. What was impressive was his girth. She could barely fit her fingers about him. And oh, so hot. A lash of her tongue wetted his skin and provided lubrication as she increased her speed. Her other hand she cupped about his tight sac, easing a careful but reassuring squeeze.

She eyed the fists at his sides. His eyes were closed. His body tense. Close to release already? But she'd not had all her fun yet.

Relaxing her grip, Saskia slid up his body and slicked her wetness over his erection, painting him with her wanting heat. Yes, there. Just the right pressure in just the right spot. The glide of him over her clit served to heighten the stirring hum in her core.

Unable to resist, she bent to lash one of his nipples then followed with a gentle nip.

"Saskia!" That opened his eyes. "I said no biting."

"I can't help it, Jack. I want to eat you up."

"Eat this." He pumped his hips so his cock nudged roughly against her folds. "But no biting. Promise me?"

She winked at him. "You trust a thief and a grifter with a promise? Okay then, I promise."

She bent to take him in her mouth and the big Irish bull was reduced to a wanting, pumping, groaning mass of muscle and musk. No man could concentrate when a woman took him by the head, literally, and showed him exactly how she felt about him. And Saskia wanted him to know that she liked him, she wanted him, and…she trusted him. At least, with her naked body. Oh yes, he could have his way with her any time.

"I'm going to come," he managed tightly. "Come on up here, Saskia. I need to be inside you. I've got a condom…somewhere…"

"No worries, Jack Angelo." She shifted along his body and settled onto his cock, teasing at allowing him in. "I am on birth control."

"Good, because I think I left that condom in London. Put me inside you."

"You sure?" She wiggled on top of him, knowing it was torturous to his needy erection. "Maybe we fool around a bit more…"

He gripped her by the hips and with a precise aim, the man entered her. Slowly, but oh so surely. His entrance stole away her teasing words. Saskia could but moan and enjoy every single inch that slid into her, filling her, becoming her. When he was hilted, she rode him, and was surprised when the man's fingers found her clit and slicked that in accompaniment to her rhythm. Most men were not so aware that a woman needed such stimulation to get off. Bonus points for him!

She could feel him step toward the edge. His muscles tightened as if leather straps. His body trembled. The fingers at her hips gripped firmly. And when his other fingers squeezed her clit…just so, Saskia hit the peak and exploded along with him. He jammed himself into her, hips rising from the sofa. And she let out her held breath and a flutter of laughter as the orgasm won.

* * * *

Later, snuggled in the blanket on the sofa, their naked bodies entwined, Jack edged close to sleep. Or maybe he was slipping out of a light nap? Didn't matter. His mind had just been blown. That sex had rocked him left, right, up and down. The woman was incredible.

And she felt like a warm length of flames that he wanted to never let go of. Especially since the chill air in the room had already cooled the top of his head. Any part of him not covered by the blanket, which included his left foot, was not happy. Everything else? A bit of all right.

Something had happened here tonight. This wasn't the first time they'd done it. But it was the first time he'd known and wanted the woman in his arms. And it didn't feel like just another fuck. It had felt so good. And right. Even though he knew he'd only be working with her another few days, then *hasta la vista*, bye-bye baby, on to a new life.

A life he couldn't imagine right now without someone like Saskia riding along with him. Wasn't that crazy? He never fell for women so hard. And he was not going to trip into such a fall this time. He was just lingering in the feel-good following sex. Yeah, that was it. He wasn't turning into a softie.

Although, his dick was. It had gotten a workout.

What he did know was that it was going to be hard to walk away from Saskia after the bank job. Did he have to? Could they keep this going? If life played out over the next few days the way he'd planned, she would be difficult to insert into that timeline.

But he could make room for her later. Hmm…

Maybe it was best not to think about it too much. It would only bring up anxiety and put him off his game for the job. So he cuddled her a little firmer and kissed the crown of her head, and surrendered to the sleep that captured them both until morning.

Chapter 11

The next morning Saskia left early to pick up some supplies. She'd need to present Clive with some semblance of a poison. And it had to be convincing. The drug store had provided what she'd needed. Now, she returned to the flat and was greeted with the lush scents of oregano and tomatoes. Bless Jack's nonna.

The scent was almost better than the sex they'd had last night. Almost, but—no, who was she kidding? What they'd done last night could never compare to a good meal, warm or not.

"You are a regular housewife," she called as she headed to the bedroom to grab the blanket and wrap it around her shoulders.

Returning to the kitchen, she sat on a stool and pulled the small bag of supplies from her pocket. She could tell him what she was going to do, but that would then require further explanation.

Yet she had to tell him everything. Because if she did, he could get that information to the right people. People she wasn't able to contact because she was in deep right now. And they needed to know.

It was her best move. She would make it.

"Jack, I have to tell you something."

He looked up from the pot of pasta that she figured was as much a heat source to him as it fulfilled his weird need to cook. "Shoot."

"Come over here and sit for a minute, if you can."

He replaced the pot lid, tossed aside the pot holder and sat on a stool next to her. She leaned over to kiss him and he responded with a long and lush kiss. The man could be as focused on her mouth as he was on his pasta. Mmm, she liked kissing him. And sharing skin with him—she had to focus.

"What do you want to tell me?"

"I've been thinking about what you asked me. About what the take for this job will be."

"The five hundred thousand we were each promised."

"Right. Shows up in our bank accounts the moment Clive sends the text that the job is complete. That's how the man works."

"You didn't seem overly interested in my concerns when we discussed this before. What's changed?"

"You did do research on the previous heist Clive headed, didn't you?"

"As much as I could." He shrugged. "The Belgian heist, right? It didn't make any major news outlets, but I did find a brief police report online. Something about breaking in and not taking a damned thing. But I figured the report got it wrong. You had to have taken something. Isn't worth the risk of prison otherwise."

"That's just it. The reports were true. We didn't take anything on that heist. Not unless Clive took something so small we didn't remark it."

"Then why even break in? I don't understand."

"I didn't either. But I'm beginning to wonder if maybe we break in to leave something behind."

"I'm not following you."

And she was having a hard time, herself, with this theory. But it made weird sense to her. "I'm pretty sure we're going to walk out empty-handed tomorrow night. No bills, no gold, not even booty from the safe deposit boxes."

"Then why are we bloody putting ourselves out to do this?"

"The payoff?"

He shook his head. "Clive must know something we don't."

"That's what I'm starting to think. And while it shouldn't bother me and I shouldn't ask questions..." She paused and Jack lifted a brow. He was listening, which is exactly what she needed from him. "What if Clive is serving someone other than himself and us?"

"Go on."

"He's not the man on top. I think he's working for someone else. Maybe. I don't know. I've not seen proof of it. It's conjecture. Listen, tomorrow's heist is the same setup as the last one. We go in. I break into the vault. Clive breaks into the safe deposit box room. Whoever gets in first, that's the vault we rob. Last time I made the vault in forty minutes, and as soon as I opened the door, Clive appeared and said we were finished."

"Had he broken into the safe deposit room? What did he take?"

She nodded. "I didn't think to ask him about it at the time. Or rather, I didn't want to. Just trying to keep my head down and do the job, you know? But now I'm more suspicious after his request for the poison. He said it wasn't related to the heist. But how can it not be related?"

"You never got the poison though, so...?" He tugged out his phone.

"What are you checking?"

"Huh? Oh, nothing, thought I felt it buzz." He set the phone aside, screen down.

But Saskia knew he'd been checking his texts. Had he looked into the results from yesterday's fouled exchange? She hoped he had.

"So you think Clive is putting poison in...a safe deposit box?" Jack prompted.

"It's one option. I briefly wondered if he was planning to release the toxin, and leave us behind, choking and fighting for our lives. But that doesn't make sense. If he didn't need us along, they why not do the job himself? Or..."

"Or?"

"What if he's got a hit list?"

"Of bank executives?"

"I don't think so. That would require he leave the poison in a desk or an office. It is a possibility. I'm thinking off the cuff here. What if it's someone who has a safe deposit box there?"

"Did you supply him poison for the last job?"

"No. But that was my first job with Clive. He could have had it made previously. I just think... If there was a way to check who owned safe deposit boxes in the Belgian bank that we hit weeks ago. Then to check that list and see if anyone, well...died. From poison exposure."

She waited as Jack moved the information around in his brain. She couldn't get any more obvious than by stating what needed to be done.

"It's an idea," he offered. "But how will knowing that help us tomorrow?"

"It won't. And we don't need help. I just would like to know exactly what the man is up to. And if I'm providing poison, I don't want to be involved in anyone's death."

"Poison generally leads to death. The client who was supposed to sell it to you? You think he's still alive? And if not, do you think you're innocent of that death?"

"Don't put it like that, Jack. I've never killed anyone. And I never will. Not unless my survival depends on it. Besides, I don't have the poison Clive asked for. But I have to give him something." She tapped the paper bag. "I picked up some ingredients this morning."

"You're going to make a poison?"

"I'm going to make a fake poison. Something that will look like what he thinks he's getting and it will give off a noxious odor that will keep him from inhaling. It should come off as the real thing."

"That could work. But what if your theory is correct? If someone doesn't drop dead—then he'll know you tricked him."

"Right, but depending on who he is targeting—if that is what is going on—it could be days or even weeks before that person returns to the box and comes in contact with the"—she made air quotes—"poison. By then, we'll be long gone."

"But I'll never know what Clive—" Jack swiped a palm over his jaw and nodded. "Right. A fake poison. That should work."

"I gotta think about this. Make sure I'm making the right move." She got up and wandered over to the window.

And behind her, she heard Jack flip over his phone and type in a long text. The man was easy. Thank goodness.

* * * *

A new twist had been added to his assignment. Or maybe it was the solution. Putting poison into a safe deposit box in hopes of murdering someone was a clever feat. But not out of the realm of possibility. And if Clive were involved in more than mere bank robbery, it could be a means to take out someone in a roundabout manner.

Jack texted Kierce Quinn at headquarters and told him he had some information to talk to him about and he'd call in five minutes.

Slipping on his coat and gloves, he paused at the door when Saskia asked where he was headed. "Across the street to the grocery. I forgot to pick up garlic for the bread. Will you stir the pasta in five minutes?"

"Sure. Pick up some of the cinnamon buns, will you? I know I'll be craving those for breakfast tomorrow morning. Gotta start the day with carbs."

"Be right back," he said.

Trundling down the stairs and across the street, he turned before entering the grocery store and waved to Saskia, who watched from the window. She waved back.

She was a good one. He wouldn't mind taking her along with him on his adventure off the grid. Seriously.

And what was that about? He couldn't risk having her along with him when he left Helsinki. She'd be in the way. And would draw more attention to him than he needed.

Jack shook his head as he aimed toward the produce aisle and pulled out his cell phone. The store was quiet, and the section at the back where the onions and garlic were displayed was ill-lit. Here, he could talk in reasonable tones without anyone overhearing.

When Kierce answered, Jack picked up a bulb of garlic and tossed it up and down as he told him everything about Saskia's suspicions.

"That's an interesting theory," Quinn said. "I can access the list of safe deposit box owners with ease. I'll search the names and get back to you if I come up with anything. When's the heist due to go down?"

"Tomorrow night. I'll keep you updated."

"Any problems? Have you learned what the goal is?"

"Beyond the suspicions about poison, there seems to be no actual goal."

"More credence that the poison angle could be it. How's it going for you working with the crew?"

Jack set the garlic in his shopping basket. "That's an odd question to ask. You want to know if I'm getting along with the crew? Or one person in particular?"

"It's standard psychological screening," Quinn replied, but Jack sensed the nervousness in his tone. "Forget I asked."

"Forgotten." But not really.

"Right. Stay warm, Angelo. And I'll see you back in Paris soon, yes?"

"If that's where my next assignment takes me." But again, not ever.

Jack clicked off and grabbed a bottle of orange juice. It was hard to shake the weird feeling he'd gotten when Kierce had asked him the personal question. Data, intel, and details of a job were the only things required on his mission reports. Not if he was getting along with the people. And while he knew the psychological aspects of relationships between the players were key, he'd gotten by with fists and fury just fine, thank you.

He grabbed a package of Saskia's favorite cinnamon buns, and then another to be safe, and after paying, headed back across the street.

The shower was running as he tugged off his coat and he winced to know that if he wanted to shower, which he did, he'd be shivering under the cold water. Should he pull a Saskia and jump in with her? It wasn't as though she'd mind.

Rubbing his palms together, he instead answered the insistent boiling pot on the stove. Yet glanced toward the bathroom. The pasta was ready, but it could go a few more minutes. By the time he decided he should go for it, the shower stopped and he heard the *shing* of the metal rings sweep across the curtain bar.

"Just as well," he muttered.

Unable to ignore the pastries sitting beside the sink, he ripped open the package, stuck a cinnamon bun in his mouth, and then tilted the cook pot over the sink to drain the pasta.

Saskia wandered out with a towel wrapped around her body and her wet hair exposed to the chill apartment air. "You got the pastries. Great! But those are for breakfast."

Jack pulled the half pastry out of his mouth and set it aside on the counter. He then shook the pasta in the pan and swirled in some olive oil and parmesan cheese. "I didn't get the memo."

"You're a guy. Guys don't read memos."

He frowned at her obvious anger over him having eaten one pastry out of the full dozen he'd purchased. Then he immediately knew it wasn't the pastry. With women, it was never what they were nagging about, but something underneath and very difficult to dredge up that was the real problem. And a man had best be wary.

"Sorry," he offered. "I'll forgo my morning pastry in penance."

A heavy sigh from Saskia warned that the apology wasn't what she'd wanted to hear. Could he get a cheat sheet on this woman? Anything to save him from an argument. She wandered into her bedroom.

While he mixed garlic with olive oil in a small pan over the stove, he wondered what her problem was. Must be worried about the poison thing. As he would be if he were in her shoes. If she was all about not killing, why had she agreed to provide Clive the poison in the first place?

There were things about her that confused him. And not in a normal "because she's a woman" way that confused all men. Was she hiding something from him? He'd never asked her how she'd known to invite him to the crew. Or at least, Clive believed he was here by her suggestion. Which he was not. Hmm…

She emerged from the bedroom wearing an oversized sweater, which reduced her figure to a blob. Her hair was pulled up in a messy bun and she looked as if she'd just rolled out of bed. Tumbled and so bloody sexy.

Jack hissed when he put his hand too close to the burner, and flinched away.

Saskia hid a smile and settled onto the sofa. "Watch yourself. You know those stove things are for big boys?"

"Are you hungry for some pasta, or what?"

"Always. Bring me a plate."

So she wanted to be waited on, eh?

Jack stirred the garlic and slowly added in some heavy cream and salt. If he had pine nuts that would make the dish perfect, but he'd forgo them for a simple meal. Then he decided the smoked fish might be a good side, so he put a couple pieces of that on each plate, rolled on some pasta, then topped it with the creamy white sauce.

The burner phone in his pocket buzzed, and he pulled it out and checked the text with his back to Saskia. Monday. Midnight. Location info to follow.

Jonny's fate was fast coming to the fore. Jack had forty-eight hours to save him. He hated being rushed. His little brother had better appreciate all that he was sacrificing for him.

* * * *

Saskia was feeling off, and it was because of the poison issue. She'd snapped at Jack earlier, and now she felt jittery. Like a drug addict coming down from a high and seeking her next fix. Or it could have been the espresso she'd slugged down before driving to the garage to look in and see if Clive or Niles needed anything.

She'd gotten Jack to do what she'd needed. She should be feeling great about this job. Instead, she couldn't get out of her brain that condemning look Jack had given her when he'd suggested the client had died from the poison.

She hadn't been responsible for his death. She'd been fighting to protect herself.

With a nod, and an inhale to summon calm, she peeked into the garage office. Clive nodded she enter. Tugging her coat closed and zipping it up to the neck, she wandered in.

"Where's Jack?"

"After a white van."

"Good boy. He's a bit of all right, yeah?"

"Sure."

Clive leaned back in his chair, now giving her more attention than was normal for him. Eye contact, even. Saskia tried not to look away. It would only make her appear nervous.

"Did you get what I asked for?" he asked.

"I'll have it. Tomorrow."

"You sure?"

"Yes, I'm sure."

"Watch the testy tone, Sass. I don't like a woman who thinks she knows more than she does."

Before she could caution her affront, Saskia said, "Maybe it's you who is testy?"

Clive shook his head. "Maybe you and your lover had an argument. Don't fuck him up, Sass. We need him at his best tomorrow night."

"Don't—" She fisted her hands at her sides. "Why is it always the women who fuck things up? You men can be perfect assholes, you know that? You expect us to do everything for you and then when one thing isn't perfect, it's our fault. Not your overblown expectations."

"You've become too bold. I prefer the quiet Sass who did what she was told. Like on the previous job."

"And I prefer the quiet Clive."

He stood abruptly. And Saskia couldn't stop herself from flinching. She'd overstepped. Damn, why had she reacted like that?

Was this job really going to bring her down so easily?

"Whatever your problem is, Sass, solve it. Before tomorrow night. Can I rely on you?"

"Of course you can."

"Don't make me regret trusting you."

She nodded and quickly exited. Niles wasn't in the garage so she returned to the car. Once behind the wheel she beat the dashboard with a fist and growled.

Chapter 12

Tomorrow was the day, and it couldn't come soon enough for Jack. Jonny needed him. Family came first, but he was not a man to walk out on a half-finished job.

"You got that extra blanket in your room?" Saskia asked as she wandered toward her bedroom.

"Yes."

"I want it. It's freezing in my room."

"But then I'll have but the sheet."

"My room faces the north side. You can wear your coat."

Now she was just being obstinate. Jack marched into his room, grabbed the blanket, then headed to her room. The door was open, and he assumed she was dressing to sleep, and that he could catch her naked....

Saskia pulled an oversized T-shirt down to her thighs. She met his gaze, and a tiny smirk gave him some hope she wasn't going to send him to bed with an angry command.

He tossed her the blanket, then leaned a shoulder against the doorframe. "You know, we could share body heat. Then neither one of us would need the blanket."

The woman tossed the blanket to the bed and strolled around the end of the bed. She aimed for him, and he knew what was coming. In one smooth motion she jumped up to hook her legs about his waist and anchored herself to his body.

"You take subtle hints well," she said.

She kissed him roughly, eagerly. And he was all in. Knees hitting the edge of the bed, Jack spilled forward, not breaking the kiss as Saskia landed on her back. But she quickly took charge by rolling over the top of him and stretching her hands up to push his arms above his head. Fingers clasping into his, she winked at him.

"Is this the kinky portion of the evening?" he asked.

"You told me no whips and chains."

He lunged up to catch her pout with a hard kiss. She bit his lower lip. And none too gently!

"Saskia, please, I don't want to end up with bruises. But I also don't want to stop you from doing whatever it is you want to do with me. I kind of like being on the bottom."

"I promise no weird stuff. I just like to take control."

"I've noticed."

She unbuttoned his shirt and spread it open. Her skin held a touch of the ever-present chill, so when she spread her palms across his pecs, Jack sucked in a breath. It was the hard pinch to his nipple that stirred up his yelp. In reaction, he smacked a palm across her arse.

A defiant glint flickered in her gaze as she drew her tongue along her lower lip and slid her hand down his abs. He still wore his trousers and his erection strained against the fabric. When she squeezed his cock, hard, Jack bucked his hips to encourage her.

"Time to ride my big Irish bull." She bent and lashed his nipple quickly with her tongue. Working down the zipper, she was careful. And when he sprang free, it was to the hot, wet touch of her tongue.

Jack slammed his hands out to the sides of the bed and closed his eyes. This kind of torture he could endure. He'd never give up the information. No matter how long, or how deep, she took him. Not that he had any information to divulge, but it's where his brain went.

On the other hand, if he ever wound up in a situation that found him tied up and his dick exposed, she could wheedle out anything she wanted to learn from him by doing exactly what she was doing right now. The focus and intensity of her tongue did not relent as it traced the thick, pulsing vein on the underside of his cock. His gut tightened, as did his muscles all over. He could feel release building, and when she clutched his bollocks and fit her mouth completely over the head of him, he couldn't hold back any longer.

She took it all. And as his hips pumped and his body shuddered, he swore a sweet oath to all that was right in this world. It had found him. For a few brief days.

Now, how to extend those days into much longer?

* * * *

Saskia rolled over to face Jack, who winked at her. She pulled the blanket up to cover their shoulders, slid her legs between his, and snuggled her body as close as possible to his. The shared body heat was ridiculous. And much needed. Remind her never again to agree to a job in Helsinki in January.

Unless of course, Gentleman Jack was along for the ride. And the sex.

His gray eyes were clear and calm as he matched her stare. "What are you thinking about?" she asked.

"I'm thinking it would be nice if you'd come along with me after this heist."

Her heartbeats quickened, and not in a good way. "Come along with you? Where are you going?" She did want to know. And yet, she did not.

He shrugged. "Places."

"That's not enough incentive to get a girl to follow in your footsteps. Even if you are a good fuck."

He chuckled. "Not sure where, exactly, my path will lead me, but I know I'm leaving things behind."

"What does that mean?"

"I'm, uh…going off the grid."

Yeah, she knew that. Unfortunately. But she was surprised he'd confessed as much to her. He really must trust her. Good going, Saskia. And…not. "You're no longer going to pull off heists or beat people bloody?"

"Heists? Maybe. It's in my blood. You know?"

She did know that. The idea of never again pulling a heist? Impossible.

"I don't like the violence," Jack explained. "It's not me. Not anymore. A bloke can change."

"So can a girl. But living off the grid is not easy, Jack. There's a reason they call it living the hard way. You need a plan."

"I'll have one soon enough."

"Soon enough is not a plan. Such a move requires a lot of thought and preparation. Do you have someone to relocate you?"

He shrugged, unwilling to offer too much information.

"And you think I would leap blindly into that adventure with you?" she asked. "Maybe I like what I do? Don't you think I have talent?"

"You are beyond talented. In the ways of disguise and sucking a bloke's cock."

"I think you definitely prefer one over the other."

"Let's just say, I'm not ever going to refuse your need to be on top."

Nor would she turn away an opportunity to have sex with this man. Their between-the-sheets adventures were fun, and hot, and satisfying. But what if the man were in her life all the time? And she could jump him whenever the mood struck. She'd never been a girl to have a long-term boyfriend. Not because the idea of it didn't appeal. She'd just never met a guy with whom she wanted to spend more than a few days or weeks.

Never trusted a man enough, if truth be told. Because those she trusted always left her.

Could she go on the lam with Jack?

"Just for a little while?" he queried.

"Live the hard life? No more heists? It's in our blood, Jack."

"I know, but…" He exhaled and looked toward the ceiling. "I can't tell you everything. I intend to go dark. I don't have a choice." He tilted his gaze toward her. The rough-tough thug had quieted, and the pleading in his eyes captured her need for connection in ways she couldn't comprehend. "Come along with me, Saskia. See if we like spending time with one another."

"Maybe."

"After tomorrow night, I want to take a few days to get out and away. Then I'll call for you. What do you say about that? You can walk away anytime you want."

"What if I walk away and tell someone where to find you?"

"That's a choice you need to make. I trust you won't. And if you do?"

"Gentleman Jack will come looking for me and apologize first?"

He clasped her hand and kissed the knuckles. He *would* come after her if she thought to betray him. As was just.

Saskia rolled to her back and glanced out the window. The faintest green glow from the Northern Lights danced high in the corner of the window.

"I'll think about it," she said.

Because she did have to give such an offer some consideration. She never thought she'd fall for the tough guy with more issues than she had, but it had happened, despite his quick temper and need to always protect her. Or was it because of those reasons? It couldn't be because of the sex. Sex was a big part of her liking him, but she knew the bloom of lust was always quick to subside, and then the couple had to deal with being around one another and sharing and emotions.

"Tell me something," he said in the quiet of the early morning. "Do you know who you are? I mean, beyond all the disguises and the charades. Who is Saskia Petrovik?"

That was a stupid question. She knew who she was. Maybe. It was easy to slip into a role. She'd been doing it all her life. Could she bare herself for him? Tell him that she desperately wanted family. That she knew her parents were out in the world somewhere. Living their own lives. Unconcerned that they'd left their twelve-year-old daughter in her grandmother's care over seventeen years earlier? Had they ever contacted Grandma Petrovik to ask about her?

Didn't matter anymore. At least, it shouldn't. She had shoved away the longing to see her parents again. They'd taught her skills. And she had survived.

But every time Jack said family came first, it stabbed her in the heart.

"I'm Saskia Petrovik," she said firmly. "And I'm tired. We've got a busy day tomorrow. I'll talk to you in the morning."

"Dream about where we'll go after we leave this frozen tundra, will you?"

"Any place that's warm."

"That's my girl."

Actually, she was no man's girl. And he'd have to learn that sooner, rather than later.

Dispelling a sigh, Saskia closed her eyes and ran through the ways she would reveal her truth to him without sending him fleeing. Because she needed him to know her. All of her. Only then would he know just how impossible it would be for her to accept his invitation.

* * * *

The crew was meeting at three in the afternoon to gather their equipment and go over the plans for the job. It was ten a.m., and Jack had finished his third cinnamon bun, along with half the juice. What he needed was a juicy medium-rare steak to carry him through this day, but there was only rice and pasta in the cupboard. He'd whip up some macaroni and cheese for lunch.

Saskia had left to retrieve coffee. The Kaffecentralen down the block brewed a fist-in-the-gut blend. She'd promised to bring him back two.

Meanwhile, his phone rang. It was Kierce Quinn at the Paris ECU headquarters. A place that he'd never be able to point to on a map, but he knew it was somewhere in the sixteenth arrondissement.

"Speak," Jack said as he corralled the pastry crumbs on his plate.

"Your suspicions panned out. An Italian dignitary with ties to ISIL died from poison four days ago. He had a safe deposit box in the Belgian bank that your crew hit two weeks earlier."

"Is that so?" Jack straightened. This was remarkable information. "So our theory is correct? Clive intends to strike again. Leave poison in someone's safe deposit box. Have you run a list of names for the bank here in Helsinki?"

"I'm doing that right now. Whatever happens, Jack, you can't let Clive leave poison in anyone's box. Or you can. You just have to know which box he leaves it in."

"So this whole safe cracking bit is a coverup to hide the real crime of murder." Jack shook his head. "Seems an awkward way to go about it. Why not take the guy out on the street or in his home?"

"It is a perfect crime. No need to stakeout a crime scene or even approach the victim. All the man needs is access to the victim's safe deposit box."

"Two keys are needed to access those boxes. Even if the target's key was stolen, Clive would still need another to open the box: the bank's copy. And apparently, they were not drilled open because there couldn't have been any signs of entry at the last heist or it would have been in the report. He had both those keys."

"Exactly."

"He must have a contact inside the bank. In order to access that key?"

"What information have you gotten from Petrovik?"

"What information should I get? She's one of the crew. Clive keeps her in the dark as much as the rest of us."

Quinn paused a long time. "Right. Uh...right."

Weird pause. But the guy was weird. A geeky gamer who couldn't be any more than twenty-two or three who spent all his time at headquarters and most of that online. Jack wasn't sure Quinn had a friend or even a home outside of work. "What are my orders?"

"Dixon says you need to keep us online during the heist."

Hunter Dixon was his boss, the man in charge of the Elite Crimes Unit. "I can do that, but you'll have to maintain radio silence. I don't want to give Clive any reason to suspect. Or for that matter, Niles and Saskia."

"Right. As soon as you know that Clive has planted the poison, alert us. We'll send local authorities to round him up."

"And the rest of the crew, I presume."

"That's how it works. You'll be out in a few days, I'm sure."

"Great." As one of the crew he would be arrested and incarcerated. The local police wouldn't know he was a member of an elite crimes unit. And they wouldn't know even after his bail had been posted and charges had been dropped against him. "Keep me posted, Quinn. Over and out."

Jack set down the phone and caught his forehead against his palm. He couldn't afford to sit in jail a few days. He had to leave tonight after the heist. He had an appointment scheduled to remove the chip at the base of his skull early in the morning. The surgeon would be at the meeting place for only a short time; if he didn't show, he'd lose that opportunity. And after that? Back to London to find Jonny.

And then, off the grid.

If he didn't alert the ECU to the completed heist, he could leave, and get on his way. The ECU would still have the evidence on Clive and his crew—which included Saskia—and could go after them.

And what did Jack care? He'd done his part. He'd uncovered the real crime behind the heists. As far as he was concerned, he'd done his job. He didn't need to stick around and clean up the shrapnel.

The door opened and Saskia walked in with a tray of four coffees. She set them on the counter, then kissed him. A long, deep, cold kiss. He pulled away and tapped her nose. "You're an ice queen."

"Let it go, let it go!" she sang.

"I don't understand that."

"I'm actually glad that you don't. It's a line from a song featured in a kiddie movie."

"Do you go to a lot of kiddie movies?"

"There are some you can't ignore. The coffee is black as Hades's bellybutton today. It'll give you a wicked buzz."

"I generally like to relax and run through the plans on the day of a heist," he said, "but anything to stay warm."

"I have to decide which disguise to wear." Saskia grabbed a cup and veered toward her bedroom.

A while later, Jack wandered into the bedroom and sat on the bed to watch as she browsed through a lot more clothing than he thought a person who should be traveling light should own.

"I'm going with the nondescript white male look." She pointed to the black skull cap and waggled a black moustache. "Gotta blend in with the boys. What precautions do you usually take?"

"Keep my head down and my cap pulled low. Dark clothing. An awareness of my surroundings without being obvious. But as the driver I'll have to worry about the vehicle too."

"Yeah, and did you notice?" She pointed toward the window. "It started raining. And the weatherman predicts it'll rain through the night."

"That can't be good in this cold climate. How does it actually rain?"

"I don't know, but it's going to be slippery later. Have you driven on ice?"

"Of course." Jack sipped his coffee to hide his grimace.

"You haven't. That's okay. I have, but it's been a long time. Just take it slow and don't slam on the brakes or you'll end up slipping and sliding like a drunk goose."

"Have you seen many drunk geese?"

"I'm from Russia," she stated, as if that was answer enough. And, strangely, it was.

She laid out a black turtleneck sweater and black leggings. Primping at the wig, and not missing a single detail. He did love to watch a master at work. He couldn't walk away from her. And if she landed in jail? Hell, he couldn't let that happen. Could he?

"Have you considered my offer?" he asked. "Because I'll be heading out as soon as we walk away from the bank."

She tugged back her hair and snapped a rubber band about it to make a ponytail. "You know you have to drop Niles and Clive off at the airport."

"Right."

"And you don't fly?"

"Nope. Gotta keep my feet planted on the ground."

"How does a quick escape work with the ferry?"

"It's not easy, but I don't have as far to fall if anything goes wrong with the boat. Unfortunately, the ferry doesn't leave until morning, so after I dump the van, I'll have some waiting around to do. Will it be with you?"

"Jack." She pulled the skull cap over her hair and propped her hands at her hips. Behind her, the daylight framed her in a soft light. "You asked me who I was last night."

"And did you figure that out?"

Her smile was anything but mirthful. "I've always known who I am, Jack Angelo. Just as I know who you really are."

He didn't anticipate the punch, so when her fist swung through the air and clocked him up under the jaw, Jack dropped his coffee cup and his body soared to the left. The momentum toppled him off the side of the bed and he landed on the floor, groaning at the surprisingly powerful force behind that punch.

Saskia stepped over him and leaned down. "I know the first stop you'll make after you dump the van and head on your merry journey to go off the grid. I know, because I followed you there the other day. That surgeon will remove the chip embedded at the base of your skull."

Jack gaped, and shuffled up to his elbows.

"Don't be too surprised," she said. "You know how people like us work. Everything is covert. You can't trust anyone, not even yourself."

"How the hell do you know...?"

She gripped his shirt and yanked it so his shoulders strained to hold the position of subservience beneath her. "I'm with the ECU, Jack Angelo. And you're my job."

Chapter 13

Jack jumped up from the floor. His muscles reacted for combat, his arms arching and fists forming, but he cautioned himself. He never hit a woman. Unless that was his only option.

But what she'd just told him!

"You are with the ECU?" he asked, utterly stymied. "I don't understand? What the hell?"

"I need you to know this going forward. So we're on the up and up." Saskia pulled off the knit cap and tossed it onto the bed. "You're my job, Jack. The Elite Crimes Unit had a suspicion that you'd go AWOL sooner rather than later, and they assigned me to make sure that doesn't happen."

Jack ran his fingers over his scalp. Processing what she was saying proved difficult, and yet, at the same time, he well knew that the ECU had him under surveillance. All the time. He wore a damn chip, for fucks sake! And he lived in an apartment the ECU had assigned him. He drove a beat-up old BMW the ECU had given him. And he received a minimal salary for his work.

Yet still, they could have no idea why he wanted out at this particular moment. Could they? No. He'd been careful. He hadn't made any traceable calls, written anything down. All the texts from those holding Jonny had been received on a burner phone. Had the ECU managed to hack into it? Anything was possible. And with expert hackers at the helm? He should never doubt that they knew every step he took.

Saskia had been assigned to make sure he didn't leave? Was she supposed to convince him staying in the ECU would give him the best life, make everything all romance and roses?

Now that he considered it... Was she seducing him in order to ensure his alliances remained to the ECU?

She had been very forward sexually.

"I thought if I didn't fulfill my contract to the ECU I was to serve the remainder of the prison sentence," Jack said. Or end up six-feet under. "Why did they send you to do this? Whatever *this* is. Are you screwing me in hopes I'll fall in love with you or something?"

"What? Give me a break. I don't need to seduce a man to make him do what I want."

"Yeah? What is it then? Are you going to bring me in so they can lock me up and this time throw away the key?"

"I don't have that information. What the ECU decides to do with you is classified. I've only been told to keep you from going off the grid. That's my real assignment. Yours is the heists. You don't know what a bitch it has been serving Clive for a month just waiting for the ECU to send you to me."

"I can't believe this! They *expected* I'd run?"

Impossible. He'd only been contacted about Jonny last week. Could the ECU be involved? If they were, what kind of fucked up—

"I followed you to the surgeon's place the other day," Saskia said. "Did you make an appointment to have that chip taken out?"

He squeezed a hand at the back of his neck. He couldn't feel the tiny chip, but had been conscious when it had been planted at the base of his skull with some kind of injection gun. Just like chipping a dog.

How had he not noticed a tail when he'd gone to meet the doctor? Of course, she couldn't have looked like the woman he would expect to see and get suspicious about. She'd probably been wearing a disguise. She was a goddamned chameleon!

"How do you think you're going to stop me?" he challenged. "Are you going to physically detain me? You haven't the chops for that, little girl. Even if you do stop me now, nothing will prevent me from leaving sooner or later."

Though it was now or never for him. He was all in. Because he had to be for Jonny.

"Why the escape, Jack? You agreed to serve your time to the ECU in exchange for getting out of prison. You owe the ECU." Straightening, she crossed her arms. "I gotta tell you. I thought you had more integrity than to ditch a contract."

That one stung. Jack prided himself on integrity. As larcenous and bloody as it had been. But he was a man of his word. Only, that word always favored family first. "You don't know me."

"Oh yeah? I know you've got a thing for me, and you want me to go on the lam with you."

"I suggested you tag along for a while. We like fucking each other. That's all."

She paced before the window. But when she cast a knowing smile at him, Jack had to caution his needy heart. "If you stay with the ECU, you can fuck me whenever you like."

"Really?" He shook his head. "That's how you're going to do this? Prostitute yourself to achieve success?"

Saskia inhaled sharply and shook her head. "It's not like that. I would never do that. And don't you dare accuse me of such. Jack, I—" She fisted the air. "I know the urge to run is strong. I've felt it once in a while, too. But then I get smart. What's so terrible about your life that you have to abandon it? I mean, you're doing something you enjoy, aren't you?"

"You think I like busting faces and breaking ribs?" Jack strode out of the bedroom, incensed that her opinion of him was so low.

Saskia followed and grabbed his arm. He roughly pulled away, not wanting to be near her. She'd revealed herself as the enemy. And he—he needed to get out of here and think about this. Get his head on straight.

And make a call to London before everything went bonkers tonight.

"Clive doesn't trust you," she said.

"What the hell do you care? Apparently that's not even your job, is it?"

"It is and it's not. Clive is leery of you, Jack. He told me."

"So what will he do? Poison me? I doubt that. The man hasn't the bollocks. Besides, if you ask me, his suspicions lie with you. And apparently for good reason. But I don't get it. You're not working the heist? You have no stake in catching Clive out with the goods?"

"That's my secondary mission. You are my first."

"Christ. I need some air."

"You have to stick around for the heist, Jack!"

The job was to occur tonight. He would drive getaway, and secure the break-in along with Niles. And yet, he'd already reported to the ECU his suspicions regarding what the focus of his assignment had been: to learn what Clive was doing during the heists. Anything that happened from here on was not on his ticket.

"Jack, stay here and talk to me!"

He grabbed his coat and shoved his feet into his shoes. "You don't get to tell me what to do! In fact, maybe I'll make sure Clive's trust for you fails. How would you deal with that?"

"We're working for the same team. At least until you decide to go AWOL. Jack!"

He slammed the door behind him and clattered down the stairs, cursing himself for such a childish comeback. He wouldn't do anything to endanger Saskia because—

No, he wasn't going to think it. To do so would acknowledge how much he cared about the woman. Because he did. He'd asked her to go along with him and he'd meant it.

She had scammed him. Played him from the moment he'd set foot on the ferry to Helsinki. Stupid, idiot bastard that he was.

"Bloody hell, this mission is cocked up."

* * * *

Saskia tossed a shoe across the room and slammed her body down onto the lumpy sofa cushions. She shouldn't have told him.

She had to tell him. Maybe?

Part of her had wanted to tell so she could solicit his trust and confidence. They were working on the same team! They had that in common. And she had divulged information that Jack might like to know so he could alter his path. He didn't want to get sent back to prison.

Unfortunately, she might have just given him a reason to never trust her again.

And she might have blown the mission.

She should have followed him out of the apartment and tracked his every move. He could be headed to the surgeon's office right now, to have the GPS chip removed. After which, she'd never find him.

But no. She knew Jack Angelo. Not well. But she knew his pride and his heart. He had committed to this heist and he would see it through to the end. And on the brief report Saskia had gotten as an e-mail a few days before she'd begun following Jack, the ECU psychologist had indicated he didn't believe Angelo would take off until the mission was complete. He never left a job unfinished. The man was a stickler for integrity.

He needed air right now. Had to be his reason for storming out. It would be wise if she let him boil until he settled to a simmer.

And now that it was all out there, and he started to think clearly, they could work together during the heist and nail Clive. The man intended to poison someone. She should have asked Jack if he'd called in to the ECU with the information about the poison.

She'd been deep undercover and hadn't communicated with headquarters at all, save for immediately following the previous heist. She'd initially been assigned to work with Clive because the man had completed a heist before the first one she'd worked and he'd walked out with nothing. And then after she had joined, nothing for a second heist. The ECU had thought it best she go deep, keep contact minimal. Because they had no clue who Clive was connected to and how close they were watching.

Only the day before she'd been alerted by the ECU that her mission had been altered—that they were sending in a new man to work the heist case—had she broken that deep cover. She'd been pissed about the altered mission, but also intrigued. Keep an eye on one of her own? What did they expect him to do, exactly, besides going off the grid? And why was he so valuable to them that they'd make the effort of trying to keep him on board? Jack hadn't shown her any remarkable skills that she believed the unit would find singularly valuable.

Unless there was an aspect to this assignment she didn't know about. Very possible. The ECU liked to keep back details. *Need to know* were three words that drove her crazy.

A lot was going on, and Saskia suddenly felt as if she hadn't a finger on a single bit of what was happening in her orbit. She wasn't sure about her position with Clive. She had no poison to hand over to him; she'd have to concoct the fake this afternoon. And she might have lost any ground she might have gained with Jack.

"I need to call the ECU," she muttered. Yet a call-in would be like signaling her failure. "Right. Not going to make that call. I can do this. As soon as the heist is complete I'll stick to Angelo like glue. He won't have a chance to go AWOL. And with luck, we'll have confirmation on what Clive is up to. He'll be arrested, and the case can be closed."

She nodded, drawing up the confidence she needed. She could do this. She would do this.

* * * *

Jack had picked up a plain white van at a used car lot across the city. Every chrome part on it was rusted and the muffler was dangling, but the engine was clean and the heater worked. Now he sat parked, the engine idling, in a supermarket parking lot across the street from where he'd been staying with Saskia. The rain had stopped, and no ice had formed on the roads, yet the weatherman on the radio had suggested everyone stay in tonight because that's when the storm was coming.

A rain storm in January. In Helsinki. Bollocks. But he could drive on ice or snow. Didn't matter.

He thumbed his cell phone, vacillating on whether or not to call the ECU and demand an explanation for the shite he'd just learned about. The call would only put them on high alert. They couldn't know that Saskia had revealed her role in this case to him.

So why had she? She wasn't stupid. Very smart, in fact.

He had to stop going over this, thinking it would give him answers that weren't there. There was a new snag. But that didn't change the fact he'd started something here in this icebox and he was going to finish it.

He'd never leave a mission half finished. And despite his mental arguments that he'd served his purpose, if he walked off the crew now, he'd raise too many red flags and Clive might call it all off, thus negating the chance to have him arrested.

So he called the ECU and connected with Kierce Quinn.

"I was just going to call you," Kierce said. "I've got the list from the Helsinki bank of all the safe deposit box holders. There are quite a few names that stand out. Dignitaries, celebrities, foreign advisors and council. Funny how a little bank in the middle of the tundra attracts so many heavy rollers, eh?"

"Just tell me what you've got, Quinn."

"Right. When I take into consideration the previous victim's political ties, I was able to narrow the list down to five possibilities. Oh, and there was another heist before the Belgian job that Clive did. Same MO. No money taken."

"And why am I only hearing about that job now?"

"It was on the dossier. Are you okay, Jack? Feeling all right?"

"Of course I am," he said huffily. He'd read the dossier. Briefly. Those tiny little files on his cell phone screen were a pain to read. "I'm sure I saw that information. Now don't get off track."

"Okay." The least convincing reassurance Jack had heard.

He didn't want to blow it with Kierce because the guy would go straight to the top and—hell, did it even matter anymore? They knew he was going to run. How incredible was that? Now the challenge was to make sure they couldn't follow him. And that included Saskia.

"I've run the list for the first bank and come up with a name," Kierce said. "There were actually two people who had safe deposit boxes in the first bank that have died within the last month. One was a little old lady who owned a dozen cats so I marked her off."

"So you're saying Clive is making hits on people through their safe deposit boxes," Jack interrupted. Because if he didn't lay this out, Quinn would talk up a storm. "Why?"

"He has to have a boss. Which has always been the ECU's suspicion. Someone pulling the strings. Can you find out if he has a hit list?"

"Yeah, that's an idea. We're pulling the heist tonight."

"We need you to stay in contact the whole time, Jack. We've got to have eyes on Clive Hendrix."

"Why don't you—" Jack rubbed a hand over his mouth. He'd almost asked why they didn't get Saskia to do that. But then, she'd have eyes on him as well as Clive. Busy woman. Very busy. "Yeah, all right. I'll stay in touch. Text me the names you've got."

"I just did. Now that we know Clive Hendrix is murdering people the stakes just sky-rocketed. You've got to nail him. And the only way to do that is to have proof he's placing poison in a safe deposit box. As soon as you've got that confirmation, we'll send in the local authorities. I'll have the Helsinki police and Interpol on standby."

"Brilliant." But he could only think "shite." With Interpol in the area that would make his escape more difficult. But not impossible. "Talk to you later, Quinn."

He didn't wait for a reply and clicked off and tossed the phone onto the passenger seat.

Turning around to inspect the empty back of the van, he knew they'd have room to fit in the drill and three people back there. And no haul from the bank's vaults?

"Genius," he muttered of the method used to make a hit. But also a logistical nightmare for him. He'd have to find a way to catch Clive in the act tonight. With the poison in hand. Which wasn't going to be real poison. And he wasn't sure if he could trust Saskia to have his back.

He tugged out the burner phone and reread the last text. Less than two days until Jonny was dead.

It would take him a good day of travel, via boat and train, to get back to London.

Jack shook his head. "Looks like I'm going to have to conquer my fear of flying."

Chapter 14

If he'd thought driving on icy roads would be a breeze, Jack now realized how mistaken he had been. This drive was going to take nerves of steel. It had rained all day and now the streets gleamed like glass. It had taken him five minutes to drive the distance of two blocks. Few cars were out and about, and if they were, they slid and slipped as he was. And slamming on the brakes was out of the question.

After driving into an alleyway devoid of CCTV cameras, he got out and pulled out the black shoe polish he'd purchased before buying the car. He swiped it over the back and front plates, making it impossible to read. Later, he'd drive out to the junkyard behind an old warehouse that once manufactured fish nets and crush the thing. It would be his final act in this game.

That is, if he got the goods on Clive tonight. And he'd need Saskia's help to do that. He hadn't spoken to her since he'd stormed out this morning. His anger had cooled and he was now in work mode. He hoped Saskia was in the same place.

Waiting at a red light, he texted Saskia and asked if she needed a lift.

She immediately texted back the middle finger emoji.

"All right then. She's good." He tucked away the phone but didn't shift into drive, even when the light turned green. Because his conscience screamed for him to pay attention to what she hadn't said. "No, she's not good. We're not good. I have to talk to her before the job."

He checked his watch. He had to pick up Clive and Niles in an hour.

Saskia's flat was five minutes away.

And, thanks to the ice, twenty minutes later he made it to her place. Scrambling up the stairs, he hoped he hadn't missed her. As he opened the door, he ran right into a young mustachioed man with dark hair tucked under his knit cap.

Jack grabbed him by the head and kissed him long and deep.

Saskia initially struggled, slamming a palm against his chest, but too quickly she grabbed the front of his coat to keep him at her mouth. Her kisses were always true and needy and everything she needed him to know at that moment. She was angry with him. She wanted him.

When she shoved him against the doorframe, he grabbed her hand and held it. She exhaled and gave it a squeeze.

"I'm sorry I stormed out," he said. "You laid a lot on me."

"I had to tell you."

"You didn't have to. You probably would have been better off had you not."

"I needed you to get details to the ECU about the poison. And I wanted you to give a good long think to your plans for later."

"Which I did. Why couldn't you contact them about the poison?"

"I've been deep undercover. Haven't wanted to risk the call because I suspect Clive has been monitoring my phone."

"Smart. I talked to Kierce Quinn."

"Paris office?"

"Yes. He checked a list of safe deposit boxes from your Belgian job. A foreign dignitary died from poison four days ago. They traced his steps back to a visit to the bank two days before that."

"Shit."

"Same with the heist previously."

"The one before I stepped in?"

"Yes, another dignitary. Quinn gave me a list of possible targets in this bank." He patted his pocket. "I need to catch Clive in the act of putting the poison in a box. Did you, uh…"

"I made a fake," she said, and then winced. "We can't convict him on the grounds of possessing a fake poison."

"We only need intent. But for good measure we need his hit list. Or the people he's working for."

"I suspected he's answering to someone higher up, but he's so closed. I've never had a chance to learn much. And you were right. He's suspicious of me. I've been asking too many questions. I hope I haven't blown my cover."

"I'll have your back. Promise."

"So…uh, does that mean we're good?"

"We are. Can we work together tonight?"

"I wouldn't have it any other way. But are you going to skip out after the heist?"

He shrugged. She knew his thoughts.

"Then we'll never be completely good," she said. "Just so you know."

"I can live with that. What I can't live with is knowing we might end tonight. After the job. You going your own way and I mine?"

"It all depends on you, Jack."

"What if I want to continue seeing you?"

She leaned against him and looked up into his eyes. He felt like a high school jock with the cheerleader swooning over him. Something he'd never experienced, because what bloke went to school when he had to run a smuggling business for his father?

"Can we separate work from pleasure?" she asked. "Because I don't think this can work any other way. And I'm not sure I can do that. Work is my life. And according to you, this work is no longer your life."

He dropped her hand. Everything she said was true. How could he walk away from this life and expect that he'd get to take along a prize such as her? It was an either-or choice. And he'd already made his decision.

Sometimes he just wanted to kick family in the arse and walk away. But not today.

"Family comes first. Always," he said. Then he grabbed the doorknob. "We should go. Clive and Niles are waiting."

"I guess so." She grabbed a coat and a backpack that must have her tools and safe cracking equipment in it, then walked out ahead of him.

While they descended the stairs, Jack's phone rang. It was Kierce Quinn.

"I've got something interesting for you."

"Speak."

"There's a particular name on the bank list who stands out. Maksim Tamm, a delegate of the Estonian Parliament. He's been a leader in enforcing sanctions against arms trading. The gun runners hate him. And, surprisingly, to me at least, he's a known heroin addict."

"Why is that a surprise to you?" Jack had to ask.

"Well, he's such a powerhouse in standing up against arms deals, I just, you know..." Quinn sighed. "I know. They are all corrupt. So. Investigations into Tamm's habit have never been able to pin down his dealer in order to hold that against him. Nor, I suspect, have they tried hard. It would serve as leverage, though, to get the real intel from him."

"What does that have to do with anything?"

"If Clive is supposedly inserting a poison that resembles white crystalline substance into someone's box, I'd make a guess it would go unnoticed in the box of that person who may happen to keep other white powder in there."

"A possibility. But who keeps heroin in a safe deposit box?"

Saskia paused and turned to look up at him. Jack lowered his voice, but he wanted her to hear.

"A national dignitary who can't risk it being found in his home?" Kierce suggested.

"Maksim Tamm. I got it. Thanks, Kierce, I gotta go."

"What was that about?" she asked as he paralleled her down the last flight of stairs. "From headquarters?"

"The name I was given is Maksim Tamm. He has a box in the bank. And he's into heroin. Quinn seems to think he might keep his stash there. A good way to slip in a little poison?"

"Yes, this poison I was supposed to give to Clive could resemble the drug. My fake? It's possible. I'm a little nervous about the fake, Jack. What if Clive knows it's not the real thing?"

"Is it that easy to determine? I mean, he's not going to open it and sniff it. Won't that kill him?"

"Inhalation will kill. And he will know that."

"Then you're good. You going to be positioned at the vault all night?"

"I am."

"Then I guess I'll have to find a way to keep an eye on Clive."

* * * *

The van slid to a park behind the accountant's office next to the bank. Saskia released her tight hold on the door handle. They didn't have to worry much about people being out tonight. Only fools would risk their lives driving around on glare ice.

On the other hand, Niles had pointed out two police vehicles as they'd slowly made their way here. Jack intended to drop them off, then park elsewhere and return for the drilling.

Clive was the first out through the back door and he landed on the icy alleyway with finesse and without a wobble. The man had slipped on rubber shoe treads that were edged with steel teeth. A necessity when living in northern climes that Saskia had used on occasion herself. She wished she had on a pair now as she slid out of the seat and onto the ice rink. Using the side of the van to steady her steps, she moved slowly. The men hefted out the drill and Clive acted as an anchor to keep them from falling on their asses.

"You're on, Sass!" Clive called.

Yes, she was supposed to pick the lock on the accounting office's back door. But she was only halfway there. Taking a chance, on her next step she lunged forward and slid the last six feet up to the door. Just like an Olympic skater. A perfect ten!

"Good show, Saskia," Niles commented as he struggled to maintain hold on his end of the wood slat shipping container.

She looked to Jack who did not make eye contact with her. He hadn't answered her question about them managing work and pleasure. He'd opted to toss out the word *family*. She suspected that whatever was pulling him away from the ECU involved his family. And while that was all well and good, she got an inkling that he was struggling with the decision. Maybe? No matter. Any hope of them continuing their affair seemed dismal. There was nothing romantic going on between the two of them. Just some hot sex and—no, she wasn't going there. It had been sex. Nothing emotional. She wasn't going to pine for him like some school girl. She was here to do a job. Two jobs, actually. And she didn't intend to fail either one.

Slipping a torque key into the simple five-pin lock, she then inserted a diamond pick and raked the pins. Once. Twice, she raked the thin pick over the pins. Could she get so lucky as to not have to shiver and concentrate on counting the pins as they dropped? Three times, and...click and twist. Nice.

Opening the door, she stepped inside and crept forward through the dark back office lined with metal file cabinets and out into the front area where customers were served. The store was dark and no one was inside.

Giving the all's clear whistle, she ran back and closed the door behind the men, but Jack caught it before she could close it all the way.

"I have to move the vehicle," he said. "Out of my way."

Saluting him, she stepped aside and let him through.

"Trouble in paradise?" Clive asked from right beside her.

She hadn't felt him get so close and Saskia jumped at his sudden presence. "What do you mean?"

"There's a certain icy tension between the two of you. Do I need to know what's going on?"

"There's nothing going on."

"Don't lie to me, Sass."

She was over this man telling her what to do. Just a few more hours and she could walk away from him. With hope, for good. "As you've suspected, we had a thing, now that thing is over. We're good though. Won't be a problem tonight. I promise."

"I hope not. Do you have what I requested of you?"

"Of course."

He held out his hand and looked over his shoulder. Niles was occupied setting up the drill at the base of the wall. An initial anchor hole had to be drilled through the concrete with a smaller drill bit, which he would start before Jack returned.

Making a show of pulling on her thin thermal gloves, Saskia then held up a plastic baggie that contained a small glass vial between her and Clive. "Be careful with it. Wear gloves. I wouldn't even take it out of the baggie without a respirator on. This stuff is deadly when inhaled."

"Thanks, Sass." He made a grab for the baggie, but she snatched it away. "Right. Gloves." He reached into a pocket and pulled on a latex glove; then she gave him the plastic bag. He tucked it in an inner coat pocket. "You never let me down."

He turned and went to stand over and behind Niles, observing as he worked.

Saskia rubbed a hand up and down her arm. She did not wear a thick coat, only a thermal long-sleeved turtleneck, along with black leggings and her hair was up and under the wig of a short, brown boy's cut. The knit face mask she wore as a cap at the moment. The mustache glue had dried and she didn't notice the smell anymore. The contouring makeup gave her a five o'clock shadow and mottled skin that looked like teenage flare-ups.

Glancing to the back door, she briefly wondered if this was it. Maybe Jack would use this moment to take off and never return. And she'd lose him, and then whose ass would be in trouble? Should she have gone along with him?

No, she trusted he would work through this heist. It was his job, after all. A job that meant so little to him, he'd leave and risk imprisonment again.

"Don't let me down, Jack," she whispered.

* * * *

Ten minutes later, the slam of something against the door alerted Saskia. She looked up from the mesmerizing spin of the drill bit as Niles punched through the concrete wall for the anchor hole. The back door opened and Jack stepped inside, shivering and complaining about the cold and how he should have strapped on ice skates.

"The next time I agree to a job in the bloody bowels of Scandinavia," he muttered as he passed without glancing at her, "somebody slap me."

Niles chuckled, but Clive only sneered.

This was going to be an interesting evening.

Chapter 15

An hour later, Jack's hands were numb after taking them off the drill. He shook them out and paced behind the crew as they waited for Clive to move the drill away from the opening, which was now approximately two and a half feet wide by one foot high. More than enough room for them all to slip through and into the darkened depths of what should be the bank's utility room. They had drilled through the thin brick wall of the accountant's office and then one and a half feet of concrete on the outer bank wall.

If they would have drilled directly into the safe room from the basement, Jack estimated another three hours of drilling to get through the thick, reinforced concrete. This way had cut considerable time off the task.

He'd glanced over his shoulder while drilling to find Saskia pacing. Every time she'd meet his gaze, he'd look away. He didn't want her to get inside his head.

Not that she wasn't already deep in his thoughts and his very being. Would it be worth it to stick around and see what could develop between the two of them? It had been a fling between the two of them. Asking her to go along with him had been a foolish thing, spoken while he'd still been riding the high of some great sex. Now that he knew the truth about her? He wasn't about to stake his entire future—and his freedom—on a wish for something that would never come to fruition.

Hell. He was starting to think words like *fruition*. What was wrong with him?

Maybe she *had* turned his head and his heart a little too far for him to disregard this time. She was a singular and intriguing woman. And her body was so hot, like it had been meant for him, and him alone. He did want to know her better, longer and—

"Jack?"

He jerked out of his thoughts and saw that Saskia was the only one left in the room.

"Right. Was just calculating when I should head back out to the vehicle. It'll need time to warm up again. Did you uh…hand over the you-know-what to Clive?"

She nodded. "Fingers crossed it isn't questioned. Can we do this, Jack? I mean… You know?"

He pulled her against his body and kissed her hard. There was that strange feeling again. The one that made him wonder why he couldn't have the life he wanted and Saskia as well. Because she fit him. And that had never happened with a woman before.

"I need you tonight," he said quietly. "We have to work together. We've got to find out if Clive has a hit list. And I will have to catch him with his hand in the cookie jar."

Her fingers clenched against his chest as she processed that information. She nodded. "I'm here for you. I'll be at the vault. But I can take a break, maybe wander down to check on Clive."

He nodded. "Give it half an hour, then take a break to stretch. I'll find a reason to walk around inside after that. Saskia." He bracketed her face with his palms. "I need to be able to contact you after this."

Her eyebrow quirked. "I've got your number."

"It'll be trash in a few hours."

"Right. Going off the grid," she muttered. "Unless I can stop you."

So she wasn't on his side. Never had been, never would be. Because she couldn't be. Her alliances were to the ECU. He didn't blame her for that. It would just make his task of keeping her in his life more difficult.

"Would you speak to me if, after I do make it out and go black, I find you later?"

She nodded. "Let the games begin, Gentleman Jack." She kissed him, a slow, lush contact between them. "But I warn you, I'm good at what I do."

Dropping, she entered the drilled hole and disappeared.

Yes, she was good at what she did. But so was he. He could work with that.

Crouching before the drilled hole, Jack inhaled the dusty wet cement odor then forced his wide shoulders through the tight squeeze and into the dark room. An empty mop bucket sat near the hole and beside that a torn-up mop. Must have gotten tangled in the drill bit when he'd punched through. Niles stepped aside as Jack stood. The door to the small supply room was open and Clive was gone.

"Clive is making the rounds," Niles whispered. "Verifying camera locations and—"

"Good to go," Clive's voice suddenly said through the doorway. "All cameras exactly where we marked them. No night guard. Everything quiet and dark, save one light above a desk highlighting a dead plant."

With limited vocal communication from here on out, Jack knew his job was merely to wait. He was the getaway driver. And, he should probably get back to guarding the office in which they'd entered. But he'd verify everyone was in position before leaving.

The crew slinked down a hallway and toward the safe room, which wasn't even a room but a vault door at the end of the hallway. An interesting open plan that had been designed to highlight the safe door to those patrons who could view it through a glass wall from the lobby. It made him nervous. Any of their headlamps might be viewed by a passerby out on the street if they turned their head just so and the flash was magnified by the windows.

But they'd planned for that and would work in the dark until light was required. And Jack doubted too many would be out wandering the streets at two a.m. risking a broken neck by slipping on the icy surface.

Saskia stopped before the safe door and, with a flick to turn on her headlamp, inspected the setup. "Richardson 2700. Just as expected," she said softly. "Always good to be right about something for a change."

She nodded to Niles, who knelt before the safe and opened his mini laptop. He would provide her with the technical data and she would do the hands-on cracking work.

Jack appreciated a safecracker. It was a profession that very few could master and only with years of study and the best teachers. Generally, from a family member or close friend of the family. He'd never had the calm patience to sit there and listen for pins dropping or wheels catching. He was the rough-tough muscle, and that suited him fine.

For only one more night.

Clive looked to him and then tapped his watch. With a nod, Jack turned and headed back to the storage room. He turned once to see Clive head toward the basement door. As he climbed through the hole, he vacillated with the options of returning to the alley with the vehicle, setting off the alarm and fleeing, or simply driving away into the icy darkness.

He wasn't sure which of the three he'd choose, even as he opened the back door and, bracing himself against the wind, skated down the alleyway.

* * * *

It would take up to an hour or more to crack this safe, of which, Saskia was prepared for the ordeal. She thrived on this game. There was no digital keypad. All old school. Her fingers, in latex gloves, moved the dial while she listened through the stethoscope to the inner clicks and gear shifts and hoped for the fence to drop into a notch. The sound was purer to her than any music.

And Niles was the perfect assistant. He didn't talk much, and when he did it was almost as if he could foresee her need to know what number she'd last given him or if she'd given him contact points. He graphed all the info. If he spent any amount of time manipulating safes himself he could excel. But they'd had this conversation last heist. He didn't like the hands on. It was all about the numbers to him and reading the grids.

Saskia had grown up cracking safes and picking locks. She hadn't realized it wasn't something normal kids didn't do until third grade when her teacher had been upset she'd accidentally locked the supply closet, in which she'd left the days' treats. Saskia had told her she could get it open. The teacher had laughed. Until thirty seconds later, and with a bent paperclip and the end of a slide ruler, the lock had been picked.

Needless, her teacher had been worried about Saskia and had sent a note home with her that day. That note had never made it to her parents' hands. Not that they would have been too concerned. They had been the ones to teach her the skills she'd enhanced and studied over the years.

As well, an early love for playacting, in the bible study classes she took because her grandmother insisted, had instilled a deep love for dressing up, pulling on a new character, and ultimately walking through the world in various forms designed to trick, and manipulate.

A chameleon, her grandmother had called her. And she was proud of that. But there were times Saskia would wonder if her grandmother would be proud of her today. The reason she had been recruited by The Elite Crimes Unit was for her disguise talents. And the fact she'd tried to sign onto a bank job with an undercover operator. When given an ultimatum by the ECU, she hadn't had to vacillate on prison or working for the law for more than a few seconds. It had been a means to continue what she loved doing, and not getting caught for it.

But she may have to get caught tonight. If Jack was in contact with the ECU they would likely want him to report their every move. And they could send in authorities to arrest them. They'd nab Clive and Niles, and also Saskia and Jack. She didn't worry because the ECU would spring her free in a day or two. But she wasn't certain they had enough on Clive right now to warrant arresting him.

Jack seemed to be more involved in this relationship, whatever they had going on, than she. But was that right? Or was she too afraid to admit to herself that she was interested in him beyond a few quick fucks.

Go along with him to live off the grid? Too risky. It was…no, she had a sweet life right now. She only owed the ECU another four years. And then? Who knew? She might choose to stay on with the ECU. Because for a woman who only knew how to survive by cracking safes and playing the long game? She wasn't sure she could manage living the hard way.

Rumor had it the ECU had recently recruited a thief who had been attempting to live the hard way. But with little persuasion she had succumbed to the lure of her former life and agreed to work for the Elite Crimes Unit.

Just went to prove you could take the criminal out of the system but he'd always find a way back in, by pick or by swinging fists.

And thinking about swinging fists, Saskia wondered how Jack was faring. "Sass?"

She startled out of her thoughts and met Niles' gaze. "Huh?"

"You've been paused over that safe dial for five minutes. Everything cool?"

"Oh. Uh, yeah. Sorry. Just…working out scenarios in my brain. Read the three numbers I've cracked so far?"

Niles read them and she nodded, making a mental note to focus. She'd simply have to trust that Jack would have her back.

And that was not an easy thing to do. Because the man wanted out, and if he felt trapped she was sure he'd fight and flee, leaving her to battle it out in the carnage.

"I need to stretch my legs." She suddenly remembered she'd promised Jack she'd look in on Clive.

"What? No, you've only got two numbers left."

"Give me five, Niles. Work out the average on the contact points I've given you so far, yeah?"

"That is not part of the plan."

Why was he being so obstinate tonight?

"It is now." Saskia rose and made show of stretching a leg and then the other. "Be right back."

Chapter 16

Surprisingly, as the night grew longer, the air seemed to warm. It wasn't a noticeable feeling on his skin. Jack hadn't stopped shivering since arriving in Finland, and was sure he wouldn't thaw out until he left the country. But the ice on the roads seemed to be melting just enough to provide traction and not send the vehicle sliding across the intersection when he slammed on the brakes.

A man on a bicycle pedaled past him, waving and rolling onward, as if it wasn't two in the morning and he wasn't riding outside in ten below weather. Must have chains on those thick rubber wheels.

"This is a nutty place," Jack muttered as he circled the bank block. He didn't note any other vehicles—especially not police vehicles—and then pulled into the alleyway. But if the ECU were on them tonight, they had to be in the area. Waiting for the signal. The all's clear.

He rubbed the back of his neck where the GPS chip had been embedded. They knew exactly where he was right now.

Once parked, he turned off the ignition and checked his phone for texts. Nothing about Jonny. And Kierce Quinn hadn't contacted him either.

"Wait and see mode," he muttered glumly.

Sucking in a dry breath as he entered the chill night air, he slipped, literally, inside the accounting office's back door. Wandering up to the front window, he looked out over the street. Calm and quiet. Save the bicyclist who turned at the corner. Was the bloke an insomniac or just crazy?

"Gives me new appreciation for London's wacky weather," he said. The British Isles were having a heat wave right now with temps in the forties.

Confident all was clear, Jack crawled through the drilled hole. He was a tight squeeze, for his shoulders and biceps, which he managed only with his jacket off. No suit and tie tonight. He wore a dark pullover shirt and dark trousers. He wasn't going to advertise to any CCTV cameras.

Entering the main hallway, he saw Niles and Saskia down the hallway, kneeling before the safe. If she cracked that in another half hour he'd give her a standing ovation. She was working old school. She hadn't brought along a drill, which would provide a sight for her to peer in with a borescope and watch the inner mechanism as she twisted the outer combination dial. She worked by touch. He liked that.

He'd taken a moment before they'd entered the bank to touch her, to make contact. He would still take her along with him if she wanted to go. Yeah, he'd be that stupid. He'd have to set her up in a hideaway until he'd finished his business in London, but then, off the grid. Completely.

Did he dare tell her everything? He'd already alluded to her about a family issue. He'd wanted her to know there was a reason he was doing this, and it wasn't simply because he no longer wanted to fulfill his contract to the ECU. He'd never walk away on a bargain unless the stakes were so high he had no choice. And they were high. Jonny's life was in danger.

So he'd walk away from a reasonably good thing and take on the unknown. And he wasn't about to let a pretty face trip him up when he was so close.

But close to what, exactly? Freedom? He wasn't stupid. If he went off the grid he'd never live another day as a free man. The years and future decades would see him always looking over his shoulder, wondering if the next time he said "hi" to a passing stranger it would be the law looking to bring him down. It was possible to lose oneself in the world. But only for so long. And he suspected the ECU would be a determined foe, not ceasing their efforts to ensure he was punished for leaving them when he still owed them work.

Rock and a hard place, bloke.

Unsure whether Saskia had yet taken a walk downstairs, he decided to play a hunch that she had not and aimed for the safe deposit box room in the basement. Down the eight stairs, then a swing to the left as he'd walked that day he'd been here to check the place out. And he got a surprise.

The vault door was open wide. A beam of light wavered from within as if a flashlight were moving about.

Knowing he'd be catching the predator while at the feeding hole, Jack had to be cautious not to surprise him. Tilting his head left to right and loosening his muscles, he then flexed his fists and approached slowly. He cleared his throat as he neared the door. The light beam brightened to indicate someone was nearing the door. Jack quickened his steps and made it to the door just as Clive slipped out. He only had a moment to scan the back wall of the room. No open box doors and nothing out of order.

"Jack. What are you doing down here?"

"Everything is A-OK upstairs, so thought I'd take a look around." He noted the edge of a gas mask peeking behind Clive's hip; he'd tucked it in a back pocket. "How you doing down here? I see you got the vault open. You beat Saskia."

"I had expected to. The vault door down here was an easy crack."

"Then why even bother having her work the safe upstairs?"

Clive's brows crimped and Jack could feel the man's tension. He wasn't going to answer that question. And he didn't expect him too. He knew what was up. And the man didn't have anything in hand. Also, expected.

"It's a good thing you came back in," Clive said. "Time to pack up shop and get the hell out of here."

"Uh, okay. I guess that was the plan. First room we crack, then we're out. You need help carrying out anything from the room?"

Clive dug into his pants pocket and pulled out a small silver box that might hold a piece of jewelry or it could even be a prized possession in and of itself. "Nice, eh?"

"That's it? Doesn't make sense."

"No questions, Jack. I answer to someone else. This is what they wanted."

Ready to ask "what the fuck is that gas mask doing in your pocket," Jack paused as Clive hefted the silver box and caught it smartly on his palm. So he changed his question. "That's it? That's the job?"

"You just got paid half a million. What do you care?"

"Then why the—?" He gestured in the direction of the safe. He wasn't going to get answers, but he wasn't going to not try. "I don't get it."

"You don't need to. Are you dissatisfied with the little amount of work you've had to put in, in order to earn your keep tonight?"

"No, but—"

"No buts." He gave the vault door wheel a spin. Taking out a cloth, Clive wiped the stainless steel, despite still wearing gloves. "Get the van ready."

Clive started to walk by him and Jack caught his palm against the man's chest, slamming him against the wall. "I need to know what the hell is going on before I go anywhere."

Now that he stood so close to him, and got a good look at his face, Jack thought Clive's eyes looked glossy. And his smirk was slippery, almost loose. It was a weird thing to notice. But the man was normally so tight and in control. Did nerves do that to him?

"I don't like your sudden switch in alliance, Jack."

"It's not a switch. I'm your man. No worries. But a bloke has a right to know what he's involved in."

"Jack?" Niles wandered down the hallway, tugging earbuds from his ears so they dangled on the cord about his neck. "What's up with you two?"

"Jack's not happy with his paycheck," Clive said. "You happy with your paycheck, Niles?"

"Hell yeah. And Saskia got another number. We've only one left to go."

Clive roughly tugged away from Jack's grip and held his gaze in the dim light. But he spoke to Niles. "The job's done. We're heading out. Jack was just on his way out to start the van. Right, Jack?"

He had no proof that Clive might have left something—poison—in one of the boxes. But that didn't matter, because the ECU could alert the bank and order a search after the fact. Which meant he couldn't call in an arrest on the man tonight. The only thing they'd have on him was the small silver box. And he had no proof that hadn't been a plant, something Clive had brought in along with him in the event one of them did ask what was up.

Shite. The job was not finished.

But Jack's choice had been made.

"Yeah. I'll go get the van started," he said, and wandered off, shoving his hands in his trouser pockets.

Behind him, he heard Niles say something about this becoming a habit, leaving without taking a thing. Clive's chuckle echoed down the hallway. There was something weird about that man that he couldn't quite place a finger on.

Swinging around the corner of the stairwell, Jack topped the main floor and stared down at Saskia, still intent on her job, completely unaware that it was all for nothing.

He'd been close to roughing up Clive in an attempt to get the truth out of him. But that would have blown his cover. Good thing Niles had shown when he had. Yet now, they still had next to nothing. Not without a thorough search of all the safe deposit boxes in that basement vault.

He'd failed the ECU. It didn't feel right walking away. He never left a job incomplete. But Kierce Quinn's research had narrowed it down to a single box, or at the most, five possibilities. They could easily locate the target within minutes. Jack tapped the earbud to turn it on.

"You in?" Kierce asked.

"Yes. And now I'm out."

As Jack bent to crawl through the hole in the wall he looked back, wishing he'd walked up to Saskia and told her that he was sorry. He should tell her that he felt a certain way about her. And that certain way was new and exciting to him.

Now, it was too late.

* * * *

Not terribly surprised at Clive's announcement the job was complete, Saskia put up a good argument. She only had one number left! She just needed another fifteen minutes. But Clive was insistent.

She packed up her tools, wiped down the safe door and floor for fingerprints, even though she wore latex gloves, and followed the men toward the exit. On the way past the stairs leading down to the safe deposit room she wondered if Jack had opportunity to see inside. She'd heard voices from below and Niles had gone down to take a look. If Jack had gotten a visual on the box, or even the area where Clive had been working, it could help the investigation.

Had he already called it in to the ECU? Would they hear police sirens soon?

A weird nervous energy hastened her steps toward the supply room. Even knowing she had a get-out-of-jail-free card didn't make her any less eager to get the hell out of Dodge. She needed to confirm with Jack where the mission status was as soon as they could find a moment alone.

After the crew made it through the drill hole, Clive announced they would leave the equipment behind. Standard procedure. They'd worn gloves while drilling, but Niles made a sweep with alcohol wipes over the drill to be safe. The accountant's office was closed until Monday, same as the bank, so they didn't expect any of the equipment to be discovered until early that morning. That gave them well over a twenty-four hour head start.

After working up a sweat sitting before the vault door, Saskia braced for the chill air, and held the back door open for the men. The van's exhaust fumes stirred up a gray cloud around them as Clive climbed in the back, followed by Niles. Saskia walked around to the passenger side and slid in.

Jack was not behind the wheel. And even as her intuition screamed and jumped and cursed her for an idiot, she tried to rationalize.

"Jack must be around the corner," she said.

"Taking a piss in this weather?" Niles said. "His wanker will freeze off."

But Clive wasn't laughing. Nor was Saskia.

"The bastard is gone," Clive said. He met Saskia's gaze in the dim light and she shrugged, but she knew her reaction had read as genuine to Clive. And now the real challenge would begin.

Chapter 17

"I'll drive," Saskia announced to the men in the back.

She slid over to the driver's seat and put the van in gear. Nice of Jack to at least keep it running and warm. Though, why she was finding ways to pat him on the back was beyond her. He'd abandoned her.

Or rather, he'd done exactly as he'd planned to do, and he hadn't lied to her about that.

When exiting the back of the accountant's office, Saskia had noticed the ice was beginning to melt. Driving shouldn't be a problem. And they couldn't afford to sit here too long. Jack could have called in to the ECU and thus, the authorities. And until she knew exactly what Clive had placed, or taken, from the safe deposit box room, she had to keep him away from police hands.

"And here I thought if anyone went AWOL on the team, it would be you," Clive said as he slid onto the passenger seat.

What the...? Seriously?

"Thanks for that vote of confidence," she said as calmly as she could manage. Her heartbeats banged drums. Betrayed by two men in less than five minutes. How was that for payback? "I have done nothing to deserve your distrust. If anyone should be asking for explanations, it's the people who have no clue what is going on. Why we walk out on heists without a single bill or gold brick in hand."

"It's all about the process of going through the motions and making others believe they've been robbed. Or at the very least, infiltrated. You knew we'd pull out as soon as one of the two targets had been breached. Same as with the Belgian job."

"But I was so close to opening the vault. We could have taken loads. Was the reward you took from the safe deposit box room so much greater?"

She turned the vehicle, heading for the airport, where both Niles and Clive were destined. She was too, but now she had the van to get rid of. She needed more information from Clive.

"You must have gotten master keys for the boxes, eh?"

He didn't answer, but she could feel his scrutiny on the side of her face. She'd said too much. Had destroyed the confidence she'd earned by acting curious about something she should have no curiosity over. Maybe? Most individuals involved in a heist were kept in the loop. It was how trust was earned.

On the other hand, she knew well that Clive was a need to know kind of guy. If the man did have a master key to turn the lock on a safe deposit box, he would ultimately have to have the key that matched the box too. And those were only issued to box holders. Unless someone had made a copy and Clive had obtained it. Made the most sense. He must have gone into the room with a key, knowing exactly which box he wanted to open. To take something out?

No, to leave the poison behind.

"Is this how all your heists go down?" she dared to ask. "In and out. Keep the crew in the dark?"

"You insist on complaining when your bank account just got five hundred thousand fatter."

He had a point. And a smart person would not push the issue. She shouldn't. This wasn't even her main focus. Jack Angelo was. And he had a head start that she couldn't allow to grow too long. She had to call the ECU and have them track Jack while they still could. But she couldn't do that—couldn't even risk a text—in Clive's presence.

"Why the sudden curiosity?" Clive asked. "You've done the exact same thing with me in Belgium. Why do you care now?"

He was starting to think. And that wasn't good for her.

She made a wild gesture with her hand and gave a shake of her head. "Hormones!" she managed. "I'm just a mess tonight. Sorry. You know. You're right. I don't care. I'll get the cash and that's all good with me. I really need an aspirin, is all."

"Fresh out." Clive turned to face the road.

Had she wheedled her way out of his suspicion with that stupid excuse? Unlikely.

"We're headed to the airport?" Niles asked from the back. "Aren't we doing to dump the van?"

"Saskia can handle taking care of the vehicle," Clive said. "Right?"

"Of course. I know the junkyard where Jack was taking it. He arranged for another getaway car to be parked there. Unless he's moved it. I didn't know his plans included ditching us."

She sighed. At least she could be honest about that much.

She swung the van in toward the airport. As she pulled to park at the drop-off, she checked the rearview mirror. Her mustache was still in place.

Clive grabbed her wrist, tightly, and leaned in. "I can trust you, yes, Sass?"

Preventing a wince was impossible. "Of course you can. I don't understand why you would have reason not to."

"Maybe those hormones of yours will make you do something stupid."

"The only thing I want to do is dump the vehicle then get a ticket out of the tundra. Seriously."

He nodded, yet his grip remained firm. "You know the way to contact me. Wait a week, then send me your details to the online drop box. The payment for tonight's job will show in your account in three days, after I've confirmed nothing is out of order."

"What could possibly be out of order? I've done the work. We made a clean getaway."

"It's how my employer likes things to go," he said. "Don't worry, Sass. You trust me, yes?"

No. Not at all. "Of course. I would have never done job number two with you if I did not. Forget my stupid questions. I really need a nap."

The man chuckled and opened the passenger door. The back door opened and Niles jumped out, slamming the doors behind him. He didn't say goodbye. It wasn't his style. He was already inside the airport when Clive got out and wandered off. He turned and watched as Saskia made her way out of the drive-up area.

Why didn't the man trust her? What had she done to alert him? Because he'd questioned her alliances before she'd spouted off those curious questions. And the other night he'd been suspicious too.

It wouldn't pay to rack her brains now. She had to dump the vehicle and find Jack. And as far as deep cover went, she was no longer in it.Pulling out her cell phone, she called the ECU headquarters and connected with Chester Clarke, the tech guy stationed in London, whom she worked with whenever she needed real-time support and backup. It was late, but he was there more often in the evenings than early mornings.

"Saskia. You are on dark mode. Waiting for us to contact you."

"Can't wait."

"Is there an issue?"

"Just help me, will you, Chaz? I need a track on Jack Angelo."

"The Helsinki job? Right." She heard clattering on the keyboard. "Kierce Quinn, out of Paris, has been working with that asset. Here's the info..." He must have been scanning the dossier on the case. It had been well over a month since Saskia had contacted anyone at the ECU. "Has Angelo still got the chip in him?"

"As far as I know."

"Your job was to keep him in the unit. Saskia, did you lose him?"

"He's...not immediately locatable. I need you to check with Kierce Quinn to see if Angelo reported anything regarding a poison drop-off during the heist tonight."

"You don't have that information?"

The accusation was obvious in his tone. Saskia fisted her fingers. "I was busy cracking a bank vault. Didn't have time to stand and chat while also trying to keep the target unaware of my alliance to the other asset. And I've got a vehicle to dump. Just call me back when you've got a location on him." She hung up.

Ten minutes later she—or rather the man she appeared to be—handed the owner of the junkyard a stack of bills and stood back as the van was loaded into the crusher. She would not walk away until she saw that piece of metal get compacted. It was never wise to trust that those she hired could manage a job without supervision. And she wouldn't risk anyone snooping in the van. Not that they'd left any evidence behind.

The junkyard owner seemed oblivious. Chewing on the end of a smelly cigar, the smoke from it curled about his frothy red beard. He pushed the big red button on the crusher and metal began to crunch and tear and compress. Sounded sickening, but much better than the sound of a compressed spine or broken bones.

What would Clive do to her if he discovered her duplicity? Why was she letting that man get to her like this? They'd completed the job with but one tiny snafu. Clive had apparently gotten what he'd wanted. And she had been left standing high and dry with no evidence that he had planted the poison.

And if Jack had that evidence she had no way of knowing what he'd done with it unless Chester Clarke could learn something from the Paris operative.

Fifteen minutes after seeing the van reduced to a rectangle of metal and chrome, she thumbed for a ride at the side of the highway. Jack had not left a vehicle near the junkyard. A trucker pulled over and offered her shivering ass a ride into town. It was only five miles, but she handed him a fifty and thanked him when he dropped her off.

Standing two blocks down from the apartment she'd rented, Saskia answered her cell phone. Chester had a location on Jack.

"That's close." She glanced up the quiet street. And she knew exactly where it was. The surgeon's office. "What about Angelo's report to Quinn?"

"No contact. And Quinn was expecting to hear from him. Find Jack Angelo, Saskia. It is imperative."

"I'm on it. I'll report back when I've got him."

Chester clicked off without saying goodbye. And Saskia wanted to ask why it was so imperative. If an asset went off the grid, then why not let them? What was it about Jack Angelo that was so important to the ECU that they'd put her on his ass to keep him?

Not that she'd managed that one very well.

She wasn't going to beat herself up over this. Chester's info placed Jack nearby. She hadn't lost this one yet.

Saskia jogged toward the surgeon's office which was a few blocks beyond where she'd been staying. She had no weapon, save a small jackknife that she'd brought along in case it had been needed during the heist, so she pulled that out from the backpack but kept it folded in her palm. She was deadlier with her fists and fast moves.

It was easier walking the streets now that the ice had begun to melt, but also sloppy. The air smelled fresh, as if awakening from a long, moldering slumber. Why she noticed that was weird. She really needed a vacation.

Should she have taken Jack's offer to go off the grid seriously? *Could* she? Not anymore. The offer had surely been rescinded. But she'd never thought that her life could be different than it was now. Freedom was a concept, not a reality. And if she didn't get Jack in hand her current freedom would dangle from a thread.

"He had better still be here," she muttered.

Approaching the nondescript office door set into the brick wall, she counted the time from when the crew had exited the bank and now. A little more than an hour. Which is why, after kicking in the door, she wasn't surprised to find a dark office.

Flicking on the light switch, she scanned around the small, dank reception area. The smell of alcohol lured her back to another room where she found a surgical table and dented metal cabinets with master locks on each drawer pull. In the waste bin she noted small bits of gauze with bright red blood on them.

Jack had been here. And recently.

She pressed her hand to the stainless steel table. Didn't feel any warmth. But if Chester's GPS had tracked the chip here...

"He couldn't have been gone for more than a few minutes."

Her phone rang again. Chester said, "He's moving. Heading south of the position I originally gave you. I've got you on radar. You're less than a hundred feet from him."

Him? Or the chip now removed?

She had to work fast. Saskia headed out the door and turned left.

"The other way," Chester said.

She swung around and ran, boots splashing in the puddles.

"It's moving rapidly," Chester reported. "Must be in a vehicle. It's going to pass right before you..."

She heard the approaching car. Shoving the cell phone into a pocket, Saskia picked up her speed. As the nose of a brown sedan appeared from the left, she leaped for the hood and slid across it. Managing to grip the windshield wiper stopped her from flying off and face-planting on the slushy tarmac. The car stopped. She slid off.

Bending forward, she lifted a leg to land a roundhouse kick to the driver's side window. It didn't crack.

Saskia opened the door before the driver could lock it. Reaching in, she grabbed the driver, a bald, stout man whose heft made it impossible to lift him out of the seat. Instead, she yanked him toward her by clapping her hands about his head. "Where is Jack Angelo?"

"Who are you, crazy woman?" His thick Finnish accent ended with a growl.

"You know who I'm talking about. Jack Angelo."

"I have no names. No names. Ever!"

"Fine. The Irishman who was just in your office. You removed a chip from the back of his head."

"No, I—"

She kneed the man in the side off his face and he yowled. Gripping the steering wheel, she saw his other hand go for the stick shift. Saskia reached in and pulled the keys from the ignition. Then she pulled the man down so the top half of him tumbled out from the car, but he was still held inside by the seatbelt across his waist.

She grabbed his head again and lifted her boot. "The next one is going to hurt. Might even take out an eye. You ever do reparative surgery on yourself?"

"He was at the office!" the man confessed. "But he's gone now."

"Where?"

"I don't know! I never ask. And who would tell me? You know that."

She did know that. And wasting any more time with this idiot would prove fruitless. Shoving him back into the car, she stomped off, tearing away the mustache as she did so.

If Jack was going off the grid he'd get out of town as quickly as possible. He could have a contact pick him up, though that would be risky. Stealing a car would be wise, but taking the ferry would be too slow. And he knew Clive and Niles had intended to fly. It would be stupid to risk running into them at the airport. As well, Jack did not like to fly.

The only option Jack could possibly go with was the ferry. No ferries ran this late at night, but that didn't mean he wouldn't be the first on the boat in the morning.

Swinging around a corner not far from her place, Saskia ran along the sidewalk and into her building. She'd turned in her apartment key before leaving for the job this evening, but she wasn't stupid.

She arrived at the door, which she'd left open a hair. Inside was empty and quiet. Using the light on her phone, she beamed it across the floor. No wet or drying tracks that Jack might have left behind had he returned here.

Her phone rang again. She did not want to confirm to Chester that she'd lost the subject, so she didn't answer. He'd figure it out. Which would not go well for her.

What next? Jack hadn't given her any clues where his destination was, despite her trying to wheedle that information out of him. She'd only gotten a redacted dossier on him when she'd been assigned this job. Minimal information. Nothing regarding the reason he'd been recruited into the ECU. The key components to guessing a man's next move were always family, friends, and history.

She had nothing.

Except.

Family is everything to me. Sometimes you take a fall for family. But always, a man is there for them.

Where was Jack's family? In London? Would he really go back to England after making a clean break from the ECU? It would be the stupidest move he could possibly make.

No, he was too smart for that. And she needed to get to the ferry station.

A text buzzed on her phone. Chester sent her a grainy photo from the airport time-stamped twenty minutes earlier. It was Jack.

Chapter 18

Hiking up her backpack over a shoulder, Saskia strolled into the airport. Half a dozen bleary-eyed travelers wandered the clean white and gray environment, looking as if they'd been lost on a strange planet that sported IKEA trees and tin-can-stars suspended from the ceiling. Behind her, moonlight beamed through the blue-glazed windows high above, giving them a deep azure gleam. It coaxed dreams one could only find from a deep and relaxing sleep.

She could use some sleep. But she'd sleep when she'd confirmed that Jack was nowhere to be found, and indeed, the only place he could possibly be was the ferry station. It didn't make sense that he would fly. He'd initially traveled sixteen hours by ferry to avoid a simple one hour flight here to Helsinki.

But CCTV photos did not lie. And Chester had been adamant he'd ID'd Jack correctly.

She approached the ticket counter where a yawning woman sat behind one of a dozen computers. She was the only one on this late shift. She must have checked in Clive and Niles an hour earlier. Would all three men find one another in the airport? Belize had been their destination. And Jack's destination?

Baffled was putting her mental state lightly.

She scanned the departures grid above the ticket desk. The woman sitting before the computer didn't smile or acknowledge that Saskia stood before her. Two flights had left within the last hour. One to Brazil, another to Amsterdam. Clive and Niles could be on either. And so could Jack.

A few more flights left on the hour. One to France. Another to London... Had he? It was Jack's home base. And as far as she knew his family was there. Of course, that was conjecture.

There was one way to find out.

Now sans moustache and looking like a woman—bedraggled at best beneath the thick white down jacket—Saskia stepped forward and assumed a shy attitude. She placed her hands on the counter and sucked in the corner of her lip. "Was a handsome man with little hair and a lot of stubble on his jaw in through here a bit ago? Jack, my—" She closed her eyes and tried to affect tears, but they wouldn't fall. Damn it! "We argued. I want to say goodbye to him. I know he's headed home…"

The woman behind the counter lifted a brow, but she was not impressed.

"I wanted to give the ring back to him," she tried. And she patted a coat pocket. "He told me it was his mother's."

"I can't let you through security without a ticket, ma'am," the woman finally announced.

"Oh, I'll buy a ticket. It means that much to me. I can't let him leave like this. He has to know I didn't mean what I said. I was angry, but also, not thinking straight. No matter what happened between the two of us, I want him to be happy. And I need to give the ring back. I can't possibly keep it."

The woman glanced to her computer screen. "The flight to London is not even half full. I can sell you a coach ticket for two hundred euros."

"Worth it," Saskia said, relieved, and also shocked.

If Jack was going off the grid, then why return to his home?

* * * *

The flight to London did not leave for four hours. And Saskia didn't want Jack to see her in the airport, so she wandered around the building, then found a place to rest in the terminal five gates down from where she'd seen Jack's long dress coat flung over a red plastic seat. He was here. He must be sleeping on a chair, maybe the pair of legs she saw jutting out from behind a support pillar.

If she'd had a disguise on her she would have wandered closer, but she'd packed light.

Setting her backpack on the floor between her feet, she leaned over and caught her forehead in her hands, and wondered if she could manage tears now. She wasn't sure she even knew how to cry. But it felt like she could. Was this how a person felt when the tears flowed? An ache in her chest, a heavy thud to her heartbeats, and an empty drop that seemed to circle in her belly?

She did not want to go to prison because she'd fucked up the job of keeping Jack in the ECU. Or worse. There was always the threat of a tombstone should an asset screw up.

Should she consider running? If Jack could do it, she could. And she happened to know a surgeon who could take out the chip with lightning speed. But she had no cash to hand. The ECU credit card she'd used to purchase the plane ticket was always monitored and strictly budgeted.

And the five hundred thousand Clive was supposed to transfer to her account? That account was owned by the Elite Crimes Unit. She never got to keep the booty from any job. All monies were either returned to the original source, if they'd come directly from a bank vault, or the ECU redirected the funds in a manner that would never be divulged.

"Well, well."

Unaware that someone had approached, Saskia looked up with a smile growing—until she saw Clive standing over her. "I thought you'd be out of the city by now," she said. "On your way to Belize. What's going on?"

"You dump the van?"

"Of course. It's now a cube. Where's Niles?"

"He went ahead to Belize. But I figured if I hung out here for a while I'd catch you."

Not good. Saskia's fight or flight response clicked to high alert. "Why do you need to catch me?"

"Because like I said earlier, I don't trust you, Sass. And I still don't trust you."

"What the hell does it matter now? The job is done."

"Did you tell Jack Angelo about the poison?"

"No." She shook her head and looked down, unwilling to look him in the eye, and trying to keep her calm. A defensive reply would only make her sound more suspicious. And the man couldn't be aware that Jack was just down the way. "Why? Did he say something to you?"

Clive pulled a bowie knife out of his coat and aimed it at her leg. How had he gotten that through security? She'd had to dump her tiny pocketknife at security and then they'd still X-rayed her.

"You're lying to me, Sass," he said in a low, exacting tone, "and I don't like liars."

"I'm not. I didn't tell Jack anything. Why would it matter?"

"It matters because Jack was asking me some strange questions inside the bank."

"I can't help what the man chooses as a conversation topic."

"Of course not. You're going to come with me. I need some answers about who you really are."

"You're fucked, Clive. You know me. We've worked two jobs together."

"And yet you've suddenly all these questions."

"I told you I'm—" Yeah, the wacky hormones defense had gone over not at all. No sense in pounding it in like a bent nail.

"You going to come along with me?" he prompted with a twitch of the blade toward her leg.

"Hell no. I'm waiting for a plane."

"You've other plans now, Sass. I've a rental out in the lot. Let's go."

She shook her head, eyeing the periphery. No one else in sight. He didn't have thugs with him. Not that she'd expect them. She could jump up, smash her palm up against his nose, and knock him out. That would give her time to grab the knife and run. To where? She couldn't go to Jack; that would compromise her. Again. And if the airport had any modicum of security, she'd have officers on her within minutes.

The smell of coppery blood filled her senses before Saskia registered the searing pain of the knife piercing her upper thigh. It cut through her leggings and tore a thick red gash in the skin. Purposely shallow and not a fatal injury. Clive didn't want her dead. He wanted to be able to move her to a different location. And then? She didn't want to consider what could go down.

On the other hand, if she got Clive out of here, she could work with that. And she still had four hours...

Clive clutched her hand. "Grab your pack. We're heading out. If you don't start walking now, I'll have to stab the other leg and toss you over my shoulder. Security will think you've fainted."

The idea of losing her mobility was not something she chose to deal with. With a submissive nod of head, Saskia grabbed her backpack, winced at the shooting pain streaking up and down her thigh, and limped off toward the exit with Clive's knife jammed into her spine.

* * * *

Jack heard the female grunt. It had sounded like she'd taken a punch, but when he dodged his head around the column behind which he'd been standing, unobtrusively observing Saskia for the last five minutes, he saw what had really happened. Clive had stabbed her.

And while his instincts were to run after them and take out Clive, he held back.

He pulled out the new burner phone he'd purchased after ditching the van behind the bank and dialed up Kierce Quinn.

"Who is this?" Quinn answered.

"It's Angelo," he said. Of course, he was off their tracking system. As planned. He needn't worry about the phone being traced. Well, he did, but Quinn wasn't stupid; he knew exactly where he was.

"We've got the London headquarters tracking you, Jack. The boss is not pleased."

"Wasn't trying to please anyone in particular. But listen. Saskia's been taken by Clive Hendrix. I need a track on her."

"What the hell did you do with your chip, Jack?"

"Quinn, this is an emergency."

"You can't be trusted now. I'm going to patch in Chester Clarke from the London office on this one. He's been communicating with Saskia Petrovik. I don't know what you're up to—"

"I'm up to trying to save one of your agent's arses. Now track her for me. I'm going to try and tail them, but I don't have a vehicle. I'll have to jack a car out in the lot. And it's freezing out there, so I'm not sure how that will go. Quinn."

"Just wait."

"Don't call the boss, Quinn. Oi. Do whatever the hell you want. Just—if you don't want to lose Saskia, you will track her for me."

He ran down the concourse. His flight left in four hours. And he intended to be on it.

Chapter 19

Saskia navigated the road heading north away from the city. Visibility had drastically decreased since they'd left the airport. A heavy fog due to rising temperatures made it difficult to see more than a quarter mile ahead of her, so she slowed her speed.

"Keep driving," Clive insisted from the passenger seat.

"I am driving."

"Not fast enough."

"Can't you see the conditions are dangerous?"

"Fuck the conditions. Just fucking drive."

"Clive, are you—" She flashed a look at him and while it was dark, his loopy smile beamed. "Are you high?"

She hadn't known the man to drink or do drugs but he was acting irrational and the knife was swaying from her head to her heart and all over the place. Her thigh pulsed, but she'd survive. Now she was really wishing for that aspirin.

"I might have taken a sniff from the box."

"The box? What the—tell me what's going on."

"Don't you already know? You and your spy Jack Angelo colluding to try and catch me out?" He chuckled, and it was a drawn out, goofy laugh. "It was easy enough to slip the poison in with the heroin."

"The heroin? I thought you said that poison was for an unrelated job?"

"And you believed me? You're more stupid than I thought, Sass. Stupid little girl who likes to play dress up. Do you put on costumes for your lovers? Are you the man or the woman when you have sex?"

She seriously hated stoned Clive. "You stole heroin?" She needed him to give her details. Arrestable details.

"The next time Maksim Tamm comes for his fix, he's gone." The man giggled again. "Serves him right for fucking with the *bratva*."

Saskia knew that name. It was Russian for brotherhood and had been used to refer to their mafia. The diplomat Tamm was making drug deals with the Russian mafia? And obviously he'd done something to piss someone off. Thus, Clive had been hired to take him out. Clever. And who would suspect a bank heist was the reason behind a murder? Twice over.

Though this second heist hadn't claimed a victim. And it would not. The powder she'd given Clive in the glass vial was inert, and wouldn't hurt a fly.

But wouldn't it have been easier just to spike the heroin before putting it in the box? Why hire a second party to go in and make a switch? She didn't have the leisure to ponder the options. She'd gotten a confession from Clive. The ECU could work with that.

"You're driving too slow!"

Clive suddenly grabbed the steering wheel. The BMW veered and hit a slick of black ice. The rear tires lost traction, swishing the tail end of the vehicle wildly.

Saskia swore as the vehicle careened off the road and into the thick snow in the ditch. She hit her head on the steering wheel and blacked out.

* * * *

Jack navigated the twenty-year-old sedan he'd hotwired in the airport parking lot onto the main freeway. He'd lost sight of Clive's car about five miles out of the city, and slowed his speed. He'd noticed Saskia was slowing down, and with the visibility nearing zero and the frequent patches of black ice, he didn't want to crash into the back of them.

He'd tossed the burner phone so he had no contact with the ECU. But as soon as he got to Saskia, the ECU would send out people to collect her. And him.

He wasn't concerned with his own plans right now. He'd seen Clive stab Saskia. And while she had been able to limp away, and hadn't left a trail of blood, she couldn't be doing well. There was no telling what Clive was up to.

Seeing the sudden flash of red to the right of the road, Jack pulsed the brakes to a sliding stop. And suddenly Clive's figure rushed into view. The man flagged him down with waving arms. Jack put the vehicle in park, and leaned over to check inside the glove compartment. He grabbed an emergency light stick and snapped it. A frantic shake mixed the chemicals inside the plastic tube. He got out of the car, holding the glowing light high. The winds whipped at his face and he clung to his open coat but the chill seared at his skin as if razor blades.

"What happened?" Jack called. The wind blew snow across the tarmac, transforming it into a white desert storm.

"She purposely drove us into the ditch!" Clive's gesture toward the side of the road was highlighted by the car's head beams. "She's hurt!"

Jack ran past the man, slipping, but he caught himself as his boots crunched onto the snow edging the ditch. He saw that the car had landed on the driver's side, sticking up in the ditch, and was half buried.

Grabbing the passenger door handle, which was level with his knees, he opened it. It was difficult to lift the heavy door with the wind buffeting him like a hurricane. And when had he last tried to open a door *up* instead of out? Struggling, he managed to slip his foot in between a space. He shoved in the light and could see Saskia was out; blood trickled from her temple and down her cheek. The keys were missing from the ignition.

Jack looked toward his car. It backed away, the headlights flashing as it turned. No way he'd catch the bastard on foot. And it didn't matter. He had to get to Saskia.

Easing himself into the car, Jack's struggles with the door and the wind made it difficult. He didn't want to step on her, so he found his footing on the passenger seat and against the steering wheel column. The door slammed shut behind him, reducing the winds to a muffled *thrum* against the car's exterior.

Jack crouched and managed to lean over the stick shift and inspect her.

"Saskia?" He nudged her shoulder gently. She felt warm and he could see her breath coming out in tiny wifts of fog. If they stayed inside this car for too long, they'd get buried by the drifting snow. There was no way to turn on the engine and thus, the heater. That bastard couldn't have known it was Jack behind him on the road. But it was obvious Clive had intended to leave Saskia here, no matter who had stopped to help him.

"Come on, Saskia, we've got to get out of here." He bowed his forehead to hers and ran his fingers along her jaw and down her neck. She was so precious. He'd punch Clive's smug face into next year for hurting her.

She jerked suddenly as he moved his touch toward her ear. Good ole icy fingers.

"What?"

"It's me. Jack."

"How did you—what the hell? Where's Clive?"

"He took off with my car. I followed you from the airport. I've got the ECU tracking you."

"But…you're supposed to…"

"Doesn't matter right now." It did, and it didn't. He was here and that was all that mattered. "What's going on with your leg? Talk to me, Saskia."

"Just a surface wound. A warning to get me to comply. It hurt like fuck, but I'll survive. But my head." She touched her bleeding temple.

"You must have hit it on the windshield when you spun into the ditch. Help is on the way."

"It is?"

"Yeah." He clasped her hand. The moment felt so wrong, and yet he couldn't imagine being anywhere else but here right now. He wished he didn't have to rescue her. She hadn't deserved to get hurt. But he was thankful he'd been close. If Clive had left her here after getting picked up by a stranger, it was likely he wouldn't have mentioned her and left her to freeze and possibly die.

"An ambulance?" she asked. "I don't do the hospital, Jack, you know—"

"Someone from the ECU will come collect us. You know how they work. Always keeping tabs on their assets. Won't even let one go unless he digs out the fucking tracker."

"But. You can't! You were on your way out. You wanted to go off the grid. Which I don't understand. Who does that by returning home?"

So she'd figured out his next move? That had been apparent from her appearance in the airport. There was no way she'd been there and had not known about his presence. She'd been following him.

"Go, Jack. Just leave. They'll find me. This is what you've wanted. An opportunity to get away. I don't know why, and I wish you'd tell me, but you don't have to. It'll only make it easier for me to deny what I know about you."

"Doesn't matter right now. I'll figure something out. I'm not leaving you here alone. But I do need to go out and set off a flare." He reached back and opened the glove compartment. A few items spilled out along with an emergency flare. Standard in this country. "You sure you're okay? Try wiggling a bit. Make sure nothing is broken."

"I'm good. But you let Clive get away."

"Hadn't much choice. We'll find him."

"Maybe. He was high on the heroin from the safe deposit box."

"Huh. I wondered if he looked a little strange when talking to him in the bank."

"Some dignitary was wanted dead by the Russian bratva. Clive was their hit man."

"Odd way of taking someone out. Much easier with a bullet. But apparently the man doesn't do guns. How the hell did he get the knife through airport security?"

"No clue. Oh, it's freezing in here."

"You sit tight. I'm going out. You good?"

"Kiss me first."

Jack leaned down and kissed her. Their mouths were cold and yet warmed quickly so he forgot about the weather outside. She clung to him, pulling him closer and deeper and he fell willingly.

He'd abandoned his escape plans in favor of rescuing the girl. And nothing had ever felt more right.

* * * *

A tow truck with a big blade mounted in front, designed for clearing snow and ice, picked up Jack and Saskia. Jack didn't ask who had sent the driver. If it had been the ECU, the driver would have identified himself. Maybe. Yet, when he offered to bring them directly to the hospital emergency room, Jack decided maybe he had just been cruising by and was a civilian.

Of course, the ECU was watching their every move via Saskia's chip. And if he were smart, he'd leave her at the emergency room and take off. But he didn't.

Much against her protests, he now sat there watching as the ER doctor inspected Saskia's forehead. She'd told him a story that the stick shift had torn through her leggings and created the gash. The doc nodded. Must have thought it sounded legit. Good thing the man was probably on the tail-end of a thirty-six hour shift. His lids were heavy and he couldn't stop yawning.

"Will she survive?" Jack asked lightly.

"A hard-headed woman," the doc offered. "I don't think you'll need stitches, but I'll send a nurse to clean and bandage both the cuts." He left them sitting in a narrow space partitioned off by beige curtains. The ER bustled. Lots of car accidents, apparently, even for the early morning hour.

"Let's leave," Saskia said, heaving herself off the bed.

"Nope." Jack stood and lifted her up, setting her back on the bed. "If you don't let them take care of you, the wounds will become infected."

"I've taken care of wounds before. There's a pharmacy attached to this building, I'm sure. Buy a jar of rubbing alcohol and I'll be peachy."

"We're staying."

She shook her head. "They're going to find you."

They both knew who the *they* were she was talking about, and Jack chose to ignore her worry. It wasn't going to get him on a plane any faster if he did. And really. Getting on a plane. Could he really do it?

"Tell me more about what Clive said to you," he asked. "The heroin and the dignitary. Did he give you a name?"

"Maksim Tamm."

"That's the name Kierce Quinn thought would be the target. I'll call it in to the ECU. But I need to use your phone."

"Yes, I didn't have a chance because Clive had a knife to my head and I was just trying to stay on the road. Lot of good that did, eh? Jack, what's up with you? You've saved me. I appreciate it. But you need to get out of here."

"Yeah? What's up with you? You were hell-bent on bringing my arse in and collecting your two hundred dollars without passing Go. Don't you want me hanging around you anymore? Is it my kiss? Was it that bad?"

"Jack, your kiss..." She sighed and her shoulders dropped; then she lay back on the bed. "Fine. Do what you want." She tugged out her cell phone and handed it to him. "I think... I need a nap." Her eyelids fluttered and she was out.

* * * *

Twenty minutes later Saskia woke because someone had bumped the wheeled ER bed she was lying on. She looked around, trying to acclimate. Beside her leg, lay her cell phone. She checked the time. Six in the morning. The flight she'd purchased a ticket for had been scheduled to leave at 7:30 a.m. Jack was...nowhere to be seen.

And she did not like hospitals. They asked too many questions.

Taking in her surroundings, she determined there were four beds with people in them; one was groaning and muttering about needing more drugs. No nurses or doctors were in sight. She was still wearing her leggings, shirt, and shoes. Her coat was hung on a hook near the bed next to the curtain on the runner track. She slipped on her coat, and stepped carefully on her leg. It hurt, but she wasn't incapacitated.

Zipping up the coat and tucking her hair down the back, she walked out into a dimly lit aisle and noted the main desk not far down to the right, so she turned left and aimed for the elevator doors. Most emergency rooms were on the main level, so she cursed when she got on and realized her best escape was where she had been. She hit the *door open* button and slipped out just as an orderly in blue scrubs and boasting tattoos along both forearms approached. He smiled at her but didn't say anything.

She swiftly passed the main nurse's station, and noticed a small café opposite it. If Jack had gone to get coffee— He wouldn't be so foolish. He had a chance. And he'd taken it.

And much as she was all for him pursuing a new life, something was not right. He was heading to London. That's not how a man went off the grid. Something must have sidetracked him. Had to be the reason. He'd been about to tell her, and then he'd clammed up. So she had no choice but to follow him, knowing the ECU would also follow.

This new information about Clive and the *bratva* disturbed her though. Would the ECU request she stay on his ass? She had no idea where he'd gone. And the less she saw of him the better. On the other hand, she'd really like to shove a blade into him and see if he squealed.

Outside in the ambulance bay, she sighted a cab and hopped in the back seat. The airport was a ten-minute drive away. Once in the airport, with ticket in hand, she breezed through security. She had nothing on her but her cell phone. A winter wear clothing shop was just opening in the gallery. With but half an hour to make her gate, she purchased a brown fleece jacket and a rabbit-fur-lined hat with the pull-down flaps that hunters liked for long treks in the cold forest. She had no makeup to change her face, but the hat covered most. It would serve.

Saskia was the last to board the plane. Head down and eyes sweeping the seats side to side, she didn't notice Jack's shaved pate. And his broad shoulders would have stood out.

Settling into the narrow seat ten rows up from the back of the plane, Saskia scanned each and every head before her. There were only about two dozen on the flight, and she couldn't see up into business class because the blue curtains were pulled and Velcroed shut. Was Jack sitting up in business? For a man who was afraid of flying that was a good place to be. He'd be coddled and could drink, even for the short flight. And she could maintain her secrecy.

But she had to be sure. She couldn't risk flying to London if the man had changed his mind. Getting up and making like she was headed toward the bathrooms, Saskia managed to slip the blue curtain aside and scan the business section—there was the top of his head—

"Ma'am, you'll have to take your seat. The captain has put on the seatbelt signs."

"Of course." She nodded apologetically and headed back to her seat.

Intending to grab a few winks as the plane took off, the exhaustion from concentrating fiercely before the vault, and then the stress from the accident knocked her out quickly. She didn't wake until the stewardess shook her by the shoulder. Saskia peered out from the froth of rabbit fur surrounding her face at the smiling woman.

The stewardess repeated, "Everyone has disembarked. You'll have to leave now, ma'am."

"Right. Sorry. Fell asleep. Thanks for the wakeup."

Ten minutes later, Saskia stood at the taxi pickup. She hadn't seen Jack. He would have made a beeline for a cab, unless someone was picking him up. Either way, this was the place where he'd get in a vehicle. Had she missed him?

"Damn it."

Pulling out her phone, she hailed a cab, and got in the back seat. Chester answered after three rings. "You're in London," he said. "Where's Angelo?"

"He's here, but I lost him at the airport. Can you give me a list of Angelo family members, Chaz? And addresses if they live in or near London."

"You think he's visiting family? Doesn't make sense."

"Probably not to you, but just do it for me, will you? I'm heading into the city center to find something to eat and… I'm tired. I need more sleep."

"I'll get you a room and order room service."

"Thanks, Chaz. Text me the details so I can give the driver the address. Is there anything else?"

"What else could there be?"

"What's being said about me and my failure to bring in Angelo?"

"Nothing. Not that I've heard. I've been tasked to keep tabs on you. We'd hoped you'd lead us directly to Angelo."

"Can you tell me why the ECU is so eager to catch the man? You wanted me to convince him to stay in the unit. What's so valuable about him? If he wants to leave, then why not just drop the hammer and take him out, as promised, if he ever fucks up?"

"I don't have that information, Saskia. You know that. You want to talk to Hunter Dixon?"

The leader of the Elite Crimes Unit. She'd met him once. Liked him. He was American, and talked with what she thought of as a lazy cowboy accent. He wouldn't give her any more information than she'd already received. Need to know, and all that bullshit.

"No. I'm fine. But it's important I get that info on Jack's family. Whatever you can find for me."

"I'm on it. I'll text you the results. I just sent the location of your hotel. And… I'm communicating with Kierce Quinn in the Paris office. Jack checked in a few hours ago on a burner phone. He's already tossed it, so I couldn't get a trace."

"Did he give them the info I relayed about the *bratva*?"

"*Bratva...*" Chester muttered as if he were thinking, or perhaps typing while he thought. "Yes, Quinn made that connection. Where's Clive now?"

"Hell if I know. After we went in the ditch, he abandoned me. Didn't see him at the airport either. Can you track him on CCTV?"

"I'll have to do something. We need to keep that man in our sights."

Saskia yawned. "Just let me know what you need next from me. I'll be online."

"Will do." The connection clicked off.

Saskia relayed the texted address to the cabbie, then let her head drop onto the seat. Jack had said something about Clive taking off in his car. Where to? Was he hell-bent to make sure she didn't survive? He could have left her out in that freezing car to die. And he probably would have had she not been so fortunate that Jack had tailed them from the airport.

But the fact remained, Clive Hendrix was at large.

Chapter 20

Jack was always startled by the homey living room, decorated in crocheted doilies and frilly porcelain-faced dolls—and the muzak that was always playing from an unseen speaker. The weird background music gave the room a feeling of a doctor's waiting room, but set in some old granny's home.

And the granny in question was a demure Chinese woman who could be pushing a hundred, for all he knew. She was half as tall as he and might go hurtling through the air should he lean over and blow a puff of air at her.

But she was a shrewd business woman, whom he had trusted for years with his secret stash savings. Her clientele list was short, and secure. She kept money, did not launder it, for a small fee. And her methods were—well, Jack would have never gone with her had she not been vetted by a friend years ago. For she kept all deposits in shoe boxes. Yes, he'd left two million pounds in a shoe box with a little old Chinese woman.

And he trusted her completely.

But now, as he waited on the Barcalounger covered in enough doilies to make him itch, he tugged at his tie. The woman's granddaughter had greeted him at the door, after the secret knock, and his verifying the code, and had offered him tea while she retrieved her grandmother. He'd refused the tea. He was still feeling the whiskey from the airplane. It had been the only way he'd been able to manage the flight. Three quick shots downed and swallowed. He'd tilted his head against the seat, gripped the arms as the plane had taken off, and hadn't released that tight grip until it had landed.

But he'd survived. Wonders did not cease.

Dressed in a bright red kimono splashed with embroidered green flowers, the old woman entered the room. Her eyes lit up as she spied him and she bowed ceremoniously toward him.

"You are returned so soon, Mister Angelo."

"I, uh—what?" Jack looked up into her sweet, unwrinkled face. It had been years since he'd last been here. "No. I haven't visited in a long time."

Her mouth pursed as she shook her head. Gleaming black hair had been pulled into a neat bun and secured with red-lacquered sticks ending in gold dangles. "You are wrong, Jack Angelo. I spoke with you two days ago. In this very room."

Jack stood abruptly. The woman did not startle, but instead followed his gaze upward. She pressed her arms akimbo and gave him a look that he wondered might laser out his pupils.

"You must be mistaken," he said. He'd never been given her name, so he was not sure how to address her. "I was in Helsinki a few days ago. Are you sure? You didn't give my box to someone else?"

Her shaking head batted the gold dangles against her hair. Now she wrung her hands together. "It was you. Very sure of that. Same face. Same voice. Same yellow tie."

Jack stroked his tie. Someone had been here, impersonating him? He didn't have to think long to land a guess on the ECU. If they had suspected he'd go AWOL, he would not put it past them to make that escape as difficult as possible.

"Show me my box," he insisted.

With a nod, the woman scampered out of the room. And Jack ran his fingers along his jaw. "Fuck."

* * * *

Saskia walked out of the hotel and turned into an alleyway. She'd managed three hours of sleep. She felt rested, but couldn't wait to really sleep.

Yet she was in London for one reason, and if she didn't get on that man's ass immediately the trail would go colder than Helsinki in January. Not that she had a trail. She was waiting on Chester to return with information about Jack's family. He'd said a name... Jonny. Could be a brother. Would Jack stop in to visit him? Had they a job planned? She had to cover every angle.

As she turned the corner to head down the street, a man assaulted her, clasping her about the shoulders and whipping her body back around the corner into the alleyway.

But she didn't fight.

"I found you," she said, unable to hide a smile at seeing Jack again. Even if he had slammed her against the wall so hard her shoulder blades tingled.

"If that's the way you want to play it." He dangled before her what looked like a dog collar with a thumb-sized black box attached to it. "Will you wear this?"

Saskia assessed the collar, and could only come up with one result. "Is that a signal blocker?"

He nodded. "Made it myself. Just for you."

"Aw, a gift from my guy. It's not exactly a fashion statement." She gazed into his eyes, which held hers as if a vice. A clutch she didn't mind at all. So maybe there was something undeniable between them. "Go for it."

He wrapped the leather strap about her neck, placing the GPS-blocking device at the back, closest to the chip embedded at the base of her skull, then fastened the clasp in the front of her throat.

"Kinky," she offered.

The man's smirk stirred her thoughts to visions of actual kinky foreplay. "You into that stuff?"

She waggled a brow at him. "I'm into anything you're willing to try."

"Let's start with this."

And then he kissed her. Hard. And claiming. There was no way she was going to struggle free from the sensuous attack that she wanted more than she needed to breathe. He tasted like whiskey, and she was all right with that. Wrapping her legs about Jack's hips, the movement pushed his shoulders against the brick wall. His grip on her ass squeezed, pulling her tight against him.

The man kissed like he walked through the world. With confidence and a certain power that no one would take for granted. And she matched his greedy want with the same clinging, demanding need. If she never got another kiss from this man, she felt sure her world would crumble. Something about him, the compelling need to always be close, tight and inside him, would not allow her to relent. They belonged together. But in a weird way that defied tenderness and cuddles. Rather, they smashed together and clung with a vengeance.

So when he broke the kiss and forced her down from the cling she felt as if the world had suddenly been pushed off its axis. It took her a moment to gather her equilibrium and look to him questioningly.

"I saw you board the plane. Was too busy pushing down the whiskey to settle my nerves to approach you." He grabbed her hand and started walking swiftly down the block. "I have things I want to tell you," he said. "But I need distance from where you're staying."

She agreed. The ECU probably had cameras on them right now. Not even probably, but surely. She swept her gaze about the building fronts and the traffic signals, spying the CCTV cameras that were everywhere. Chester at headquarters could access those cameras with an ease that made her head spin. And he was surely already aware that her GPS was being blocked, so that would put up an alert on his end as well.

Jack tugged her into the lobby of another hotel scattered with frothy green plants. They walked swiftly past the reception desk, angling down an aisle that passed a restaurant boasting hand-fed veal, and a few boutique shops whose windows glittered with rhinestones and platinum. They exited another door that was on the opposite side of the block where they'd entered. He was weaving and she followed.

Ten minutes later, after twists, turns, and a double back, Jack slowed his pace. The neighborhood was less city and quainter, yet the vehicles were BMWs and shiny SUVs, so Saskia guessed it was an elite neighborhood. They entered a deli advertising vegan meats. One side of the small shop featured half a dozen tables set in the hazy winter sun beaming through the windows.

Jack nodded she go find a table and he went to the counter to purchase coffee.

Saskia sat at a table away from the front window that looked out to the street, in sight of another CCTV camera. She scanned the menu above the deli counter, curious about what, exactly, was a vegan meat. Wasn't that an oxymoron? And not at all appetizing.

She tugged at the dog collar. It wasn't tight, but the new leather did itch. She'd keep it on. For Jack. Because right now her alliances held a sharp split and sat at opposite ends of the scale from one another. The ECU had been good to her and she had no reason to betray them. And yet Jack. Well...Jack. She wanted to do right by him. This was the first time she'd felt inclined to help another person because she trusted him. Trust wasn't an easy thing. Her and Jack Angelo? That felt comfortably easy.

He returned to the table with two coffees and a dessert bar topped with a froth of chocolate frosting. But Saskia was suspicious. The signs on the walls warned her to be cautious. She leaned over and sniffed at what looked luscious and gave off a strong cocoa scent.

"What's wrong? You don't like vegan food?" Jack asked.

"How can meat not be meat?" She prodded the chocolate frosting, then licked her finger. Tasted like chocolate. "Is this vegan too?"

"I believe so. No milk products used. Give it a bite. Because when I get into it there's going to be no more sharing."

Taking a bite, she had to admit it wasn't bad. Certainly not cardboard.

"It's not the cinnamon buns from Helsinki, that's for sure." She pushed the plate toward Jack.

He made good work of the treat in three bites. And for some odd reason, the sharing of the treat seemed to bond her closer to him. It was silly thinking. Swooning teenager stuff. But she'd never had such a feeling about a man before, so she went with it.

Careful not to catch her chin in palm and gaze doe-eyed at him from across the table, Saskia propped her elbows on the table and spoke in low tones. "So? You wanted to tell me something? Because even if they can't track me, it's only a matter of time before they mark my location by the cameras. Chester Clarke is the one who arranged my hotel stay. There's not a step I've taken since landing in England that hasn't gone remarked by the ECU."

"I know that. And yes, I'm risking my safety coming to you. I had to do it, Saskia. I…couldn't walk away from you like that."

The schoolgirl inside her swooned. But she maintained a calm façade, nodding he continue.

"This is what you need to know. I had to go AWOL for my family." He hunched forward so their faces were close and their conversation was private. A lunchtime crowd had started to file in and the noise in the deli had increased, which disguised their words well. "My brother specifically."

She'd been right to suspect he was here for his family. Saskia wondered what Chester had found. But maybe Jack would fill her in now.

"My brother is in deep shit with a dangerous bunch. They're no Russian mafia but they won't blink an eye to cut off fingers, hands, or even heads. I've got less than twenty-four hours to come up with a million pounds to save him from getting decapitated."

Saskia spread her fingers about her neck, just below the leather collar. Decapitation was a very distinct threat.

"I used this assignment in Finland to visit the surgeon to have my chip removed," Jack said. "Only, I didn't expect that the ECU would be one step ahead of me. How could they know I'd plan to go off the grid?"

Saskia shook her head. "I don't have that intel, Jack. And trust me, I'd tell you if I did."

"I believe that. They know too much. But that can only mean they have information about my brother and his situation. They have to. Are they involved? Is this some kind of test? They are arseholes, if it is. But it doesn't matter. I'm here to save Jonny. Family first. Always."

Saskia nodded, bleakly wishing she'd had such a family to stand up for, criminals or not.

"You have a means to get the cash?"

"That's the problem. I was feeling confident after the flight landed, until I arrived at the—you don't need to know the location. My stash that I put away before I was sent to jail? It's gone. Someone who looked just like me took it all two days ago. I think the ECU got to it. I was counting on that to get Jonny out. Now I've got to swindle the big bucks. A million in less than twenty-four hours? It'll never happen. I might have to go in big guns blazing and take everyone out to save him. But I don't want to do that. I just…" His sigh rippled down Saskia's spine. His angst was apparent. "I can't do that anymore, Saskia. It's not me."

Gentleman Jack had become the epitome of the moniker. And in his line of work, that wasn't optimal. Saskia laid a hand over his on the table. "I have some money, Jack."

"I can't take your money."

"You can. It's like yours. A secret account that I put together before the ECU found me. My rainy-day stash. It's all online, but I can liquidate it quickly."

He swiped a hand across his jaw and looked aside. His eyes tracked to the camera outside and across the street. She knew exactly what he was thinking. They couldn't stay here much longer and remain out of the ECU's view.

"How much you got?" he finally asked.

"Enough to cover your brother's ransom. I can have it in about…" She worked the angles she'd have to go through to gather the money from the various stashes she had all over the world. "Ten hours? I'll have to go online and move things around."

"I need cash."

"It'll result in cash. Promise."

"It's too risky for you. The ECU will know your every move."

"Not if I keep the kink collar on."

He smiled at that. "Why are you doing this? If you do this, Saskia, you can't turn back. You'll be as much an ECU target as I am."

She sat back. Why *was* she offering to sacrifice the freedom she'd earned and had never thought she'd want to lose?

Did she love the man?

No. Love wasn't that easy or quick. Was it?

The two of them felt comfortably easy.

"I don't know, Jack. Maybe I just want to help. Maybe I want to be something more than the chick in the costume who does what she's told. Maybe I like you a little more than I should."

He clasped her hand and leaned across the table, compelling her to move in closer until their foreheads touched. "I can't promise you anything," he said. "I don't know what tomorrow will bring. I don't even know what the next hour will bring."

"I get that." And if she jumped, she'd not surface the same person in the same situation or the same comfortable lifestyle. Ever. And that thrilled her beyond belief. "Let's do this. I just need a safe, quiet place with a laptop and a wifi connection."

"My family has a safe house in Brixton. We'll hop a cab."

"Really? The cameras will pick up our every move."

"We're leaving out the kitchen, and, you won't be looking like yourself when we do." He nodded over his shoulder and the first person Saskia noticed was an elegant woman in a fur coat with her gray hair pulled up to reveal diamond earrings.

"You think so?" she asked.

"I'll distract her. There's another reason I'm called Gentleman Jack. Niles would be jealous."

He tugged his suit coat and adjusted the yellow tie. His wink was devastating to her swooning heart. And Saskia suddenly felt one hundred percent sure she'd made the right decision.

Chapter 21

It hadn't taken more than a few sweet words to get the elegant woman to trade her coat for Saskia's and to give up her heels. Saskia emerged from the bathroom looking like half a million bucks. And Jack had procured a knit cap and left his suit coat behind, tucking his tie in a pocket. It was warmer in London but only by about thirty degrees. He was still going to feel the chill.

And he did as they exited through the kitchen and out the opposite side of the building.

"Where we headed?" Saskia asked as they ran down the alleyway.

"Brixton," he said. "Instead of the cab, we'll catch a bus."

"Really?"

He smiled at her sudden surprise. Surely the woman had had to flee tricky situations before. As he emerged from the alley he thanked a god he wasn't sure had ever had his back for the double decker that was just starting to leave the stop. He tugged Saskia along and they made the bus much to the shouts of the driver that they couldn't enter while he was moving.

As he sat on a seat at the back and twisted to scan the surroundings, Jack noticed Saskia tapped her ear. "I thought you said you weren't in contact with them?"

She wore an earbud issued by the ECU. The only way to communicate beyond cell phones. It also had a tracker, yet the jammer she still wore should block communications.

"I got a buzz," she said, and then paused as she was obviously listening to someone through the ear piece. "Chester," she mouthed to Jack.

"Shite, the blocker isn't working. Take out the earpiece."

She put up a palm and listened to whatever was being said in her ear.

Michele Hauf

And Jack clenched his fists. He didn't deal with Chester Clarke too often, despite knowing that Clarke was stationed somewhere here in London. Jack preferred to deal with Kierce Quinn, a much younger, though still adamantly cocky young gent who could speak in bits and bytes.

"I am on the job," he heard Saskia say. "What are you telling me?"

Jack would give his right leg to be in on this conversation. If she didn't relay it to him, he was out. It was the wisest choice. Right now, all he could be concerned with was Jonny. With or without Saskia's offer to donate the cash he needed.

She nodded. Looked to Jack. Her eyes didn't convey anything to him. The bright red lipstick she had borrowed from the woman in the deli had smeared just a little on the corner. Still, she looked amazing.

Jack looked away. Eyes on the surroundings, he reminded. Keep alert. Suddenly Saskia joined him on the bench and sat close, leaning in to speak, "I'm off your case. They've officially marked you AWOL."

"I got that. Now what?"

"I'm still on the heists. Chester tracked the first dignitary who died of poisoning and they sent out an agent to interview his wife. She gave some damning information about a man connected with the Russian *bratva*. Confirms our suspicions."

"So Clive really does work for the mafia."

"Yes. The ECU needs me to lure him out so we can bring him in and extract a confession."

"We don't know where Clive went."

"Apparently, he followed me or you here."

"He's in London? The wanker."

"Headquarters thinks he's on our tail."

"No. We're clean. I'm sure of it. Save for the bloody earcom you're wearing."

"I do work for the ECU, Jack. As for Clive, I didn't notice him on the flight. And I'm guessing you weren't in top form to have a look around in first class."

Jack gaped at her but she was right. He'd been a nervous mess."We're getting off at the next stop," he decided. Though their destination was still on the other side of the Thames. "We go on foot from here. And with better disguises. Unless…"

He waited for Saskia to confirm what he suspected. That she was out now. Her alliances had to remain with the ECU. She couldn't risk helping him any longer.

"I'm good," she said. "I told Chester to keep an eye out on CCTV for Clive and alert me when he had him. Until then, I'm my own agent."

"What did he say about the GPS blocker?"

"He's knows I'm with you. The earbud doesn't have GPS. And I've been ordered to take the blocker off." She tapped the front of the leather collar and shrugged. "My fingers are too cold right now. Can't operate the complicated mechanism. This is our stop. Ready?"

Yes, he was.

* * * *

Saskia noticed that Jack had a manner to him when walking out in the open on the sidewalks. His head was constantly shifting side to side, his eyes sweeping the area. He seemed to have radar for each and every CCTV camera. They were few and far between in this neighborhood that edged the Thames River. They'd just passed through a marketplace busy with people, which had relaxed Jack's shoulder. An asset always felt better in a crowd. Easier to go unnoticed. Yet also a challenge if they were trying to track someone.

Having abandoned the fur coat for a cheap slicker a few blocks back, Saskia had pulled her hair back and pinned it up. Dark sunglasses and the bright red lipstick gave her a trashy look that had gotten more than a few glances from the yuppie crowd in the marketplace.

For his part Jack always looked like Jack, though the knit cap did disguise his recognizable shaved head. He'd pulled on a down jacket and zipped it up high to snug beneath his jaw and that blended with his stubble so cameras would have a difficult time defining his face.

They walked through a neighborhood that was less elite now, and chain link fences edged one side of the street. Brick buildings were not all open businesses, and a car in need of a new muffler blurted past them.

When Jack clasped her hand, Saskia cast him a smile. It was such an unexpected move. But it felt so good. Reassuring. But as Jack had said, he couldn't promise her anything. And she didn't need a promise.

Perhaps a bit of hope though.

With all this walking her leg was bothering her. The knife wound pulsed with every step she took. Her non-existent kingdom for an aspirin.

With a tug, Jack pulled her down an alleyway littered with a few broken wood pallets and fluttering sheets of yellowed newspaper. Once again, he shoved her against the wall. But this time the shove didn't hurt. Instead, it owned her as Jack's kiss took away the question she'd been about to ask.

Just when she began to question her alliances he always seemed to pull her back in. Tug on the rope and keep her close. Just as she had done with him in Helsinki. And it was working on her. She'd already gone beyond the point of no return with him. She knew that.

When he ended the kiss, she sighed. A smile glinted in his gray eyes. But really, they were bluer now that she really looked. Yeah, the irises resembled a cloudy sky. She'd not really noticed them before. Hadn't wanted to make that step. The eye color stage. Because that was when things got serious.

So, she had stepped into serious now.

Jack's face suddenly changed. He winced.

Saskia heard the *whizz* of something passing by her head. And the impact of whatever that something was hitting the brick wall. She tasted spattered bits of brick on her tongue. Reacting, she dropped her body weight to the left, gripping Jack's shoulders as she did so and brought him down with her.

Now she noted the red dash across his cheek and over his ear.

"You've been hit."

* * * *

"Sniper," he barked. Pushing her aside to sit up, Jack scanned the area. Across the street, the buildings were only three stories tall, but that could have been the only origin of the shot. "I'm going after him."

To her credit, Saskia didn't argue, she followed.

Jack didn't worry about running head-on into another ambush. A sniper generally took the shot, then got the hell out of there. He had to have been trying for a kill shot. In the brain. But who was he working for? Was this how the ECU took out their operatives who thought to go off the grid?

Dashing across the street, he flipped the bird at a honking car as it put on its brakes to avoid hitting him. Saskia blew the driver a kiss and caught up to Jack, but he wasn't slowing. An alleyway between two buildings led him around the back of a laundromat. And he saw a man jump off the metal stairs hugging the building, glance over his shoulder at him, and run.

A long dark backpack was slung over the runner's shoulder. A rifle case. He leaped for the top of a dumpster set up against a fence, and made the landing, but the lid wasn't metal, and his footing slipped on the plastic cover, toppling him backward to land on the ground with a yelp and what was either rifle parts breaking or bones crunching.

Jack landed the man's chest with a knee and swung a fist up under his jaw. Saskia stood back, keeping lookout.

"Who do you work for?" Jack asked.

The man spat blood at him.

"Is that so? Well, I'm right sorry about this, bloke, but I'm going to have to do some rearranging with your ribs and kidneys."

The next blow connected his knuckles with the man's right kidney. He groaned and spat up more blood. But then he did something odd. He said something in Russian, and then smiled a wide and bloody smile.

"Oh shit!" Saskia plunged to the ground and slapped her palms to each of the man's cheeks. "He just said he'd see you in hell. His mouth is starting to foam. He had something in his cheek. Cyanide. Don't touch it!"

The two of them stood back and watched as the shooter's body flopped uncontrollably a few times. Foamy spittle drooled out of his mouth and his eyes rolled upward. And then he collapsed. Dead.

"We have to get out of here." Jack turned to assess the surroundings.

Cars swished by on the street down the alleyway. They stood behind an older apartment building, but he didn't see any movement behind the curtained windows.

Saskia bent and tore open the shooter's shirt.

"What the hell?" Jack asked.

She tapped the black tattoos on the man's chest. "This will tell us who he is and who he is working for. I suspect it's *bratva*," she said. She tugged out her cell phone. "I need to take some pictures and send them to Chester."

"Don't send it to Chester from here. He'll locate us."

"I'll wait until I get to the laptop and send it to an anonymous drop box. But we've got to move on this. I need a report on what the tattoos mean."

"You don't know?"

She shook her head. "But I do know they are mafia. We've got to call this in. We can't leave him here for the police or even the journalists to find."

"There's a phone booth down the block."

Saskia stood and walked swiftly, but she called back. "You got some change for the phone?"

He tossed her sixty pence.

She caught it and said to him as he paralleled her, "I hope that safe house is as safe as you think it is. Because now we've got the Russian mafia after us too."

* * * *

The safe house was a flat in Brixton, where, Jack pointed out to her, not three blocks down from the infamous prison he had served two miserable yet boring years. It wasn't a fine neighborhood, but Saskia had grown up in a similar sort. She followed Jack down a row of gray, blocky buildings. The distinct scent of trash rose even on this chilly day. Flames flickered in her periphery, and she noted a gang of teens huddled over a rusted barrel fire, warming their hands and lighting firecrackers.

Up three floors and down a dark hallway, Jack punched in a digital code on the apartment door. The tech surprised her, especially for what was obviously low-rent housing, but then she realized it must have been added by the renter. Jack's family? How strange was it that a family had to have a safe house?

Not so strange, she knew from experience, as she followed him inside the flat which was colder than it was outside.

"No one keeps the heat on unless the place is being used," he commented as he walked directly to the thermostat. It clicked as he turned the dirt-smudged dial. "No food, either, but I don't anticipate us needing to stay very long."

"It could take me hours. You got a laptop?" she asked, plopping down on a wobbly chair before a small pockmarked kitchen table. "I need to send those photographs of the shooter's tattoos."

"Should be one in the bedroom safe. I'll be right back."

When he returned, Saskia noticed the blood that had dripped onto his white shirt collar. It smeared down his cheek as well. She got up and snapped a few paper towels off the roll by the sink and wet them. Jack plugged in the laptop and turned to her.

"Sit," she said, and then touched the towels to his cheek.

"I can do that," he said.

She shoved him so he landed in the chair behind him, then bent and carefully dabbed at the cut on his cheek.

"Saskia."

"Jack, will you let me do the girlie thing, here? I won't be able to concentrate until I know you're okay."

"I'm bloody good. It was just a nick."

She glided the towel over the top of his ear that had taken the most damage. Just skin torn off. Nothing major. "It's lucky for you the sniper was such a terrible shot. But since when are snipers so poor to aim? This doesn't make sense."

He inhaled through his nose and nodded.

"And he wouldn't have done the suicide thing if his job was only to wound you."

"I was thinking the same thing," he said. "That's a major sacrifice for something so minor. He missed. He had been sent to kill."

"Yes. But which one of us?"

He clasped her wrist, stopping her from her care. "My bet is on the ECU, and me."

"I'm not so sure after seeing those tattoos. The ECU is after the *bratva*, not working with them."

"You have a point. But that just makes everything a bloody mess."

"Well, you're no longer a bloody mess." She kissed him quickly, then turned and tossed the soiled towels into the bin beside the stove. And Jack grabbed her and pulled her onto his lap and kissed her deeply.

"Thanks, Saskia."

She shrugged, like, sure no problem. "Why do you call me Saskia and not Sass?"

"You don't like being called Sass."

"How do you know? I've never said anything to you about it."

"You didn't have to. I pay attention. Every time Clive called you Sass you cringed. Not so much when Niles did it, but a little. You hate the name."

That he had figured it out touched her right in the heart. Felt like a hug that she hadn't known she needed. Saskia wrapped her arms around his shoulders and just when she would rest her cheek against his, she pulled away from the wound.

"Maybe you need to bandage that."

"It'll be fine. I'll heal."

"Not without a scar."

"Will that make me less pretty?" He shook his head as if a glamourous woman shaking out her hair.

She laughed. "I think scars are supposed to add character. And you are not a pretty man. You are handsome."

"I'll take handsome." He nodded toward the laptop. "You going to work your magic?"

"Yes, I should hurry. I can send the photos to an anonymous drop box online so the ECU won't be able to track the IP address back here. What's our deadline for the cash situation?" She turned on his lap and opened the laptop.

"Midnight. I'll get a call beforehand with the drop-off location."

"That gives me eight hours to gather a million bucks. I can do that."

"Can you?"

"I really can."

She twined her fingers together and twisted them outward as she readied herself to tap into the accounts she'd hidden in case of emergency. This was not the kind of emergency she'd been planning for, but the sacrifice felt right.

But first things first... She grabbed her phone and emailed the photos to her drop box account.

"You hungry?" he asked.

"Starving."

"There's a shop on the other side of this apartment complex. I'll run down and grab us something. Might even scrounge up some hot coffee."

"I'm in!"

He kissed the crown of her head, then opened a closet by the front door. He pulled out a leather jacket and muttered something that sounded like a thanks to his father. "Back in two shakes." He left her alone with a lock of the door behind him.

Saskia sent the drop box link to Chester with the message:

Is this how you bastards treat one of your own? Sniper shot at Jack. Or me? Is it ECU or bratva? Tell me what these tattoos mean.

She typed in the address where they'd left the dead man and sent the files.

"And now to make some magic happen."

As the first account flashed up on the screen, Saskia turned to look out the curtained front window. He wouldn't leave her again. Would he? He couldn't. She had the cash he needed to save his brother.

"Come back, Jack. I'm in this now. And I need you."

Because she wasn't sure what her status with the ECU was anymore. But it couldn't be remotely the same as it had been twenty-four hours earlier.

Chapter 22

Four hours later Saskia had set up a cash pickup not far from the safe house. She located a trusted fence she'd worked with in the past, who worked as a sort of money launderer. He would cobble together her money from three locations, and for a fee, bring it to her. Perfect.

What she was giving to Jack was a good portion of her secret savings. But if she couldn't do something good with it, then why let it sit around waiting for discovery by the ECU and eventually having it stolen out from under her?

Tossing aside the empty bag of vinegar and pepper crisps, she wished that Jack would have brought back something solid and not just snacks. Her stomach did not like the sugary soda pop at all, so she switched to the bottled water. In the living room, Jack paced. He'd been good about not disturbing her while she'd wrangled her money. She turned from the laptop to announce she was ready—when her laptop rang.

"Who the hell is that?" The look Jack gave her said he knew exactly who it was. She'd not expected a hack into the laptop but she wasn't surprised.

"Sorry. But I'm going to take this."

It was Chester Clarke at the ECU. He started right in. "We've ID'd the tattoos on the sniper. They indicate the man was a torpedo for the Siberian brigade of the *bratva*, as you'd suspected. Torpedoes are contract killers. This brigade can be connected to Clive's actions. Clive must have reported Angelo, or possibly you, to his higher-ups, and the hit was called in."

Saskia eyed Jack as he waited for her to speak. "What's the next step?"

"We need you to bring in Clive Hendrix for questioning. We'll get a confession out of him, perhaps a hit list, and that will bring us one step closer to the mafia. With the sniper's body, we've only circumstantial evidence."

"I don't think Clive will give up the mafia. He's not got a death wish."

"We've methods of extracting confessions."

Saskia was sure they did. And she couldn't stifle a shudder to wonder about it. On the other hand, narcing on the mafia? She'd probably have a tough time doing that and would go with whatever the ECU thought they could dish out.

"You need to get in touch with Clive, set up a meeting," Chester continued. "We'll be there to bring him in. You have his contact info?"

"I do. What do you want me to set the meeting up for? Just to chat? That's not going to go well. The last time I saw Clive he left me for dead in a Helsinki ditch."

"Yes, a meeting. And you're going to have to go back on grid, Saskia. This is highly unprecedented. We need to be able to track you. I know you're with Jack Angelo. You're protecting him. And that's not going to go well for you."

"It's a choice I had to make. Wait." Her phone beeped, indicating another call. It didn't ID the caller, but she had a suspicion. "I'll get back to you, Chester. I think the dog just came sniffing at my door." She clicked on to the new caller and Clive's voice was cheery and not at all reminiscent of the heroin-addled bastard who had stabbed her earlier this morning.

"We need to talk, Sass."

"Is that so? What? You want to finish the job? You want to stab the other leg now?"

"I was high, Sass. I'm terribly sorry. Honest. I don't know why I did that. I get crazy when I mainline."

"If I had known you had an issue with drugs, I would have never worked with you." She noticed Jack's keen interest, and mouthed "Clive." "Where are you?"

"London, of course."

"I thought you were going to meet Niles in Belize?"

"I needed to make things right between us before I could go. I followed you."

Of course he had.

"That's pretty extreme just to apologize."

"I didn't say anything about an apology. I want to make things right. I need you for the next job, Sass. Your skills…"

"Are apparently useless for your modus operandi. We never take anything, Clive. You don't need me to tap into the main vaults. What the hell?"

"I'll let you in on the real operation if you'll come meet me."

"Tell me now. Over the phone."

"Too dangerous. My people like to keep tabs on me."

The *bratva*. Ugh. Saskia wanted to drop the phone right now. Because if the mafia got a line on her, she would not live to see tomorrow. But then, they had already sent a sniper after either her or Jack. She was in deep. And that was not cool.

"You think a face to face meeting is going to be any less dangerous?" She made show of blowing out her breath. She was stringing him along when she knew this is exactly what the ECU wanted. But it felt wrong. And so dangerous.

Of course, that was what she did. Face danger and give it the middle finger. But danger had never come tattooed and reeking of the mafia before. Damn it, she hated this.

Meeting gazes with Jack, she looked for something, anything, in his eyes. And she found there a deep respect and certain confidence that shimmered through her system and straightened her spine. Is that what love did to a woman? That was definitely going on in her heart right now.

"Where?" she asked Clive.

"In Peckham on the Left Bank." He read off an address to her. "In an hour?"

He was in a hurry. And she had a pickup in less than an hour.

"I'm not familiar with London. I can make it in an hour and a half."

"That'll work. Come alone. I know Jack is with you."

"We've…recently parted ways," she said, thinking if Clive knew about the sniper hit, he might assume Jack had been taken out.

"He's gone? Where?"

"Not sure. Something happened. And that's all I'm going to say."

"Very well. Sass. I want you to trust me. You're key to the crew. I need you."

"You're going to have to prove it by making up for stabbing me." She clicked off and set the phone on the table.

"That bastard wants to meet?" Jack asked.

She nodded and stood, stretching her back muscles from side to side and feeling the painful tug in her thigh again. The longer she sat, the achier her muscles grew. She needed to stay on her feet.

"The first caller was Chester. He wants me back online with them." She tapped the phone. "The sniper was with the *bratva*. A torpedo."

"Hired killer," Jack said, and then whistled lowly. He rubbed the cut on his cheek. "They should get a refund for that cocked up job."

"Right? Chester has been able to connect Clive to the *bratva* as well, and he's assuming Clive made the call for the hit. The ECU wants me to bring Clive in. And wonder upon wonders, Clive followed us here."

"He's in London?"

"Someplace in Peckham."

"That's not far from here."

She nodded. "I can't seem to shake that guy. He's like a tick that I can't crush."

"You arranged to meet him. You're not going alone."

"He thinks you're gone. I tossed that in, in case he believes the sniper hit his mark."

Jack nodded. "Good call. But you're not going alone. I'll be close."

"I want you there. I don't trust Clive as far as I can spit. I think he's going to try and take me out." And the shiver up her spine echoed that statement. "We need to move. I've got the pickup soon."

"Right. But first." Jack strode down the hallway and into the bedroom. "Come here!"

She wandered into the white-walled room. The twin-size bed boasted an old patchwork quilt that looked like something Saskia's grandmother might have made. It was a strangely homey touch that made her gasp and put her fingers to her throat.

Jack sorted through some items hanging in the closet and produced a black vest. "Kevlar," he said.

"You want me to wear that?"

"You're not leaving without it on. And I'm going to arm up." He tossed her the heavy vest, and then bent to push aside a shoe rack that revealed a medium-sized safe. Two minutes later, he checked the magazine on a Ruger and then tucked it in his waistband. "Now, we're ready."

* * * *

The pickup was a breeze. Jack almost stopped Saskia from reaching out the car window for the plain brown leather attaché handed over from a parked Volvo. She had cobbled together a million pounds to ransom his brother. A million pounds that he didn't have to pay her back. A million she had saved for whatever sort of emergency or backup plans she had made.

He couldn't do this.

She turned to him, attaché in hand, beaming. "Drive, Jack. We're done here."

The Volvo drove away and for a moment Jack felt helpless. And grateful. And lost in the woman's smile.

"Jack?"

He shook out of the strange wonder. Saskia laid the attaché on her lap and rapped her fingers on it. "Come on. We've gotta head to the next meeting. The one where I get dead."

"Don't say that." He pulled into traffic from the parking lot and signaled his turn. "I'm going to have eyes on you the whole time. And you've got Chester in your ear, yes?"

"Yes, the ECU should be on the scene. You know this will lead the ECU right to you?"

"There's no place I'd rather be right now." He cast her a wink, but the lighthearted move didn't ring true in his heart. He was nervous as hell that the ECU would scoop him up and take him away. Or take him out.

It could happen. It *would* happen. He crossed his fingers it didn't occur until after he'd gotten Jonny back safely.

"The only place you want to be right now is at your brother's side," Saskia said. "So, you going to write me an IOU for this, Jack?"

"The money? Of course."

"I'm kidding. This is a gift. I have more."

"You do? How comfortable are you?"

"I would never call keeping money in overseas bank accounts comfortable, but I'll survive. It means a lot that you'll take this from me."

"Like how so?"

"Like..." She turned on the seat and faced him. He kept his eyes on the traffic but he could feel her scrutiny on the side of his face. He wanted to lean over and kiss her. "Maybe I like you more than a little," she confessed. "Enough to trust you with my secrets, anyway."

"I've told you that isn't wise."

"I think it is. You might not want to show it, but you feel the same way about me. I have a confession, Jack."

"Bring it."

"I've never been in love before. Never had a relationship that made me want anything more than club-hopping and sex from a guy, you know?"

"Why are you bringing this up?"

"Because. Maybe... This could be love. I don't really know what that is though," she said. "No one has ever said it to me. But then, who knows? Maybe I am in love."

He swallowed and glanced at her. She shrugged, offering wide, bright eyes. God, she was beautiful. And talking about love and all that crazy stuff? He wanted to get behind it, but he was like her. Love wasn't tops on his list of experiences. Women had been rather fluid in his life. One or two might have hung around for a few months, but never anything permanent. It was difficult to have a relationship when a guy was a thug. And even harder when his life belonged to a black ops Interpol organization.

Not that he couldn't have relationships. He'd just...never taken the time for one. It had always been family first.

But his family had grown distant. And yet, why did he feel Saskia was akin to family?

"I just freaked you out, didn't I?" she asked. "Sorry. That was my mistake."

"No, it's cool." He pulled down a dark road. It was nearing ten in the evening. They were cutting it close to the midnight exchange for his brother.

"I think we both feel kind of the same, yeah?"

He smirked. "Yeah. The meet location is just ahead. I'm going to drop you off and park a few blocks up the way, then return on foot. You call in to Chester now and get your backup."

"Will do."

She slid the case under the front seat. Tugging off the scarf from around her neck, Saskia arranged it over the part that still showed, concealing it.

Jack's phone rang and he answered abruptly. "Midnight," the voice said. "The dock in East Tilbury. You know the one."

Yes, he did. It was a place he and Jonny had once smuggled in stolen artifacts for the Downs gang. An unassuming, wooded area that hid a few old, unused docks nowadays.

"Got it," Jack said. "My brother better be there. I've got the cash." He hung up. "The exchange is by the river."

"Really? A dock?" Saskia asked.

"It's on the Thames, out of the city in East Tilbury. Down the way from Coalhouse Fort. It's about an hour drive from here. If the traffic cooperates."

"Then you should leave for the dock now," she said, zipping up her coat to cover the Kevlar vest. "I'll have backup." She tapped the earbud.

Jack waited for her to make arrangements with Chester. The ECU would likely send a sniper out to keep an eye on Clive, though it sounded as though they wanted him alive. The local London police would be called to make an arrest. But they'd have to surround the meet on the sly so as not to alert Clive. Best scenario was if Saskia could keep him talking and not allow him to take her to another location.

"Ten minutes," she said to Jack. "I should head out. I'll see you after midnight?"

"I'm not going anywhere until I know you're safe."

"Jack."

"Hey, let me do the guy thing here, will you?"

She smiled at his turning around what she'd said to him earlier when she'd cleaned up his wound.

"You mean the rescuing knight?" she asked. "You've done that once already when I could have frozen to death in the ditch."

"Maybe I need more practice." He leaned over and pulled her to him with a hand to her nape. The kiss was warm and firm and the best thing he'd ever experience from here on out.

Because the moment he walked away from Saskia and handed over her cash to the men holding his brother, his future was uncertain. No way could he turn back and pretend everything was still the same.

As he pulled away from her mouth, but not so far that he still couldn't kiss her quick, Jack said, "Family."

"Is waiting for you," she affirmed.

"No. It's right here." And another kiss was just the thing to keep him from saying more mushy, romantic stuff. His heart was feeling it, but it felt weird to put it into words. Especially a tough guy like himself. "You're my family, Saskia. Don't forget that. Now go. I've got your back."

She nodded, bowing her head quickly and sniffing as she got out of the car. Had that been a tear she'd sniffed back?

"This romance stuff is crazy," he muttered, pulling slowly down the street to find a parking spot. "It'll be the death of me."

* * * *

Saskia stood at the open end of the alleyway, hands in her pockets, knit cap pulled down tightly to keep away the chill. She didn't need a disguise.

In her earbud, Chester spoke calmly. "We're on, Saskia. I've got a man up high and a team of London constables on the other side of the building. Unmarked. We don't want to spook the man. Keep him talking and allow the constables to move in."

She didn't reply. He wouldn't expect her to.

So she had three men at her back? Correction: four. Jack was somewhere. She wished he'd gone on to the dock to rescue his brother. But he still had time. And knowing he was watching her right now lifted her shoulders and straightened her spine.

Maybe she had fallen in love with the bloke. Too bad there wasn't a way to know what the next few minutes would bring. It would be a crime if, after finally realizing she had fallen in love, she lost that by death.

A man strode down the alley toward her, his gaze flicking left and right and up high, taking in the surroundings. Clive noted every crook and cranny. His hands were shoved in the slim pea coat he wore, and on his head a tight-fitted knit cap—much like Jack's—concealed his silver hair. He neared and she shook her hands out at her sides to show him she wasn't holding a weapon.

"Sass," he said as he closed their distance. "I'm glad you came. So I'll do you the favor of making this quick."

Fingers tightening, Saskia's heart dropped. That didn't sound at all favorable from her side.

Clive stopped five feet before her, hands still in his pockets. "The sniper's bullet was meant for you," he said.

Her jaw dropped open.

"I've suspected you were duping me since the poison you gave me turned out to be nothing more than a compound of salt and fertilizer. I tasted it." He pulled a hand out of his pocket.

She looked high for the sniper, but sighted no one.

"You're with some secret organization," Clive said. "My employer filled me in. Thanks for nothing."

The impact of a bullet to the Kevlar vest at such close range pushed her back and threw her off her feet. Saskia felt as if her spine had been punched out through her back. She struggled to stay on her feet, clutching at her gut.

A hand gripped her by the hair and pulled her head up. The gun barrel hit hard against her temple.

Chapter 22

Jack swung his head around the corner of the print shop, where Saskia was to meet Clive. He'd heard Clive talking but couldn't make out what he was saying. As he turned and shifted his shoulder to stand halfway unprotected by the building, he saw Clive's hand pull out of his pocket. The object gripped in his hand was a gun.

Jack aimed down the alleyway, arm high and outstretched. He looked through the pistol sight. Saskia took a bullet to the gut. He didn't flinch. She was wearing the Kevlar vest. It would hurt like a bitch and leave bruising, but she'd survive.

It was when he saw Clive's hand move upward that Jack swore inwardly. Clive's motions seemed to move so slowly that Jack could make out every minute fraction until the gun connected with Saskia's temple. Clive's finger had slid off the trigger and just as Jack watched that movement, he squeezed the trigger of his gun.

He watched Clive's gun go flying. Clive flinched and yelped, drawing to his chest a bleeding hand. Saskia wavered and stumbled backward.

It had been a risky move, but it paid off.

Swinging into the alleyway, Jack raced toward the twosome, unconcerned for whatever backup the ECU might have on the scene. All he saw was Clive and Saskia. He wasn't about to let her stand alone before that crazed bastard any longer. He collided with Clive and snatched him by the collar. The man groaned, gripping his bleeding hand.

"No apologies this time," Jack said.

He connected his fist up under Clive's jaw, a knockout punch—or it should have been. The man tumbled backward, his weight pulling Jack forward. He released the bastard to fall. Plunging to the ground beside the moaning man, Jack pummeled Clive in the ribs, gut, and collarbone with punches. He didn't feel the pain of impact. He was merely returning to him the suffering he'd given Saskia.

"Stand down, Angelo!" a male voice said from above and behind him.

Jack didn't listen. Saskia's shoes appeared near Clive's head and she begged him to stop. And it was only her voice that managed to connect with that broken part of him that didn't know how to solve anything but with fists and fury.

Pulling his punch, Jack froze over Clive's body. The man lay unconscious and bleeding. Chill air swept Jack's face. His heart squeezed because he sensed Saskia standing over him. Witnessing him losing his shite. Behind him, he sensed others stood.

"Cuff him," a female voice ordered. Not Saskia.

Two London police officers knelt and Jack stepped back as they cuffed Clive.

"Both of them," the woman ordered. "Angelo too."

A pair of hands gripped one of Jack's wrists and tugged his arm to twist his hand around behind his back. It wasn't a surprise. He'd suspected it could go down like this. The ECU had known he was with Saskia and wouldn't miss the chance to also take him in hand.

Jack looked to Saskia. She clutched her gut but her expression was wild.

"No," she said to the woman Jack had yet to see. "He helped us bring in Hendrix. You can't take him in!"

"You don't get to tell me what to do," the woman said.

And as the plastic ties zipped about Jack's wrists, he turned to face the female with the deep and powerful voice. He knew her. She'd been the woman who had come to him after he'd been taken out of his jail cell. Tall, blond, and sexy as hell, but with an iron bar for a spine. Lucinda Marks, the Commander of the Elite Crimes Unit. The buck stopped with her; her word was all powerful.

"This shouldn't surprise you, Angelo," she said to him.

He lifted his chin. All he could think was that he'd failed Jonny. Twisting his hands within the tight zip ties, he wished they'd cuffed his wrists before him instead of behind him. At least then, he might have escaped. Now? He had to figure a way out of this.

As the officers roused Clive and lifted him to a stand, Jack was tugged away and down the alley. Behind him, Saskia argued with Lucinda Marks, the woman who could change a man's life for the better or the very worst.

Shite. He had to break free. Jonny needed him. But would he risk a sniper bullet to the skull again if he did so?

* * * *

Saskia swore at Lucinda Marks. She'd met her once and had never liked her, despite knowing she was the one who'd organized the ECU because she believed criminals deserved a second chance. Where was Jack's second chance?

When it was obvious that no one was going to cuff her, Saskia stepped back from Marks. Her gut ached and she wanted to bend over and cry, but there was no time for feeling sorry for herself. It had to be nearing eleven, probably past that time. Jack's brother had less than an hour.

"We'll need you to come in for a debriefing," Marks said as she brushed a sweep of blond hair from her perfectly made-up face. The beige wool coat that swept to her ankles must have cost a pretty penny. "You want a ride to headquarters with me?"

Saskia shifted back her shoulders, standing strong. Best not to run off and draw the sniper's bullet after her. He'd made himself known by leaning out the window and waving to Marks. "I'll get there on my own."

"You don't know where it is," Marks said. "Come on, ride with me."

"There's something I've got to do first."

Lucinda's gaze cut through Saskia's bravery. Ice Queen must be the oath most often whispered behind her back.

"You can do whatever you want with me in an hour. Just give me one hour," Saskia stated emphatically. "I'll explain everything then." She turned and rushed down the alleyway where the police cars were pulling away.

A glance over her shoulder saw Marks shake her head toward the sniper. He'd been called down. Whew! She was giving her the hour?

Hard to know.

"What's going on?" Chester asked.

Touching the plastic device in her ear, Saskia almost pulled it out to toss aside, but a moment of wisdom stilled her. "Got a date with a man who needs my help," she said. "You can verify to the Commander that I'm not going AWOL. I swear it to you."

"This is irregular, Petrovik. The Commander wants you back at headquarters."

"Soon as I can make it. Promise!"

A glance down the street spied the rental Jack had parked. Saskia dashed up the sidewalk, and once inside the unlocked car she confirmed that the attaché was still half-hidden under the passenger seat.

Leaning under the steering wheel and peeling off the plastic shell that protected the wiring, she prepared to hotwire the vehicle, but she needed a screwdriver or something to jam into the ignition. She opened the glove compartment and found inside a travel-sized tool kit. Perfect.

Forty seconds later the car purred to a start. If she turned off the ignition she might never get it started again, so she had to make this work. Jack had mentioned an old dock just out of the city. She had no clue where that was.

As she pulled away from the curb, keeping one eye out for police cruisers. Thankful for the car's online GPS system, Saskia asked for directions to East Tilbury.

* * * *

Jack allowed the officers to escort him into the back of the police cruiser. Hands behind him, he slid to the opposite side of the back seat and sat directly behind the driver. He caught sight of Saskia running toward the parked rental as they pulled away from the curb. He didn't turn his head to watch her. Didn't want anyone to pick up on his curiosity and go after her.

He knew what she was going to do. It gave him a moment of relief. Of gratitude.

And then he fisted his hands until the zip ties dug mercilessly into his wrists. But one thing to be thankful for was that his shoes laced up. He'd be out of these zips in no time. He began to thread a lace through the plastic strip.

As for Saskia's goal? The people holding Jonny would never make the exchange to a woman. And she had no clue where the actual dock was. He'd only mentioned a dock a ways down from Coalhouse Fort. That could be any number of places.

As the cruiser stopped at a red light, Jack met gazes with the driver in the rearview mirror. If the ECU wanted to punish him, they would have to take him in hand. Or they could let him go through the system and end up back in prison.

Either way, it was now or never to tilt the odds in his favor.

Chapter 23

"Marks has had me put a tail on you, Saskia," Chester reported as she parked the vehicle.

She peered through the driver's window toward the old wooden dock that was a half a football field away, across a snowy field. Didn't look like anyone was on it. This had to be the right one. After pulling onto three docks beyond the city limits, none had looked old or abandoned. This one had a sign posted telling people to keep out, that the area was unsafe. And there was a fort nearby. Maybe an old army fort? Had to be the one Jack had mentioned. A rusted yard light flickered off and on at the top of the dock. It stayed off longer than the few seconds it was on.

Snow flurries whipped before the parked car in a diagonal veil. And the wind whistled. It looked wicked cold out there.

"Saskia?"

Drawn back to the moment, she touched her ear, aiming her focus on what Chester had said. She was being tracked? "Yeah, I expected that. Whoever is coming for me... Can you hold them back a bit, Chester?"

"What are you doing?"

If she couldn't be honest now, she'd only miss her opportunity to help Jack.

"I'm finishing something for Jack. It's the reason he went AWOL. He never would have left the ECU if he didn't have to. He's a good man, Chester. But his family comes first."

"We can't protect Jack Angelo anymore. And your assignment is complete. Whatever you're up to—"

"Won't take much longer. Then I'll turn myself in, and let you guys do what you will. I owe Jack this much. He saved my life, Chester. He deserves a good turn. I'm going radio silent now. Sorry. It's got to be done."

After pulling out the earbud and tossing it to the floor of the car, Saskia grabbed the leather attaché, and stepped outside. Still wearing the Kevlar vest, more for the heavy warmth of it, than anything, she winced as each movement stabbed her in the ribs. The hit must have broken a few, surely. At the very least that pain distracted from her thigh.

The brisk wind was picking up. She turned to the side to block it from beating at her face. Scanning the area, she decided she was the only one idiotic enough to be out here on such a foul evening. But she saw a small light nearing the dock. A boat?

Shrugging up her shoulders to stir a little warmth around her neck, she scampered across the snowy field and then strode down the dock, attaché in hand. The boards creaked and she could feel their give. Decades of water and weather had softened them. One step could break through the aged wood. She angled her path toward where she noted the nails formed a line, and hoped that was where the support beams beneath were.

A searchlight from the approaching boat cast across the end of the dock. Another sweep, longer and holding on her for a moment, momentarily blinded her as it crossed over her face. She waved, thinking whoever was in the boat was expecting a brutish man in a suit and yellow tie and not a small woman fit out in down jacket and bulletproof vest.

She had to take the chance they would not turn around.

This was a far cry from Helsinki's docks. And much warmer. But right now Saskia's blood felt like ice. A dip in the drink would not bring the night to a pleasing end. She should have had a weapon. At the very least, a knife to defend herself. But she wouldn't need one if she remained on the dock.

If the ECU were indeed on her ass, they could arrive at any moment and fuck up the exchange. She rushed forward to stand but three feet from the end of the dock. The boards under her shoes wobbled and groaned, and the wind bruised her cheeks. It was difficult not to stand there, hands down at her sides and shoulders hunched up around her neck as if a frightened and cold waif.

Another wave lured the boat closer. She counted five men in the boat. Not good odds. Was one of them Jack's brother? What did he look like? Similar to Jack? Who were the people who held him? What had Jonny Angelo done to warrant a million dollar ransom?

Did any of those questions matter? Not really.

A man in a dark leather jacket and gloves stepped up to the side of the boat while another at the prow stabbed a massive hook onto the dock to hold them there. At the back of the boat another man reached out to grip the dock with gloved fingers.

"Who the bloody hell are you?" the dark man called in a distinctive Irish accent.

"A friend of Jack's," she called against the wind. "He wasn't able to make it, but I've got it." She slapped the attaché. "A million pounds. Where's Jonny?"

The man turned and looked behind him. It was then she saw the man bound from shoulders to hips with thick rope. His face was bloodied and bruised and a gag wrapped around his mouth. He wasn't wearing winter gear and had to be an ice cube after a blustery trip down the Thames.

"Hand it over!" the man said with a gimmee gesture of his gloved fingers.

"Put Jonny on the dock first!"

The man smirked and shook his head. "You heard her, boys. Put the boy on the dock!"

Saskia watched as two men lifted Jack's bound brother. Just when it looked as though they would heave him up onto the dock, she felt the attaché being swiped out of her grasp. The man in charge had plunged forward to grab it. Of a sudden the man with the hook disengaged his weapon and gave a shove. The boat motor growled to a roar and the boat pushed away.

And Jonny was...

Saskia didn't see him on the dock. Had they not released him? She counted the silhouettes in the boat. There were only four. Where was he?

She plunged to her knees and leaned over the edge of the wood dock. Under her palm, a thick chunk of weathered wood splintered and gave way. As she caught herself, her head lunged forward and she saw him. Hanging from one of the thick support posts. A big rusted hook held a loop of rope, dangling him mercilessly. His head rocked as if he were screaming, but Saskia couldn't hear over the wind and waves. Half his body was submerged in the icy waters.

Saskia saw no way to get him loose unless she had a knife. She could free him if she were able to lift him a good foot to pull up the ropes from the hook.

A wave of icy water stirred by the boat's wake washed up against the dock, covering Jonny's gyrations, and splashing her face.

"Shit!"

This was not the job she'd signed on for.

But falling in love with Jack Angelo hadn't been a part of the original plan either. And she did not regret that for one moment.

She'd always stood up to a challenge, and shown it her teeth. No reason to stop now.

Standing and unzipping her coat, Saskia swore against the blistering cold. She dropped the Kevlar vest at her feet and winced as the release of that hugging item seemed to pull out on her broken ribs. Without another thought, she stepped forward and dropped into the river.

* * * *

The police cruiser paralleled the Thames. Until it turned to head for Scotland Yard, it was very near the direction Jack had intended to go to find his brother. He had no idea what time it was, but he wasn't going to risk losing the one chance at saving Jonny's life. By tying his shoe laces together and sawing them across the plastic, he'd successfully broken them apart. Now to play it by ear.

The cruiser suddenly swerved and pulled up to the curb. Ahead, parked a dark limousine. Was it the same that had been parked back at the scene where Saskia had met Clive? His brain clicked and gears turned. Quick thinking honed over the years. This was the opportunity he needed. Because he wasn't headed to Scotland Yard. They were going to hand him off to the ECU. Lucinda Marks, to be exact.

The back door opened, and Jack got out. He kept his hands behind his back. The officer didn't notice. He was led around to stand at the curb while the limo light beamed onto his backside. The officer returned to his patrol car and...pulled away.

Jack lifted a brow. Running would be too easy right now. And he would not get far.

He guessed there would be a driver, armed, and Lucinda, also armed, inside the limo. They expected him to turn and walk back to them. Bloody hell, he had no plan. But he did need a vehicle.

The driver's door opened and out stepped a man Jack didn't recognize. Merely a hired hand or a trained ECU asset?

Jack remained at the curb, facing the blustery winds. He wasn't going to make this easy for either of them.

"You'll join us, Mister Angelo," the driver said in an accent that the queen herself would have swooned over. He was a hired driver, Jack decided. Mistake number one on Marks's part.

"I want a few minutes to take the air," Jack called. "You know, my last bloody breaths?"

Hey, it was all he could summon at the moment.

And where was Saskia? Was she in the limo? He could see the outline of only one head in the backseat. Had she made it to the dock? It was too much to hope for.

"There will be time later for taking the air," the driver called politely. "Miss Marks wishes to speak with you."

"Then tell her to come out here. It's a beautiful evening. I'd hate for her to miss the moon." He nodded toward the sky where the moon was full yet blurred by the snow that whipped mercilessly in his face.

The driver ducked his head inside the limo. Discussing a game plan? Or simply relaying to Marks that Jack was being a right asshole. When the driver straightened and returned to the front of the car, Jack saw the gun in his hand. Or was it?

The back door opened and out jutted a long leg clad in black slacks. She wore an ankle-length beige coat. Blond hair shone on her shoulders and appeared highly lacquered. She looked ready for a night out at the billionaire's club. And that woman would not be any man's trophy, but rather the prize all men could only hope to admire.

With a flip of her long hair over a shoulder, she placed her hands akimbo and walked up to stand beside the driver. "Get in the car, Angelo. We'll talk."

"I'd like to talk out here, if you don't mind. More of a ground zero, neutral field sort of thing."

"Very well." She took a few steps toward him. "You can put your hands in front of you. I'm not that stupid."

He spread out his arms to reveal he wasn't bound and slowly brought his hands together in a clasp before his crotch.

"Any way we can talk a deal?" he asked.

She shrugged. "I'm always willing to deal if the person shows merit. Skill. If he possesses something no other has. Something the ECU can use." The snow seemed to avoid her and her hair remained perfect as she eyed him slyly. "Are you singular, Jack Angelo?"

I want to fuck you, Jack Angelo. Those words spoken by Saskia days earlier when he only had eyes for the pretty redheaded hotel receptionist. What a ride she'd taken him on. How to make sure that ride never ended?

"I am," he offered.

Marks tilted her head. "I'm not convinced of that. Thugs are a dime a dozen. You came to us because you had the knowledge we needed regarding infiltrating banks and their security, but we've gained another agent with such skills recently. You are no longer singular."

"Well…"

"Tony."

At Lucinda's nod, the driver approached Jack. Jack put up his hands, wanting to see what the man had in store for him. As he neared, Jack saw the gun wasn't a pistol. He recognized that thing. It was an injection gun.

Tony shoved a hand onto Jack's shoulder, and from behind he pressed the gun against the base of his skull.

Jack swore. His muscles tightened, preparing for defense. And yet... If they were going to chip him again, there had to be a reason. They wouldn't chip a dead man.

The click of the injection gun preceded the skull-throbbing pain of the intrusion. A microscopic GPS chip had been forced through his skin and into the tissue at the base of his skull. It burned, but it was a pain he took with some optimism.

Tony returned to the driver's door to place the injection gun back inside the vehicle. While Lucinda stepped toward Jack.

It was now or never. "Seems like you've got the dog back on the leash," he said.

"The best place for you, Jack. You know that. You promise you won't run astray this time?"

Was she offering him what he thought? A chance to stay in the ECU? No prison? No tombstone?

Yet for all that hope, Jack still couldn't give her what she wanted. Not yet.

"I'm really sorry about this, Miss Marks, but I am a gentleman, and this is how a gentleman handles the obstacles life puts in his way."

He lunged and wrapped an arm around her neck, swinging her to face the driver. Kicking high, he connected with the driver's hand, sending what he now saw was a gun flying. Marks elbowed him in the ribs smartly. She wasn't all glamour and makeup. She was strong. Skilled.

As the driver grabbed for Jack's throat, he managed to drop his center of gravity, pulling down Marks and fisting her in the jaw. A knockout.

From behind, the driver gripped Jack about the throat and squeezed. He rolled forward, over Marks's body and flipped the driver into the street to splay before the limo's headlights. A quick fist to the man's jaw knocked him out.

Snow collected on the woman's perfect red lips. She wouldn't be out for long.

Jack slid into the driver's seat. The car was still running. And tucked down the side of the seat, he tugged out a bowie knife. Good thing Tony had preferred a pistol. Pulling carefully away from the curb so he wouldn't nudge either of the bodies on the street, he headed for the edge of the city.

Chapter 24

Jack pulled the limo up next to the rental just as he saw Saskia go over the edge of the dock.

"What the hell?"

He noticed the red lights on the back of the boat as it headed north up the Thames. They must have already made the exchange. Maybe? Something was off. He didn't see Jonny.

The gears grinded as Jack abruptly threw the limo into park and opened the door at the same time. Pulling off his coat and shedding that in his wake, he raced over the lumpy snow-capped field and to the end of the dock. No other cars were in the area. But Marks would have the ECU on his arse soon enough. Hell, they could find him now that he'd been rechipped.

Bending over the end of the dock, he nearly slipped into the drink when his palm crushed the rotting wood and the plank gave way. Leaning onto his side, he saw the situation. Saskia was in the water struggling with the heavy ropes wrapped around his brother's body. Jonny had been hung on the pier post and the water sloshed up over his chin. He was out, but his shivers were evident. As was Saskia's failing strength.

Jack pulled out the bowie knife and thought to hand it to Saskia but she didn't see him. And the winds would make calling to her difficult. He slipped over the wood planks, grasping the edge of the dock. The icy water shocked his system, and soaked through his clothing. He cursed seven ways to Sunday.

Saskia sputtered water and shouted something that sounded like his brother's name. She reached for him. Her fingers clasped, stretching, but not connecting. A sudden wave washed her out of Jack's reach and away from him.

"Grab the dock piling!" he shouted.

Michele Hauf

Another wave banged him up against his brother. Jack grabbed the slippery rope wrapped about Jonny's chest. He hadn't much time before the icy water numbed his extremities and made holding the knife impossible.

He sawed the Bowie over the thick ropes that must be used for shipping. They were as thick as the ropes that had hung in the Helsinki warehouse. Thankfully, it took but a minute for the rope to sever and loosen. Jonny's body slumped against his, yet the waves sloshed him away to hit against the piling. His head banged the rusted hook. Jack struggled to stay above water with the heavy weight against him.

And where was Saskia? Had the current pulled her out into the river? No, it would generally smash a body against the shore, which was sandy and pocked with head-sized stones. He couldn't see for the blur of snow and wind.

Gulping in air, Jack then dropped under water and clutched his brother about the legs. With one forceful kick he pushed upward, propelling Jonny into the air. His chest hit the dock and just when he hoped he'd stay, Jonny slipped back onto Jack's shoulder. Kicking furiously, he swallowed water and choked. Jack's head went under. Bubbles burned in his nostrils.

He could close his eyes and the struggle would end...

Saskia. Where was she? He couldn't let it end without giving her his all.

A wave of determination tightened in Jack's gut. Another breath, and with a kick of his feet, another propulsion. As Jonny's body rose out of the water he heard his brother yell. Jonny slapped his arms across the dock and hung there, his legs dangling in the water. The weathered dock cracked sharply. Jonny's body shifted downward.

"Climb on!" Jack yelled. "Before you fall in again."

"Jack?"

He pushed up his brother's legs. They folded and Jonny was able to pull himself completely onto the dock. He rolled over, tucking up his legs until he curled into a helpless ball.

The cold water filled Jack's throat and iced his lungs. Blinking, he went under and again the water shrouded him warmly, beckoning him to stop kicking. And he did....

It could be love. I don't really know what that is. No one has ever said it to me before.

Yeah, it probably was love. And he hadn't said the like to her. So he wasn't about to go out without making sure she heard it from him.

Kicking his legs, Jack aimed away from the dock and allowed the gentle current to whisk him along the shore. He kicked and swam. It had been ages since he'd swam in the Thames, purposely, and as a kid he'd always been the first to dive in and then come up to a float.

That's what he had to do to stay alive. Turning onto his back, Jack floated and kicked and backstroked until he bumped up against something solid. Hair slipped over his face. He turned and the movement swept Saskia's body under his. He wrapped an arm about her and kicked toward shore. It wasn't far, and he could reach out for the stones and crawl up to push her body onto them.

Dragging himself out of the water, he struggled to stand half upright. His wet clothing weighed him down, but he shook so much it seemed to keep his adrenaline pumping. Tugging Saskia by the arms, he moved her toward a strip of soaked cardboard that might have once served as a homeless man's bed and rolled her onto it.

A glance toward the dock spied Jonny lying there, motionless. And the swinging beams from two flashlights. The ECU had arrived.

Jack bowed his head over Saskia's. He pressed his shaking fingers to her neck. Heartbeats pumped. Still alive. But for how long? He pressed her chest, not knowing how the CPR thing worked but thinking he needed her to choke up the water she might have swallowed. Turning her onto her side, she did suddenly choke and spit up water.

"Yes." He clutched her head with both hands—his fingers were numb—and bowed his forehead to hers.

One of the bobbling flashlight beams approached them.

"I love you, Saskia. Don't forget that."

"Jack..."

"You're my family now. I'll never stop looking for you. Promise."

"Jack, don't leave me. I...your brother..."

"He's good. Safe. Alive. Thanks to you."

"Jack Angelo," the voice behind the flashlight beam said. "Stand and put up your hands."

And with a quick kiss to Saskia's brow, he pushed up from the ground and turned to face the light, lifting his sodden arms and splaying his hands.

Chapter 25

Clive Hendrix was not one to endure intense torture. He gave up the *bratva* after forty-five minutes. He didn't have a hit list, but would receive calls when another dignitary was targeted to have poison left in his safe deposit box.

It had been a clever scheme. One that Clive had carried out three times before the ECU had caught on and had insinuated Saskia into his crew. Four innocents were dead. The fifth had been saved because Clive had not left anything in his box after testing the poison and learning it was not what Saskia had said it was. He'd had hopes to go under, disappear from the *bratva's* radar.

And he'd been successful. The ECU turned Clive over to Interpol. As far as the *bratva* was concerned, and what steps Interpol would take—if any—were classified.

That was the information Lucinda Marks gave Saskia as she lay on a London hospital bed. An IV pumped clear liquid into her left arm, and the machine it was attached to beeped every twenty minutes, curtailing her from slipping into a deep and much-needed restful sleep.

But when the blond commander had walked in and touched Saskia's cheek, she'd grown alert and cautious.

"Where's Jack?" Saskia couldn't stop herself from asking.

Lucinda tilted her head. Her eyes were blue. Too pretty, Saskia thought. Because beneath the benevolence and beauty she suspected a diamond-hard bitch reigned.

"He's been dealt with," Lucinda offered in a much-too-pleasant voice. "He betrayed us."

"He was only doing what he had to do," Saskia said. Her throat hurt and she was fighting exhaustion. She couldn't raise her voice. "He saved me from Clive. The man would have shot me in the head."

"I had no idea Angelo was such a marksman."

"Doesn't he get some credit for that? He was only helping family. His brother—"

"We know about Jonny Angelo. We've known since before Jack took off for Helsinki. How do you think we knew to put him on the mission and assign you to watch him?"

"But… Are you involved in what happened to Jonny? What did happen to his brother?"

Lucinda shook her head. "That Angelo brother liked to skim off his client's take from smuggled guns. The ECU was not involved in his kidnap and the ransom request made to Jack. What the Angelo family manages to get themselves involved in is entirely of their own doing. But we keep tabs on them. It's necessary for the safety of our assets."

Saskia closed her eyes. Her brain wanted to sort through it all, to deduce and understand, but she wasn't able. It felt good to keep her eyelids shut. She needed to rest.

Jack had told her she was family as she lay there on the edge of the river, feeling as though an angel had pulled her up from hell. Had he said he loved her? Or had her iced brain wanted to hear that? Maybe. But she was certain he'd said he'd never stop looking for her.

Could a dead man find her?

"Just tell me he's alive," she whispered.

"That's need to know, Petrovik."

If she'd the strength, she'd grab the commander by her throat and pop her fingernails through her skin. The act of imagining it gave Saskia a smile. Bitch.

She turned away from Lucinda and her gaze fixed on the daylight framed by the partially-opened curtains. "What's to become of me?"

"While your actions went against some ECU policies, we have never been a by-the-book unit. You did what you had to."

As had Jack!

"Your alliances are still in question, though."

"Doesn't matter anymore, does it? Jack's gone."

When Lucinda took her hand and held it gently, Saskia wanted to pull away but—her warmth felt welcome. "The two of you worked well together. I won't overlook that."

What did that mean?

"You rest. I've requisitioned a four-day vacation for you. Sounds like you'll be free to check out this evening. And I've suggested your next assignment be someplace warmer. How does that sound?"

Saskia could but tighten her shoulders and curl in deeper on herself.

"Thank you for your work, Petrovik. It will not go unrewarded. But tell me one thing."

She waited for the question.

"At any moment did you consider going off the grid with Jack Angelo?"

She had. Well, she'd considered it. But had she considered it seriously? It was hard to know. But she knew what the Commander wanted to hear. And she wasn't willing to give her that lie.

"Yes," she said resolutely.

Lucinda's exhale said so much. The woman's heels clicked as she exited the room, leaving Saskia to wonder if they would ever tell her where to find Jack's tombstone.

* * * *

A week later...

Lucinda Marks had kept her word.

The hot Australian sun burned over Saskia's shoulders and arms but she could handle it. Slipping on a pair of Ray Bans, and flip-flopping her way down the gangplank toward the waiting yacht, she tucked a hand at her hip, above the string bikini bottom. It wasn't the best costume for hiding weapons, so she hadn't. But the scarf she wore wrapped about her upper thigh, to hide the healing knife wound, did have a thin leaf blade in it. Just in case.

The boat was taking dozens of millionaires on a cruise around the Whitsunday Islands. It also featured a private auction of stolen artwork taken during an embassy raid in the Middle East. Millions of dollars' worth of Egyptian pottery and even some emeralds and jewel-encrusted porcelain bowls were going on the block. And all the buyers knew the booty was hot.

Saskia's objective was to insinuate herself into the target's confidence. From there she would learn his connections and draw out a chart of all the places he received from and eventually the ECU would track the kingpin behind the operation.

She estimated a few weeks undercover as a spoiled rich girl sent on vacation by her daddy. She was meeting her "brother" on board, another

ECU asset whom she'd only been informed about half an hour earlier as she'd dressed for this excursion.

"What's his name?" she'd asked Chester Clarke.

"He's under a cover name of Finnister Wright. Billionaire owner of an auto-tech research lab. Makes race cars as a hobby. He'll be your brother."

She hadn't gotten an asset name, but it was just as well. Saskia would know him when he came up to give her a brotherly hug.

A purser and female attendant with perfect blue cat's eyeshadow greeted her as she boarded. Champagne was immediately offered, and she was told to join the party on the upper deck. The yacht would be leaving in five minutes.

Snatching a flute of champagne, Saskia thanked them and wandered into the party, which looked populated by men in yuppie gear. More than a few yachting captain hats. The requisite sun-tanned skin. (She did not miss Helsinki at all.) And cigar smoke everywhere. She was thankful for the open air. And for the fact at least three other women were on board.

One of the women walked up to her and touched her lightly on the arm. "I love your ensemble. Yves Saint Laurent?"

Yeah, so she'd invested for this costume. It had seemed the best bet.

Saskia fingered the gold clasp at the front and center of her bikini top. "Got it on the first guess. So where's the snort?"

The woman gestured over a shoulder. "Back near the bar. There's ecstasy too. Are you here alone?"

"No, I'm meeting my brother. We're shopping for daddy's birthday today."

"Sweet." The woman tilted her glass toward the crowd of laughing men. "Which one is your brother? And is he single? I'm here doing some shopping of my own. But not for art, if you get what I mean."

Saskia got it. And the slender looker with artificially-plumped lips and breasts, could probably lay claim to any man she chose today. It would be a feeding frenzy, for sure.

"I don't see him yet." Saskia made show of looking about for a man of whom she had no idea how he might look. "But he's not single," she added, because she didn't want to hamper her partner with this winner. Unless of course, he chose that impediment. "But *he's* handsome." She nodded toward a blond man who was so sun-browned he looked baked. "Nice eyes."

"That's Evert Flynn. CEO of MasterWear. Worth billions," the woman cooed eagerly. "I think I'm going to claim him. Hands off, okay?"

Saskia tilted her champagne glass to the woman as she sashayed off toward the billionaire. And when she turned, an arm suddenly slipped across her back, a hand falling to rest casually at her hip.

"Hey, sis."

Saskia's heartbeats thundered. She didn't even have to look at him. His voice. The feel of him standing so close to her. He...

...wasn't dead.

"Jack," she whispered.

"Finnister Wright," he said under his breath. Then in a normal tone he asked, "How's my sister doing? You're looking ready for some fun in the sun." He leaned in closer and whispered, "Told ya you were family, eh?"

Fighting back relieved tears, Saskia could only nod and allow the man to hug her. She wanted to melt against him, to kiss him, to grab him by the face and stare into his blue-gray eyes. To know it was him. Alive. And standing beside her. But she couldn't. Not without breaking cover.

As he pulled away from the too-brief hug, Jack winked at her. He wore a captain's hat and a white short-sleeved shirt with casual linen slacks and sandals.

"I was worth keeping around," he said quietly. "Or so the commander said. Got another chip too. Now that Jonny is safe I'm in for the long haul this time."

"Oh, Jack."

"Finnister."

"Right. Finn."

"And you are Lisa, my sister. I'll be keeping you close today. Protective older brother thing, and all."

"Please do."

"We'll have a moment when we dock later. And then?"

"Then?" Hope lifted her chin.

"Then we get to know one another again. All night long."

The End

The Thief

Find out where it all began!
The Elite Crimes Unit series by Michele Hauf

The Elite Crimes Unit works behind the scenes of Interpol—and employs some of the world's most talented criminal minds. Because as everyone knows, it takes a thief to catch a thief—or to seduce one . . .

The old farmhouse in the French countryside is a refuge for former jewel thief Josephine Deveraux. Admittedly, there aren't many men in the vicinity, but she has her cat to cuddle up with. It's a far cry from her former life, constantly running from the law, and she's enjoying her peace . . . until the intruder in the three-piece suit tackles her. He wants her back in the game, helping with a heist—and he's not above making threats to get his way.

Little does Josephine know that notorious—and notoriously charming—thief, Xavier Lambert, is after the very same 180-carat prize she's being blackmailed to steal. To his chagrin, he's doing it not as a free agent, but as a member of the Elite Crimes Unit—the team he was forced to join when his brilliant career came to a sudden end. And little does Xavier know that his comeback is about to include a stranger's kiss, a stinging slap, and a hunt for missing treasure—along with the infuriatingly sexy woman who's outfoxing him . . .

Chapter 1

Josephine Devereaux strode through the open front screen door into the kitchen. Creamy golden evening light spread quiet warmth across the aged hardwood floors. The old farmhouse had stood on this plot in the southern French countryside for centuries. She'd had the pleasure of owning it for two years.

Setting a clutch of fresh carrots pulled from the rain-damp garden into the sink, she spun at a tiny meow. Behind her, the two-and-a-half-year-old Devon Rex cat with soft, downy fur the color of faded charcoal batted at the hem of her long pink skirt.

"Do you want fish or chicken tonight, Chloe?"

She opened the refrigerator to find the only option was diced chicken, left over from last night's supper. Her neighbor, Jean-Hugues, had butchered a rooster yesterday morning and brought her half.

The cat went at the feast she'd placed on a saucer with big elf ears wiggling appreciatively. Chloe had come with the farmhouse. The couple moving out hadn't wanted to bring along a kitten on their overseas move to the United States. It had been love at first purr for Josephine.

She smiled at the quiet patter of rain. And then she frowned. "Mud," she muttered. And she hated housecleaning. She had never developed a domestic bone in her body and didn't expect to grow one.

She'd spend the evening inside, maybe finish up the thriller she'd found on Jean-Hugues's bookshelf. He always encouraged her to take what she wanted—she was a voracious reader of all topics—and she gave him vegetables from her garden in return.

Not that she was a master gardener. Jean-Hugues tended the garden, along with the few rows of vines that produced enough grapes for one big barrel of wine. Jean-Hughes was sixty, but he flirted with her in a non-confrontational, just-for-fun manner, which she appreciated probably more than a twenty-six-year-old woman should.

Living so far from Paris made it difficult to find dateable men, let alone a hook-up for a night of just-give-it-to-me-now-and-leave-before-the-sun-rises sex. But that's what grocery trips to the nearest village were for. If the mood struck, she'd leave in the evening for eggs, bread, and a booty call, and find her way out of bed and back home by morning.

Sighing, Josephine forgot about the dirty carrots in the sink and padded barefoot to the lumpy jacquard sofa that stretched before the massive paned window at the front of the cottage. The window overlooked a cobblestone patio, which stretched before the house and also served as a driveway, though no cars used it. She didn't own a car. And she never had visitors, save Jean-Hugues, and on occasion the neighbors who lived on the other side of him. They were newlyweds, Jean-Louis and Hollie, and they spent most of their time by themselves. And that was exactly how Josephine preferred it.

She picked up the book, and the creased spine flopped open to the last page she'd read.

An hour later, she had to squint to read because the sun had set. Splaying the book across her chest, she closed her eyes and breathed in the fragrance of rain on fieldstones. Chloe nestled near her foot, keeping her ankle warm. The screen door, still open, squeaked lightly with the breeze. Everything was....

Peaceful? Was that a word she was supposed to embrace? To somehow understand?

"I am embracing it. Life is good."

Or rather, more different than she could have ever imagined it would be.

She set the book down, but the sound she heard was not of a paperback book hitting the wood floor. Josephine closed her eyes to listen intently. The floor creaked carefully above her, where the bathroom was located. It did not indicate the aches and pains of an aging house. This house had settled long ago.

Curling her hand beneath the sofa, she gripped the cool bone handle of the bowie knife she'd tucked up into the torn fabric amongst the springs and pulled it out. Pointing the blade down, she took a deep breath and stood up. Moving sinuously, she crept around the end of the sofa. Her free hand skimmed over Chloe's body, comforting and promising she'd return. The cat purred but thankfully didn't follow.

Upstairs, it was silent. Josephine wasn't easily spooked by natural noises, but that had not been a natural noise. And she wasn't unnerved now. Just.... annoyed.

This was her sanctuary. No one knew where she had disappeared two years ago. Very few had known her location before that. But since then, she'd completely erased herself from the grid. Therefore, whoever was stupid enough to break in was looking to rob a random person. And they had to know she was home, which meant the intruder did not fear an altercation.

Tough luck for that idiot.

On the other hand, she had only herself to blame for leaving the ladder up against the north wall after knocking down a wasp nest this morning.

Approaching the stairway, which was worn in the center of the stone risers from decades of use, Josephine tugged up her maxi skirt and tucked in one side at the waist to keep from tangling her legs in the long, floaty fabric. The stairs were fashioned from limestone; no creaks would give away her position. Barefoot, she padded up six steps to a landing. Ahead, around a sharp right turn, rose another five steps to the second floor.

Hearing the creak of a leather sole, she realized the intruder had stepped onto the stairs. But where was he? Waiting for her to spin around the corner? He probably thought she was still downstairs relaxing on the couch.

Which gave her the advantage.

With her right arm thrust out, knife blade cutting the air, she rushed forward. As she turned the corner on the stairway, the intruder grabbed her wrist, forcing it upward to deflect the blade from stabbing his face.

Josephine yanked her arm back, causing the intruder to lose his balance. His weight crushed her against the plaster wall, and they struggled on the landing. Although it was dark in the stairway, she could see that he wasn't an average intruder—most tended to not wear three-piece suits. He was about her height and lean. She did not doubt she could take him out.

He managed a weak knee to her gut, but she didn't even wince. She rammed her head against his shoulder. He twisted his waist, knocking her off-balance. They spilled backward. Her hip landed his thigh as they slid down the stone stairs.

They landed on the kitchen floor, Josephine on her stomach, with the intruder on top of her. The knife flew out of her hand and skittered across the floor, landing before Chloe's toes. The cat bent to sniff the weapon.

"Chloe, no!" she shouted. The cat scampered under the sofa.

The intruder grabbed Josephine by the hair at her neck and lifted her head. Just when he would have smashed her face against the floor, she kicked him right between the legs. His fingers instantly released the pinching hold on her neck. He swore and dropped beside her.

Scrambling across the floor, she grabbed the knife and stood, flicking on the light switch on the wall, and moving to stand over the attacker.

"What the hell?" she gasped. "You?"

A man she knew well, and had trusted enough to let down her guard and actually date, offered her an imperious smile. He swore and rubbed his crotch. "Your aim has always been spot on, Jo-Jo. Ah fuck."

His head dropped. His eyes closed. Passed out from the pain?

Josephine inched closer and leaned over him. With the tip of the knife, she prodded him at the temple.

The man's hand whipped up and grabbed her long hair, jerking her off balance and swinging her to the floor. He slammed her knife hand on the floor so hard, she let go. Grabbing the knife, he pressed it against her left breast, right over her heart.

"I have a proposition for you, Jo-Jo."

No one had called her that in over two years. And hearing it now conjured up dread and regret. But along with those feelings, there was the sudden rush of adrenaline that always came with the game. She'd walked away from the game, and this man's world of larceny and lies. And she didn't intend to walk back into it—or be forced.

"Funny, your last proposition had me running for the hills." Away from the engagement ring he had offered like a tempting sweet. She wasn't that kind of girl. The domestic, let-a-man-own-you type. Her mother's horrible choice in men had taught her a few lessons. "Never thought I'd see you again."

He winced. "Your refusal wounded me, Jo-Jo. But I'm able to put past mistakes aside. I need you for a job."

A mistake? More so on her part than his. But with his narcissism, he'd never care that she did have feelings, and she could be hurt. Hell, it had taken her two years living alone in the French countryside to realize that herself.

She splayed out her arms and closed her eyes in surrender. "Just kill me, Lincoln. That's the only way this will ever happen."

"I assumed as much. You like living the hard way? Out here in the sticks? I'll give you that. But you owe me, Jo-Jo. For saying no."

"Seriously?" Since when did a woman owe a man because she'd refused his marriage proposal?

She closed her eyes, inhaling the cool, ocean scent of his skin as the knife's cool metal disappeared from her body. "What the hell could you possibly want from me?"

"There's a pretty bit of sparkle I need you to pick up for me. This Saturday. In Paris."

Lincoln was interested in the sparkly stuff? Since when? The man was into money laundering and securities fraud.

Did it matter? "Not interested."

The knife blade glinted from the light over the kitchen table. "One job and I'll never bother you again."

"Since when are you into jewel theft?"

"It's related to an offensive situation that could cast a black mark against my name. I'd like to remedy that. But since you know where my expertise is focused, you should also understand I have to bring in an expert for this particular heist."

The asshole could skim a million from a major stock as easily as gliding a knife over butter. It was that talent that had initially attracted her. He was Robin Hood, taking from the rich—but he'd never given to the poor. And that had been a sticking point for her, a woman who had always tried to give away some of her spoils to those in need.

An offensive situation? She couldn't imagine. And she didn't want to know.

"How'd you find me?" she asked.

"I've kept tabs on you since you went under. Did you actually think you could elude me, Jo-Jo?"

"Don't call me that."

"It's your name, Josephine." He straddled her hips, and his grip at her shoulder loosened. He let out a long, deep breath. It reminded too much of soft summer mornings spent lazing under the sheets against his warm skin. "You never did like this position," he said. "Me on top."

"You have a thing about being the one in control."

"And you don't?"

She was in no mood to discuss her preference in sexual positions, or even to converse with this man. But she remained still beneath him. The knife blade pointed away from her; he'd let down his guard. She had only to bide her time.

"You know I'm not in the trade anymore, Lincoln. If you need some sparklers, there are other options."

"Yes, but I require discretion and quality work. You're the only thief I know who can do this job. I'll even pay you."

She scoffed. "I know better. You are not a generous man. Leave."

He slapped her face. The smack rung in her ears, and Josephine's gasp burned in her throat. But she used the distraction to her advantage, jabbing her knee into the femoral artery in his thigh. Always a painful spot. The knife clanked on the stone floor. She twisted her body, slamming him onto the floor, and landed both knees onto his torso. Grabbing the knife, she lifted it above her head with both hands, aiming for his chest.

Lincoln chuckled. His dark eyes twinkled in the cool evening shadows. Yeah, that was a devastating twinkle, and he knew how to wield it. As he spread his arms out, and she felt his chest relax beneath her knees, he said, "If I know one thing about you, Jo-Jo, it's that you are not a killer."

She tilted her head and nodded. "Nope, I'm not so keen on taking life. But I don't mind causing a little pain now and then."

She slammed her hands down. The knife pierced Lincoln's Givenchy suit and nicked bone as it entered his shoulder. He growled as she stood up over him.

"Get the hell out of my home." She stepped back and glanced around the room. Chloe was still under the sofa. "Now!"

Gripping his shoulder but leaving the blade in, Lincoln stood up, staggered, yet managed a cool recovery. He swept a hand over his coal-black hair, slicked with pomade. "You will do this job for me. I will be back."

He turned and stalked out, leaving the screen door swinging out over the courtyard. Spots of blood dribbled on the floor and cobblestones in his wake.

As Josephine let out a long breath, she heard a car roll across the gravel drive. Lincoln must have had a driver park at the end of the half-mile drive. He had walked up and insinuated himself in her house as if he was a specter.

It didn't matter how he'd gained access. He'd crept back into her life. Not cool.

Josephine's instincts kicked into survival mode.

She ran up the stairs and pulled a duffel bag out from the bedroom closet. Stuffing it with shirts, pants, bras, and a Glock 42—a .380 automatic—she scrambled down the stairs, calling for Chloe. The cat scampered out from under the sofa.

"I'm sorry, sweetie, but my past just stopped by for a visit."

And she wasn't stupid enough to sit around and wait for that return visit he had promised. Because it would happen.

Ten minutes later, she'd pulled the rusty ten-speed bicycle she used for grocery trips out of the garage and pedaled up to Jean-Hugues's cottage. She handed him Chloe and bent to kiss the cat's downy-soft head. "I need you to watch her for a few days. I'm heading to Paris. I have some things to take care of."

Like finding a new place to live. The little apartment she owned in Paris's 8th arrondissement served as a safe house. It would provide cover until Dmitri, her go-to man, could relocate her.

"Is everything okay?" Jean-Hugues asked as he cuddled Chloe against his neck. He bent his head to allow the cat to nuzzle against his five-o'clock shadow. "You are not in trouble, Josephine?"

Her name always sounded whispery and sexy when he said it. Of course she'd let him flirt with her. She'd considered kissing him once—a deep and lingering taste from a wise and seasoned male—but had never gone beyond the thankful kiss to his forehead or cheek.

"No, not in trouble. Never."

She'd not told him why a young, single woman had suddenly moved out to the country to do nothing more than read and bike, and spend her evenings cooking meals straight from the garden alongside a sexy old Frenchman. He'd always accepted that she had some secrets, as did everyone.

"I'm going to pedal into town and catch a cab to Paris. I'll be back in a few days to pick up Chloe. Okay?"

"Of course, mon petite chat is always welcome. We will have chicken and eggs for breakfast, oui, Chloe?"

Josephine stroked the cat's head, then she leaned in to kiss Jean-Hugues's cheek. "Merci. I will not be long."

* * * *

Two days later, Josephine took a cab back to Jean-Hugues's place. She'd set up in the Paris safe house and had contacted Dmitri. It would take a week to relocate her to Berlin. She didn't look forward to that—she didn't speak German and the city was dismal—but it wasn't permanent. A quick layover that would provide much-needed misdirection. All that mattered was getting out of France and going under.

Again.

How Lincoln had managed to keep tabs on her was incredible. She'd been careful. Since moving to France with her mother when she was eight, she'd never been issued a driver's license or ID card. No internet presence, not even a credit card. The only phones she used were pre-paid burners. Of course, she should have expected Lincoln would not let her leave so easily. He'd been infatuated with her. So quickly. It had freaked the hell out of her. She'd refused his marriage proposal after dating only four weeks.

She wasn't the marrying type. Domesticity gave her the hives. Sharing her life with a man sounded so evasive. Since giving up thievery, she liked to keep her head down and her ass out of trouble. And Lincoln wanting her to step back onto the scene now was not keeping her head down.

She directed the cabbie to turn off the headlights so they didn't shine through her neighbor's bedroom window, then told him she'd be right out. She headed up the walkway, then stopped.

The front door was open. Instinctively, Josephine's hand went to the gun she'd tucked in the back of her leather pants. While she didn't like guns, sometimes they were necessary. She pulled out the small pistol she favored and held it pointed down near her thigh. She stepped over the cracked stone threshold.

"Jean-Hugues?"

A groan sounded from the living room. She hurried in to find the old man sitting on the wood floor before the smoldering fireplace. Blood dribbled from his forehead and had stained his upper lip. He smiled up at her, but then winced.

"Jean-Hugues, what happened? When did this happen?" It must have been Lincoln. Had to be. Had she passed him on the road coming here?

"They were here not too long ago. I am so sorry, Josephine. They took Chloe."

Heart dropping, she bent before Jean-Hugues and touched his forehead. He'd been punched, and probably cut with a ring. Not a deep cut, but it must hurt terribly.

"A man with dark hair asked for you. I told him I didn't know where you were. He had two thugs with him. Why did they take the cat?" he asked, spreading his hands. "I don't understand."

It was a means to force her to do the job. Lincoln was a ruthless bastard. Hurting an old man to get to her was beyond cruel.

"I'm sorry, Jean-Hugues. Let me get that first-aid kit out of your bathroom and we'll take care of you."

"No, I am fine. Just a cut and maybe a few bruised ribs."

"They beat you?" She stood and pressed the gun grip against her temple. "That bastard."

"Why do you have a gun, Josephine? Who were those men?"

Josephine clenched her jaw. "My past."

Chapter 2

Two days later...

The glamorous black tie ball charged five thousand dollars for entry and benefited the International Mission For More. Feeding hungry children was always a good cause, yet Xavier Lambert wondered what more meant. More money? Shouldn't charity eventually be able to achieve its goals? He'd made a point to give away seventy-five percent of his income throughout his career. Yet, did it ever really help?

If only The Elite Crimes Unit he had been forced to join could know how many charitable dollars had been removed from the system upon his removal from the system.

Didn't matter. He was doing well, and had become as close to a functioning normal person as the parameters of the ECU would allow. Or so, that is what his handlers had tried to drill into him over his past year of service. It would take a while to teach an old dog new tricks.

This new trick called "life now, like it or not" had made Xavier roll over, yet he would never beg. After a year incarcerated in an eastern Belgium prison, he appreciated the modicum of freedom he now had, granted by a digital chip embedded near the base of his skull that allowed the Unit to track him at will.

As Xavier strolled the marble-floored ballroom beneath a constellation of massive crystal chandeliers, he sipped sweet champagne and scanned every face in the room for about three seconds. That was enough time to fix them into his brain: male or female, rich or pretending, a player or a gentleman, a gold-digger or a trophy for one's arm.

He had identified the Countess de Maleaux earlier. She was wearing the diamond-strand necklace weighing a hundred and eighty carats. He intended to walk out the door in about twenty minutes with that prize tucked in his pocket.

Chanel No. 5 breezed by him. He closed his eyes and inhaled. The fragrance was common in the echelon of society he frequented. What startled him now was the scent of a natural oil like clove or lavender. Simple adornments were gauche amidst the champagne-and-caviar crowd.

Unfortunate. There were occasions where he preferred simple.

Xavier placed the empty tulip goblet on a passing waiter's silver tray and made his way along the edge of the black-and-white harlequin dance floor. Most of the waltzing couples were older; the women's faces hiked up with surgery and the men's hearts thundering from the Viagra they'd swallowed upon arrival.

He smirked at the thought. To live to be seen and admired seemed a sorry existence. He had always strived to walk the shadows, to never be seen or noticed. Growing up in a wealthy family, such social fanfare had once been integral to his existence. And yet the hundreds of carats of sparkling diamonds and colored stuff milling about the room beckoned all to observe, to admire. To invoke jealousy.

Perhaps even to lure one to take.

Because, in truth, those chunks of compressed carbon could serve a much better purpose fenced and sold for charity than resting in the wrinkled cleavage of Madame Chanel No. 5.

"How's the room look?"

Xavier tilted his head at the voice in his ear. He hadn't heard from Kierce since he'd entered the mansion and had almost forgotten his presence. Almost. The man was at headquarters, sitting before a computer system so complicated it boggled Xavier's mind. Yet Kierce Quinn could map out the floor plan of the building, access ventilation shafts and alarm codes, unlock windows, and even determine a person's temperature if Xavier touched someone with the tip of his forefinger, on which he wore a thermodynamic biometric slip.

But put the guy in a social situation—with real people instead of an online forum—and watch him quiver.

"The usual idle rich," Xavier answered quietly. He turned around to give the impression he was looking over the curved blue glass bar. He was careful never to allow others to suspect he was talking to himself. "I'm moving in soon."

"After you snatch the prize, take pictures with the cufflink camera," Kierce said. "It'll take me a few minutes to run an analysis, and I don't want to wait for your return to know what we're dealing with."

"I understand. No problem. Just the girdles?"

"Yes, the rims of the diamonds, if possible. Then I can verify authenticity. Depending on the setting, you may or may not have access. If not, do the best you can."

"They are in a prong setting." Xavier had noted the setting when he'd walked past the countess. "Girdles exposed, or at least a good portion."

"Excellent. I'm working on the access code for the garage. I've determined that's your best exit option. Should have it in five."

"Then we're on. Give me radio silence, will you?"

"They don't call it radio silence, old man. It's 'ten-four.'."

Kierce wasn't even twenty. And Xavier was not an old man. But there were days he felt it around the boy genius. He kept up on all the technology regarding safes, locks, and alarm systems. But it all moved so quickly. Had it been a good thing he'd been nabbed two years ago and taken off the streets?

He tried to convince himself of it, but always failed. Someone had narced on him and ended an illustrious fourteen-year thievery career. Revenge had never been his style, but should he learn who'd given him up? He'd consider changing that style.

One bodyguard shadowed the countess. Not a big man, but Xavier was sure that beneath his cheap suit, there were muscles trained to incapacitate with a few discreet, yet devastating, moves. The thug scanned the surroundings, and when the countess would speak to someone new, he'd home in his gaze on the conversation. If she lingered in the discussion for more than a few minutes, the bodyguard began his periphery scan over again.

So Xavier would have to chat more than a minute or two. Perhaps even entice her to give him a few private moments.

Moving across the dance floor, he deftly navigated the distance between him and the countess, whom he pinned at age sixty-two. Kierce had provided cursory research on her when he'd arrived at the party: married at seventeen; the count had died when she was fifty. She'd taken a new lover every year following until a devastating operation had left her scarred in a very personal location (botched plastic surgery was the speculation). She attended any and all events, Xavier guessed, because she was lonely. She had no children and favored private jets.

Her spangled blue gown dazzled as she delivered an air kiss to a woman in a green silk sheath and bid her thanks for something Xavier had missed. He stepped forward, bowing slightly, and took her hand before she could assess him. He kissed her warm skin, the sagging flesh spotted from sun exposure.

"Enchanté," he offered. "Countess, you dazzled me from across the room." He swept a hand to distract her attention across the busy ballroom and noticed the bodyguard's gaze also followed. Nice. "Might I beg the pleasure of your company for this waltz?"

The orchestra had launched into a Chopin waltz.

"Mon cheri, you flatter me, but I was thinking to find the little girl's room."

But his few minutes had not yet passed. "I understand." Xavier leaned in and touched the dangling chandelier earring, making sure to brush her skin ever so lightly. "Cartier?" he asked.

"Why, yes." She touched her neck where his finger had glided and he noticed the blush rise at her breasts. "How did you know?"

"I'm a jeweler," he lied. It was one of many roles he assumed on command. "Worked at Cartier a while back. Lovely place. The sapphires call attention to your eyes, but are certainly lacking in comparison."

Her body heat rose as his wrist brushed her shoulder. Kierce would get that reading as well. She was focused on him—his face, his voice, the compliments she surely received often and required like oxygen.

"I do love this composition. And the waltz is my favorite," she said.

"Then shall we?" He bowed again, grandly, charmingly. And when he looked up, the countess sighed and took both his hands.

"Just once around," she said as he guided her into a light and free stroll around the dance floor. "Oh, you are very light on your feet, Monsieur...?"

Ignoring her hint for his name, Xavier whisked her around, hugging the inner edge where dancers brushed shoulders and the swish of satins and silks harmonized with the orchestra.

A black moiré ribbon served as backing for the diamond strand, a throwback to eighteenth-century styling. Xavier considered it a bit of good fortune. No clasp to deal with, if he were lucky.

The duchess was also light on her feet, and they'd made it halfway around the dance floor when Xavier made to sweep back a loose strand of hair over her ear. It was a simple flick of his fingers to untie the ribbon necklace. As he did he leaned in to whisper in French, "I am bedazzled by you."

"Tell me your name, and I'll follow you home," she cooed.

"Uh, uh." He waggled a finger, while noting over her shoulder that the bodyguard had assumed a laser focus on him. "My wife would not appreciate the extra place setting."

The countess pouted. Xavier danced her back to her bodyguard. He waited with arms akimbo, as if to ready for a gunfight.

"A revoir, ma jolie." Xavier lifted the countess's hand and kissed it. "Merci, pour la danse."

The bodyguard stepped in. The brute's dull gray eyes narrowed. "So sorry," Xavier said to him. "I understand." He backed away, and turned to stride off, enfolding himself into the crowd.

Out of the ballroom, Xavier walked purposefully to the cloak room, which he had scoped out upon arrival. A long fluorescent light illuminated a row of purses—some worth as much as an economy car—top hats, and even canes. The pimply attendant talked to someone on his cell phone, likely a girlfriend for the purring tone he assumed. His back was to Xavier; the guy had not been instructed in effective security procedures.

Xavier pulled out the necklace, turned his back to the attendant some thirty feet away, and then used the camera Kierce had designed to look like a silver cuff link. Fitting the round aperture completely over the crown of the diamond, the ring-shaped lens was able to completely photograph the girdle. How such a thing worked, Xavier had no clue, but he liked it. Handy.

"Report," Kierce said in his ear.

"Have the prize. Snapping shots. Escape cleared?"

"Tell me when you need it four seconds in advance. I'll have the doors open."

"Ten-four."

Xavier snapped six diamonds before someone cleared their throat behind him and asked if he could help.

"Non, merci. Just needed a moment," Xavier said, adjusting his tie.

With a nod, he quickly walked out. Stupid excuse. But if he left quickly enough, the attendant would forget about it and get back to his girlfriend.

He strolled toward the ballroom. The outer hallway, which bordered the massive room, was segregated by marble columns spaced ten feet apart. It was lit only by LEDs around the bases of the columns, providing a quiet and dark aisle for escape from the bustle of the rich and famous, or even a illicit fondling session. Xavier scanned the crowd for the countess's blue spangled couture, but didn't spot her. She must have found the bathroom—

—the kiss came out of nowhere.

A woman's mouth landed on his with a firm and intentional connection. Xavier ran his hands up her back instinctively, feeling the curve of her waist under sleek silk fabric. She felt right. Comfortable. But he hadn't seen her face and had no clue who she was, so he gently pushed her away.

Even in the shadows, her aquamarine eyes flashed at him amidst lush black lashes. Dark hair was piled high on her head like Audrey Hepburn. No jewels about her neck or at her ears. Her bare red lips curved into a smirk.

"Aw, you don't remember me, Xavier?" she asked.

She nudged his nose with hers and glided a hand down the front of his suit. Again the kiss connected with his mouth and this time he let it happen. Because it was a crazy, weird thing.

She tasted like champagne and caviar. Her body fit against his as if they'd done this a thousand times before. And her heat had already given him an erection. He wished she'd slide closer, rub her hip against him to increase the intensity of his hard-on, but he wasn't about to break the kiss to give orders. Instead, he pulled her in tighter, silently indicating that he wanted this dive into the unknown.

She took the command, sliding a bent leg along his thigh and hugging her mons against his erection. Mm…. how he loved a beautiful, intricate woman who knew exactly what she wanted.

And yet. Had she….? She had called him "Xavier." So few knew him by name. And those who did? He knew in return.

Out in the ballroom, a woman shrieked. The attendees rushed to her, the commotion drowning the orchestra's rendition of the French national anthem.

When the women pulled away, she blinked at Xavier and purred. "I could never forget your kisses," she said. "I lose myself in them."

She stroked his cheek, and he noted tattoos of tiny…cats on her inner wrist. He would have remembered such tattoos had he met her before. He never would have forgotten such gorgeous gemstone eyes.

"I…uh…." If he confessed he didn't know her, he might lose the chance for another kiss.

Then again, what the hell was he doing? He didn't need this distraction. He was on a job. And the alarm had just sounded.

Damn it. She'd actually pulled him out of focus. That had been some kiss. But he had to get out of here. Whatever ruckus was exploding on the dance floor only grew louder.

"Sorry," he said curtly, and tugged at his tie. "I don't know you."

"What? How dare you!"

The slap stung his cheek but bruised his ego much more sharply. That was to be expected, but never accepted. On the other hand, now was not the time to admonish a stranger for a stolen kiss.

He needed to extricate himself before the thug scanning the crowd at the edge of the ballroom spied him.

"The kiss was great," he started, "but—"

"Yeah, whatever. Asshole." She turned and marched off, leaving him not so appreciative of her kiss after that rude oath. Women who swore like truckers never appealed to him.

"And a good evening to you, too," he said in her wake.

"Did some chick just kiss you?" Kierce asked through the earbuds.

"Oui. Happens more often than you can imagine."

"You live such a tough life, Lambert."

"Yes, well, you didn't hear that slap."

"I did, but I assumed you liked it rough."

No way Xavier was going to comment on that one.

"All but one of the photos came through clean," Kierce said. "I can read the code on the girdles. You headed toward the escape door?"

"Yes. And…"

The bodyguard who had been lurking over the countess charged around the marble column. He grabbed Xavier by the tie, and swung an uppercut to the underside of his jaw. Xavier wobbled, but maintained consciousness and, thankfully, his upright status.

"That did not sound like a slap," Kierce said.

"A new challenge has presented itself," Xavier muttered. He slammed an elbow into the bruiser's ribcage. "Give me a few minutes."

Meet the Author

Photo credit Abbey Wright

Michele Hauf has been writing romance, action-adventure and fantasy stories for over twenty years. Her first published novel was *Dark Rapture* (Zebra). France, musketeers, vampires and faeries populate her stories. And if she followed the adage "write what you know," all her stories would have snow in them. Fortunately, she steps beyond her comfort zone and writes about countries she has never visited and of creatures she has never seen.

CPSIA information can be obtained
at www.ICGtesting.com
Printed in the USA
LVOW07s1430031217
558469LV00001B/129/P